CAUGHT IN A MOMENT

Martin Dukes

Caught in a Moment

Martin Dukes

Published by

PB Software
3 Nelson Road
Ashingdon, Rochford
Essex SS4 3EJ

First Edition
First Printing June 2102

A CIP catalogue record of this book
is available from the British Library

IBSN 978-0-9569934-5-8

Printed and bound in Great Britain by
4edge Ltd, Hockley.   .4edge.co.uk

"In an infinite universe everything is possible. More than that, it's inevitable. Open up your mind."

For Linda

Chapter One

It was a Monday afternoon, the sort of sultry afternoon in early May that acts as a promise, a taster, for the anticipated pleasures of high summer. Soft scars of fading vapour trails were all that marred the perfect sky. There was hardly a breath of air to stir the leaves in the trees that broke the concrete monotony around the school sports hall. The windows of the classroom had been opened the meagre crack that was all that health and safety rules allowed.

Alex Trueman sat hunched, perspiring over his desk in one of several great trapezoid blazes of sunlight. He was nearly fifteen, a boy of unremarkable appearance except for his ears, which stuck out from the sides of his head like the handles of a sports cup and had earned him the nickname "Trophy." A desk space in front of him, motes of dust danced gracefully above Jessica Elliot's blond curled head, stirred into sudden, urgent action as she flicked her hair. Out on the playing field boys were playing cricket. From his place next to the fly-specked window Alex could see the leisurely movements of the fielders on the boundary, the sudden bursts of activity as the batsmen cut or hooked, a bowler's arms raised as he appealed half-heartedly for a wicket. It was not that Alex particularly liked cricket. It was one of the many sports that he wasn't any good at. But if he was happy to concede to them the doubtful pleasures of cork on willow, he envied them the air and the space and the freedom from the tedium of double Geography.

"Alex is a loser," was the message crudely scrawled on the scrap of paper passed to him by his neighbour to the left.

This was his friend Henry, who grinned sidelong at him to demonstrate that he expected Alex to retaliate in kind.

Turning the paper over, he took his own pen and gave the matter some thought. He might conceivably have written, "You are fifteen years old. I would have expected you to have grown out of this kind of stuff by now."

Instead, with a sigh, he wrote, "Henry is a *big fat* loser," and passed it back.

Henry frowned and chewed his pen whilst considering how to sustain this witty dialogue.

Part of Alex was aware of Mr McTavish's flat nasal tones describing the features of a central business district. He frowned. His fountain pen traced slow circles on the corner of his exercise book. There was a dead wasp at the base of the window, curled and desiccated, with half a wing missing. Alex imagined it suddenly huge and wicked, carrying him away like a dragon over the cricket pitch. Perched on its back, he smiled at the upturned faces of the players, pale with sudden shock, the wasp shadow passing dark over the umpire's pristine coat. The teacher's voice, whilst remaining audible, had become no more than a series of disconnected sounds that had no meaning. A dry marker squealed faintly on a whiteboard. A lazy bluebottle buzzed feebly at the window, but gradually those sounds dwindled in his ears as the wasp bore him away, big as a racehorse, bright as a jewel. Strange. As a boy with a well-founded reputation for inattentiveness in class the experience of daydreaming was familiar enough to him in general, but this time there was something different. It was as though time slowed down around him. Slower and slower, instants trickled by. And stopped. With a shudder Alex snapped out of it, recalled not this time by his teacher's irritated summons but by a sudden thrill of horror. The dream wasp vanished. The world stood still. Out on the field, a ball thrown from the boundary paused at the zenith of its lazy arc. Hardly daring to turn his head, Alex glanced furtively around him. The world was silent. The teacher stood immobile, pen raised, his mouth half open in mid-sentence. He had one gold tooth that sparked light as Alex rose slowly to his feet. Next to him Henry was frozen in the act of polishing his glasses. The bluebottle hung motionless in the still air above the faded globe at the front of the class. Alex surveyed the frozen world around him, the rows of statues that his classmates had become. He realised that his heart was thudding in his chest. He sat down, shook his head vigorously and the world suddenly continued with its business.

"… economic conditions," continued the teacher, as Henry carried on polishing his specs. "If you'd like to turn to page 42 in your books and have a look at the diagram."

At break Alex mentioned the strange time lapse to Henry as they waited their turn at the drinks machine. Henry was taller than Alex, but slighter, with unfashionably long hair. He was easily the brightest boy in the class, but because he had a tongue like a rapier he was never picked on by the big thick lads.

"It sounds odd alright," said Henry now, pushing his glasses further up his considerable nose. "My cousin's epileptic and he has these petit mal episodes when he's totally out of it for a few seconds."

"It wasn't like that," Alex told him. "Everything just froze. I was the only one who could move. Time stood still."

"Sounds brilliant," said Henry, who never really took Alex

very seriously. "All sorts of possibilities there. Maybe it'll happen in English. Then you can go and write stuff on Mr Keane's big old bald head."

"Cool!" snorted Alex with a nod, putting the idea away for later consideration.

"It's a thought alright," continued Henry, keeping the theme going indulgently. He was counting out change in his palm. "It's important always to turn every situation to your advantage, no matter how unpromising it looks. First rule of the SAS… or something like that… maybe it was the Brownies. No," he said on reflection, "deffo the SAS."

"Have you got any homework?" asked his mum that afternoon when he was dumping his school bag in the garage. As ever this was amongst the first things she said to him upon his return from his day's labours.

"Is there any chocolate?" he countered, coming into the kitchen and draping his blazer over the back of a chair in a manner that he knew to be highly provocative.

"There is if you left any yesterday," retorted Mum, setting down a bowl of food in front of their aged spaniel Rufus, who glanced at Alex apologetically and wagged his tail as if to say, "I'd be glad to greet you with my usual enthusiasm, but as you can see I'm otherwise engaged at present."

"What have you got on your hands?" asked Mum, wiping her own on a tea towel.

"It's nothin'," said Alex, glancing at the dense pattern of writhing forms he had earlier drawn on them in felt tipped pen. "Just a neural network of tiny metal threads so that when you touch a computer you interface with it directly and tap into the global mind."

"Really," said Mum, turning to the dishwasher. "Well get it washed off before tea, please. The global mind will have to manage without you." A thought struck her suddenly and she turned to Alex, her brow creased. "It'd better not feature on the school photo you had taken this morning. You know what your grandparents would think of that."

A tiny part of Alex's mind, one on the whole he was able to ignore, briefly considered this point and told him they would be displeased. His mum was a small, slender woman with anxious, bird-like movements and a way of biting her lower lip when distracted. She did this now, regarding her son's hands and then his blazer disapprovingly. By most standards she was rather too old to be the mother of anyone of Alex's age. Kate, his sister, was seven years older than him and in her third year at university. Rob, his twenty-four-year-old brother, was working in North London. But then Alex had apparently come along as a bit of an afterthought, or possibly a mistake, as Alex occasionally conjectured, although no one would ever admit it to him.

"I did it *after* the photo," Alex explained. "In Physics."

"Whoa!" said Mum. "Things have moved on in Physics since I was at school. Neural networks eh?" She grinned to demonstrate she was joking with him and tousled his hair playfully. "Go on now. Tea's in ten minutes, so no chocolate and biscuits for you. And go and get this blazer hung up. Do you want it to look like a piece of rag?"

Alex had no particularly strong feelings on this issue but he took it from his mum's outstretched hand and went up to his bedroom, chalking up for himself a minor point in having managed to avoid responding to Mum's question about homework. In fact there was French and Chemistry to be done. Unfortunately the worksheet that he needed in order to do the Chemistry was where he had left it in his locker at school. This would require a period of urgent attention in the ten minutes or so before lessons tomorrow. On the other hand the French revision he had been set could safely be ignored, which left the evening nicely open.

"Hmm," he said to himself, switching on his laptop and loosening his tie before slipping it over his head (an expedient that saved having to tie the knot again the following day). "What's the point in Chemistry anyway? I'm never going to be a chemist. I'm never going to be a physicist, a biologist or a geographer either."

His laptop, which had once belonged to his sister and was showing its age, took an eternity to boot up. Alex occupied this time by launching himself onto his bed in a manner that drew a squeal of complaint from the bedsprings. He rolled over to regard the ceiling thoughtfully. Above him, various models of aircraft stirred gently at the end of the dusty cotton threads from which they were suspended. Visions of his future passed before his eyes. He closed them. Now History… he could see the point in that, given that he envisaged himself as an archaeologist. There he was, in the parched desert of Morocco, leading a team excavating the remains of an ancient civilisation. He wiped the dust and grime from his brow as his trowel encountered something hard amongst the compacted sand in the bottom of the trench. He glanced around. One of his colleagues trundled a wheelbarrow along a plank that bridged a whole network of trenches excavated during the previous month. It was hot. The sun beat down on his sweating back. Sweat trickled cold down his rib. Someone in the neighbouring trench chuckled at some private joke as Alex scraped away at the sand. There it was – a tiny metallic glint. In his dream Alex closed his eyes, too, and opened them once more, taking a deep breath. He was conscious that his heart was suddenly hammering within his chest. Was this the moment? Abandoning the trowel, forgetting all his training, Alex clawed at the sand with his bare hands to reveal beautifully glistening gold, more and more of it, and the features of what could only be a royal death mask emerging from the earth like a swimmer from the ocean of ages. "Oh my god!" he murmured under his breath. "Is this it? Am I gazing upon the face of the king of Atlantis?"

That question hung in the air, unanswered as a text came in from Henry.

"Wnt 2 ply footy at mine?" was the query.

"Tea's on the table," called his mum from downstairs.

"After t," Alex texted back. Then he threw his phone into the laundry basket and rolled off the bed like a soldier lurching into a slit trench, a sudden artillery bombardment unleashing the fury of Hell all around him.

"Coming!" he shouted above the cacophony of exploding shells.

Tuesday's French test brought with it the realisation that there were a surprisingly large number of French words whose meanings remained mysterious to him. There were others that seemed vaguely familiar but hovered frustratingly just beyond the reach of his comprehension. Having set forth all his knowledge in the best part of five minutes, Alex found himself with a further fifteen to kill. Henry, he noted, was scribbling away industriously, brow furrowed in concentration. Erica, the fat girl with BO at the desk next to him, sat hunched over her paper in such a manner as to make it impossible for him to make out anything she had written. Nevertheless, she turned to eye him suspiciously from time to time and once, noticing that he had already set down his pen, gave a little sniff of disapproval. Alex sighed. In the corner of the test paper he began to draw out the outline of the continent he would create were he to be given god-like powers. Some knowledge of Geography, he had to concede, proved useful in this context. His teacher would undoubtedly have approved of the elaborate delta he had placed at the mouth of the continent's chief river. Soon, great forests of tiny trees marched along the flanks of high mountains and a Lilliputian city sprang up in a deep valley between two rocky spurs. He was putting the finishing touches to a series of lakes when he became conscious that a shadow had fallen across his world. Madame Aitken, his French teacher, was standing at his shoulder. Alex's pen paused in the act of creation. A moment passed. The shadow remained. Without turning his head or otherwise indicating that he was aware of her presence, Alex carefully wrote "le foret" next to one of the trees. There was a muffled snort from behind him and then Madame Aitken had moved on. "I wish, I wish I could just walk into this page," thought Alex, regarding his little kingdom with satisfaction. There'd be no French tests in Miroplagia – no French people either for that matter, with their selfish insistence on speaking a completely incomprehensible language. Alex glanced up at the clock and saw that there were seven minutes until morning break. The red second hand moved evenly between the numerals on its perimeter. Did it falter for a moment? Did it stop for a fraction of a second and then lurch forward once more? Alex rubbed his eyes. Time moved on. Had he imagined it?

At break he was somewhat preoccupied by the behaviour of the clock. Had he been fully in possession of his wits he would not have walked past Gary Payne carrying an open packet of sweets in plain view. Gary Payne was a large, crop-haired lad for whom Alex harboured feelings of deep loathing and resentment. Gary was a school bully in the traditional mould and had made Alex's first weeks in this school misery. Only teaming up with Henry had spared him from a regime of continual persecution. Gary had a worrying tendency toward violence and a dislike for intellectuals that stemmed from his inability to tell them apart from homosexuals. Because Alex knew more words than him (hardly a rare distinction) and was known to read a lot of books, Gary had him down as an intellectual.

"Oi, poof!" Gary greeted him, moving smoothly into his path. "Got some suck 'ave yer, Trophy?"

Since the beginning of time school bullies have been accompanied by a couple of brutish sidekicks and Gary was no exception. In this case it was smirking Mason Tennyson and wall-eyed Macaulay Pitt. Alex had a suspicion of people who had been given surnames for first names but he kept this to himself as Mason and Macaulay invaded his personal space on either side of him.

"Who are you calling a poof, you horrible knuckle dragging moron?" he imagined himself saying. "Yeah," was what he actually said, glancing warily around for possible sources of support. The space outside the tuck shop was busy with people queuing or standing about talking, but there was no one who seemed likely to intervene on Alex's behalf in what he foresaw with grim certainty was going to be a tuck mugging. Henry had gone to sign up for cricket practice after school. Nathan, another friend, was down in the lockers at the other end of the corridor.

"It's good to share, isn't it?" asked Gary, indicating Alex's packet of sweets meaningfully. Alex recognised that he lacked physical courage and didn't quite know what to do with them. It was too late to slip the colourful tube into his blazer pocket so he found himself gripping it tightly to his solar plexus region whilst a variety of emotions wrestled for control of him. There was indignation in large measure, fear in roughly equal proportion and regret that he hadn't already been to the toilet. Where was a teacher when you needed one? "I bet you'd like to let me have the rest, wouldn't you, poof?"

Alex found himself unable to speak for a moment. His mouth was suddenly dry and his tongue afflicted by a strange paralysis.

"Give!" said Gary suddenly, grasping for the sweets.

"Hey!" gasped Alex, instinctively snatching them away so that a brief tussle ensued from which there could be only one outcome. Alex was spared this by the sudden intervention of Jessica Murphy, an impressively large and assertive Year 11 girl with a face resembling a potato. For this reason she was generally referred to as "Spud," although rarely within her earshot.

"Hey! Leave him alone you big bully!" said Spud, shouldering her way past Macaulay and glaring into Gary's face. She was at least as intimidating as Gary, and with a cohort of her own pals there to back her up, Gary was suddenly outgunned.

"Come to stick up for your boyfriend have you?" jeered Gary, going on to mention a number of things he thought Spud could go and do with herself. Alex listened to this with interest now that the Gary threat was certainly quelled. As Mr Jones, the enormous Head of PE, hove in sight along the corridor, Gary moved off uttering a stream of imprecations that many people might have thought unkind or even hurtful. Spud merely shrugged and laughed uproariously with her friends, winking at Alex and giving his bum a sharp tweak before moving off towards the girls' toilet in regal splendour.

"What's going on?" asked Henry, turning up at Alex's side with masterly timing. "Do I detect romance in the air?"

"No you bloody well do not," said Alex, with feeling, conscious that his face was flushing a deep crimson. The humiliation of being rescued from his plight by a girl was almost too much to bear. "Come on, we'd better not be late for Chemistry. My homework's not going to win any awards."

Alex returned home to find a most unwelcome development, which had arrived through the letterbox in the superficially innocent form of a brown envelope. It might as well have been a letter bomb for its explosive impact on Alex's day. It contained his school report. The grim set of Mum's jaw and the glint of steel in her eyes when Alex walked in to the kitchen signalled danger ahead. Alarm bells were dinning away insistently by the time the brown envelope was brandished in his face.

"This," she said, tapping him on the head with it for emphasis, "Is your report." She paused to let Alex dwell on this prospect. "It does *not* make good reading. Let me see," she pondered as she snatched up her glasses and whipped the report out to read. "Mathematics... 3C... English... 2C... Design Technology, get this... 4D." She read through the whole list in a voice trembling with outrage. "And here's the grand finale," she said, shaking the page. "The considered opinion of your form teacher. Do you want to hear what Mr Burbage has to say about you?"

Alex had absolutely no desire to hear this now, or indeed ever, but he recognised there was no point in saying so. A display of submissive behaviour seemed in order. He hung his head. "*Alex is undoubtedly an intelligent pupil with a bright future, should he choose to exert himself,*" she read. "Get that? *Should he choose to exert himself.*"

Her face came worryingly close to Alex's as she stressed this last part. He was conscious of a little drop of her saliva on his chin, at first warm, now suddenly cold.

She carried on reading, jabbing a trembling finger at Alex's chest for additional emphasis. "*Unfortunately, Alex seems content to spend his time in lessons daydreaming. Until such time as he makes the decision to engage fully with his studies he is unlikely to fulfil his potential."*

"There!" she said, throwing the paper in the vicinity of his left ear. "What do you have to say to that?"

"It's only a grade report," he tried, after a moment's silent contemplation. "I mean, it's not a full report or anything."

"What difference does it make?" demanded Mum, ratcheting up the volume a couple of notches. "This is pretty much exactly what it said in your last full report. You promised me." She clenched her fists into tight, white-knuckled balls that Alex regarded warily. "You promised me you'd change! Didn't you? *Didn't you?*" she screamed.

There was a great deal more of this kind of thing, much of it wearisomely repetitive in nature, but there was no mistaking his mum's sincerity. In a manner that even he had to concede was all too familiar, he heard himself offering up apologies and earnest assurances of future good behaviour. He was sincere (so he told himself), he was contrite; he sat at the kitchen table with his head in his hands whilst Mum sat opposite, suddenly deflated, all the rage ebbing away from her. She looked old, tired and defeated. The skin hung loose around her jaw and her eyes were puffy and red-rimmed. Was she going to cry? Alex felt a catch in his throat. There was a frailty about her that affected Alex far more than her fury.

"I'll try," he said, reaching across to squeeze her hand. "I really will."

"You know your father'll blame me," she said quietly, reaching for a tissue and dabbing at her nose.

Alex's parents were separated. Three years ago his dad had walked out on Mum and set up house with a considerably younger and more attractive woman. Since that time this woman had in turn left Alex's father for a younger and more attractive man, which struck Alex as a delicious kind of irony.

Dad worked for an international plumbing supply company and so was out of the country for a good part of the year. As a thoroughly practical, down to earth sort of man with a passion for sport manifestly lacking in his youngest son he tended to take a dim view of Alex. He also took the view that Mum was far too indulgent of him, far too lax in her supervision. Dad would be getting a copy of the report, too.

"It's not your fault," Alex said. "I'll tell him it's all me."

He would, too. Alex felt suddenly fiercely protective of his mum and a great surge of guilt washed over him. He stood up and put his arm around her shoulders, whereupon she began to sob. Alex blinked back his own tears.

"I'll be better," he said, forcing the words through a throat that felt strangely congested.

"There's something wrong with time," he told himself later. He considered texting this sentiment to Henry but lifted his thumbs after the first character, thinking that it might make him look a bit mad. But there definitely was. He considered the unblinking eye of the clock on the wall above his bed and glared back at it, listening attentively for any sign of faltering in its soft, electric pulse. It was ten o'clock. He closed the Physics textbook he had set himself to learn by heart by the end of the next week and pushed away the page of scrawled notes. His History homework, four sides of well-presented arguments with carefully chosen references, lay complete on top of his printer. A number of abortive attempts, in the form of scrunched up paper balls, lay about on his desk top amongst a scatter of stationery and sweet wrappers. On an impulse he picked one up and threw it at the model Hurricane suspended above his head. It began to sway and spin crazily whilst motes of dislodged dust sparked in the light of his angle poise lamp.

He swivelled in his chair and subjected the clock to the closest of scrutiny. What would it be like to be a chrononaut? Which century would he choose to visit if he had a time machine? He imagined himself caressing the controls of a complex device that could, at the stab of a button, hurl him backwards or forwards through the whirling vortex of the centuries. Ancient Rome would be fascinating, of course. What about a trip to the Colosseum to see gladiators in action or a bit of chariot racing in the Hippodrome? "Cool," he said out loud.

There was something odd. Glancing upwards he noticed that the aircraft had stopped its gentle sway. "Huh?!" He lurched back in his chair.

"Lights out now, please," came Mum's voice from downstairs.

The Hurricane resumed its motion. Alex felt a vague prickling sensation over his scalp. In which order had those events just occurred? Had he imagined it?

"Alex?" called Mum when there was no immediate response.

"Okay," he called. "'Night, Mum."

"Did you get your report?" asked Henry on the coach the next morning.

"Oh, yeah!" said Alex, with feeling, heaving his bag into the overhead luggage rack.

"Bad was it?"

"You could say that," said Alex, slumping next to Henry.

"Did you get the full working over?"

"Worse than that."

"Oh my god! You didn't have the old girl in tears? You *bad* boy!"

"What about you?" countered Alex, more as an attempt to move the focus elsewhere rather than because there was any likelihood that Henry's report contained bad tidings."

"I got a 2B," said Henry with careful neutrality.

"No way! That was your best grade?"

"My worst," grinned Henry, springing the trap.

The coach was moving by now, having collected Alex and another boy from the last stop before school. Henry had a new phone, the features of which he demonstrated at some length during the journey. Two sixth form girls in the seat in front turned and wrinkled their noses as Henry broke wind ostentatiously in conclusion. Alex began to tell Henry that he thought there might be something wrong with time. He was doing this when there was sudden lurch accompanied by swearing from the driver as the coach pulled up sharply. A car had pulled out suddenly from a side street and a collision had only narrowly been avoided. Hoots and cheers from the children on the coach celebrated the moment. Only Alex remained silent. A glance at his watch revealed that the second hand had stopped moving, unless one counted a vague quivering.

"Time has stopped," he declared, his voice drowned out by the general hubbub.

Henry had heard though.

"Huh?" he said, indicating the many unmistakeable signs of activity in the world around them. "In what sense," he asked, all too reasonably, "Has time stopped? I think you'll find it's your watch that's stopped, mate."

They both studied the watch, the hands of which remained essentially motionless.

"Doh!" Alex slapped his own forehead.

"You've been giving this time thing a lot of thought, haven't you?"

It was in Mathematics, later that morning, that Alex made a vital discovery. In line with the new spirit of conscientious endeavour that he felt he owed to his mum, Alex had devoted himself wholeheartedly to his studies for the first half of the lesson. Given that he was quite good at Maths he quickly worked through the exercises he had been set to do and there were a few minutes to spare whilst the rest of the class caught up. Inevitably his attention was drawn to the clock, which in this case was hanging lopsidedly so that eleven o'clock was at the top of the dial. There were still twenty-two minutes until morning break, and in the absence of a second hand he found himself counting seconds until the minute hand ticked forward. Why did there have to be sixty seconds in a minute, or sixty minutes in an hour for that matter? Were he Emperor of the world, he might consider decimalising time. Having a hundred seconds in a minute would surely make more sense. It would simplify mathematical calculations involving chaps cycling 'x' distance in ten seconds, so how far would they go in an hour, supposing they didn't have to stop at traffic lights or drop in at the newsagents for a bag of crisps? Alex smiled to himself as he considered the meeting of leading scientists he would convene to discuss this revolutionary scheme. Outside, across the quadrangle, a pair of window cleaners was at work on the sports hall. A pigeon was caught in mid-flight, motionless, a few metres from the window. It took several moments for Alex to register this phenomenon. Then he gasped and span round, finding the classroom and everything within it likewise frozen into immobility. His biro slipped from his grasp and it was as though the tiny clatter broke the spell. The world got on with the day – the pigeon resumed its flight and Henry, sitting next to him, continued to change the cartridge in his fountain pen.

"It just happened again," he whispered.

"What?"

"You know… the time thing."

"You're crazy," Henry told him matter-of-factly, wiping inky fingers on his blazer. "Honestly. You are losing it, mate."

Chapter Two

But he *wasn't* crazy, and more than that, Alex now had a good idea what it took to stop time. He could hardly wait to tell Henry when the class streamed out at the end of the lesson.

"It's when I daydream," he said excitedly, grabbing Henry's shoulder and spinning him round to face him.

"Nuts," said Henry, tapping his head and making a whistling sound.

"Seriously," insisted Alex, with a note of pleading in his voice so sincere that Henry was obliged to give it serious consideration.

"Go on then. Explain how you, Alex aka Trophy Trueman of 9B, can single-handedly stop time."

"I know it sounds a bit unlikely," Alex was forced to concede.

Henry snorted, pulling a packet of biscuits out of his bag as they settled on a bench in the quadrangle. Spring sunshine was dappling the earth beneath a few struggling trees, the stirring shadows of branches passing across Alex's wrist as he studied his stopped watch.

"It's when I daydream," he said, tapping it thoughtfully on the bench top, on which there was an irregular scatter of crisp fragments.

He described the circumstances of the last few occasions that time had appeared to stand still. On each occasion he had been distracted, his mind moving onto a plane somewhat distant from reality, in a state that might almost be described as a trance.

"Okay," nodded Henry, absently throwing a piece of biscuit to one of several sparrows that were hopping about by the school minibus. "But nothing happened for me. How do you explain that? Time can't stand still for you and keep on going for me. That doesn't make sense, does it?"

"No," admitted Alex. "But it really happens. You've got to trust me."

"I'd like to see you prove it," said Henry, regarding him over his glasses.

And so he did. It happened again on Thursday, although unfortunately not in English, when Mr Keane's bald head was shining more glossily, more temptingly than ever. It was Maths once more, in the last lesson of the day, when Alex's concentration resources were stretched as thin as they ever were. Mrs Wade, whose own head had hair cut to resemble a German helmet, was talking about the importance of revision in her flat, nasal, northern voice. Alex, though, was setting foot upon Mars, his footprint there the very first, another giant leap for mankind. He gazed around him in wonder at the red and arid canyon, whilst behind him, reflected in the visor of his helmet, others of his crew cautiously descended from the vast and glittering spaceship. Vaguely, he was aware of the action in T16 grinding to a halt. Recalled from the red planet, Alex observed with interest as Mrs Wade froze slowly into immobility, her fingers turning the pages of a textbook. He felt no sense of panic; indeed, a sense of exultation was gathering in his breast. It was really happening. He felt the hair rise on the nape of his neck and a pulse throbbed at his temple. His mouth was suddenly dry as he waited for the spell to be broken once more, for time to lurch into action as though nothing had disturbed it. Heart racing, he pushed back his chair, the sound of it loud in the dense silence that had settled upon the room. Everything was quite still, just as it had been before. The clock had stopped at 3.34 pm. For a little while Alex stood stock still himself, waiting to see if anything would happen. Nothing did. Then, increasingly confident, he edged past Henry into the aisle between the desks and had a cautious wander around the classroom. He chuckled to himself as he surveyed his new kingdom. Such possibilities! His eyes darted from place to place as ideas suggested themselves to a mind that raced from project to glorious project. What to do first? At the back of the class sat Gary Payne, his mouth stretched wide in a yawn that revealed a glistening red cavern of opportunity. The notion of colouring in Gary's tongue was the first idea to come to mind, but then Alex noticed that there was a large piece of chewing gum between the thumb and fingertip of the boy's right hand. It had to be presumed that this was on its way to a final resting place underneath the desk.

"Hmm," said Alex to himself. Inspiration struck him. Reaching out he seized the gum between his own finger and thumb. To his surprise it was as hard and cold as a pebble. It was only with the greatest difficulty that he was able to work it loose, and then at last it came free with the same kind of suddenness that a magnet releases a nail. Once in Alex's hand the gum quickly recovered its soft, moist stickiness. Grimacing a little with disgust, Alex poked it carefully up Gary's left nostril, an orifice that was itself as stony as a statue's. Then, warming to his task, he took a felt tip pen from his pocket and wrote 'I am a moron' across Gary's narrow, pimpled brow in neat capital letters.

"Lovely," Alex said to himself, stepping back to admire his handiwork and then laughing until his sides ached.

At last, wiping tears from his eyes, he sat on the corner of a desk and considered his options. The bin next to Mrs Wade's desk proved to contain several used tissues, various bits of orange peel, pencil sharpenings and scrunched up paper. Having prised these free, Alex placed a selection of them in Gary's mouth. It felt as though about five minutes had passed, although of course the world around him remained fixed at 3.34pm. A series of experiments revealed that his other classmates, like Gary, were frozen as hard as stone. Everything was fixed in place by the same mysterious force that resisted attempts to move them. It was only by the greatest of exertions that he was able to free a few exercise books and move them about between desks. Once laboriously freed they reverted to normal book behaviour so that Alex was able to add a few witty inscriptions here and there before setting them down. When released, they reverted to stony immobility. At last, thinking that he had done enough for a first attempt, he rubbed his hands together in satisfaction. As an afterthought he crossed to the whiteboard and rubbed out the homework task that Mrs Wade had just applied there in a green spidery hand. Carefully prising the board marker from her hand he used it to write the words "How much more proof do you need?" in large capital letters. Then he returned the marker to its owner and sauntered back to his place with a broad smile of satisfaction.

It was time to get things moving again. But how? This was an issue that Alex had neglected to consider, dazzled as he was by the possibilities of his new powers. He settled into his seat and blinked his eyes. He dropped his biro a few times without effect. He clicked his fingers. Nothing happened. Or rather nothing continued to happen, much as before. Alex frowned. He snapped his fingers. No result. He cleared his throat. He said Shazzam, Abracadabra and Alleeoop, all with no effect whatsoever. He closed his eyes tight shut and opened them one at a time. He stuck his fingers in his ears and banged his forehead on the desk.

"Jesus!" he said when this didn't work either.

He felt a gathering wave of panic. What if he was stuck like this? He gasped. Tears were starting in his eyes when suddenly, after a vigorous shake of his head, the world started moving again. Myriad familiar sounds reached his ears once more, the almost imperceptible creaking of chairs, the click of pen on ruler, the low murmur of illicit conversation. Mrs Wade continued to turn the pages of her book, before adding to what she had written on the board, unaware as yet of Alex's addition to the board behind her.

"… And if you get time," she continued to say, "You might try exercise 4a on page 28 and… let me see…."

Sounds of alarm had been issuing from the rear of the classroom even as she uttered these words, and the last of her musings were drowned out by the sound of Gary Payne lurching to his feet, spitting, swearing loudly and clutching his nose.

"Gary Payne," she roared, throwing the book down on her desk. "I will not have language like that used in my lesson. Where on earth do you think you are? And get your filthy finger out of your nose. This instant, I say!"

"I'm sorry, Miss," came Gary's strangled voice from behind his hands. "I've got something stuck up my nostril."

"Well, you'd better go to the toilets and get it out!" she snapped. "And what the dickens have you got written on your head?" She narrowed her eyes as Gary stumbled past her. "Well, I've seen it all now. Don't expect me to argue with you on that score, you silly lad."

There was uproar in the class during the whole of this interlude, of course. Alex, whose initial relief at getting things back to normal had hardly yet worn off, thought his ribs would surely burst because he was laughing so much. Tears were streaming down his cheeks. Everyone was roaring and hooting with mirth as the unfortunate Gary hurried out into the corridor. Henry, though, was staring transfixed at the board behind their teacher. The look on his face when he eventually turned to Alex was one of wonderment.

"That was you," he breathed. "Wasn't it?"

Alex could only nod

"Alright. Enough, enough," said Mrs Wade, waving her hands ineffectually.

Henry was giving Alex a searching look.

"I'll tell you after," muttered Alex, dabbing his eyes with a tissue.

He felt like he was walking on air. Great waves of power surged through him. He was a phenomenon, a wonder of science, or nature, or magic or such like. Amazing. How could life ever be the same after this? He had god-like powers. Let Gary and his pals mess with him now. They could look forward to some sneaky, and most importantly, totally un-attributable retribution.

"That really, really *was* you, wasn't it?" Henry asked him as they sauntered towards the coach park at the end of school.

"Mmm, hhh," affirmed Alex gleefully, with a glance behind to see that no one else was in earshot.

"That is *sooo* weird," said Henry with a low whistle. "If I hadn't seen what you wrote on the board I'd never have believed it. Oh my god! That's the weirdest thing I ever heard of. Wow! How do you do it?" He turned to Alex earnestly. "Do you think you can show me?"

"You mustn't tell anyone," Alex told him. "Absolute top secret. D'you promise?"

"Yeah, yeah. Of course," Henry assured him, nodding fervently.

Alex told Henry all about it, every last detail, whilst they waited for the Cardenbridge coach. Henry listened, nodding thoughtfully as Alex recounted the problems he encountered in getting things moving once more.

"I'll try it myself tomorrow," he said. "Adventures in freeze frame, eh. What a scream! Double Physics should be as good a chance as any." He frowned. "You'll have to be very careful though, Alex."

"What do you mean?"

"Well, if there are too many hilarious and unexplained incidents happening to people you don't like, people are going to start asking questions, aren't they?"

"I guess so," shrugged Alex, feeling vaguely resentful that Henry was raining on his parade but conceding that he had a legitimate point.

Alex could hardly sleep that night. He lay awake long after midnight whilst the day's events replayed themselves in his mind. As yet he had barely dipped his toe into the vast ocean of possibility. Alex was not an especially mischievous boy but a strange and wonderful power seemed to have been bestowed upon him. It seemed ungrateful not to exploit it. As the clock on the wall above him ticked off the slow minutes of the night, Alex rehearsed the things he would do the next day: things moved, things looked at, things drawn or written upon, forbidden places visited. His restless mind teemed with delicious possibilities.

But at first they came to nothing, which was perhaps a good thing, all in all. Hollow-eyed from sleeplessness he shambled into school on Friday morning. His mum, who tended to be over-anxious regarding his health, had been all for keeping him away from school. For once, and to her surprise, Alex was insistent on struggling in regardless. She put it down to the new attitude he had promised to adopt with regard to his studies and squeezed his arm fondly as he hurried off to the end of the road where the coach stopped. Alex could hardly stop himself from running, despite the stubborn headache that had established itself above his left eye. If he had to drag himself there on his hands and knees that day he was going to school. Henry, when he joined him on the coach, was almost beside himself with excitement, having practised daydreaming since the moment he awoke.

And yet double Physics proved to be a big disappointment. Henry and Alex daydreamed with a single-minded inattentiveness that earned them both a stern rebuke from Doctor Brean, Head of Science. To no avail. Time proceeded with the tedious regularity for which it was famous. French and then Art followed break, but although Alex daydreamed with unheard of intensity, nothing at all came of it. Two chastened and downcast boys sat gloomily at lunch, listlessly toying with the sausages that were such a rare treat nowadays and which their peers were devouring with enthusiasm.

"I can't understand it," said Alex, regarding a suspiciously dark baked bean disapprovingly on the end of his fork. "It worked perfectly well yesterday."

"And I got a demerit from Hot Lips," grumbled Henry, referring to the Art teacher, Miss Houlihan. "I'm beginning to think you made it all up."

"Oh *are* you now?" retorted Alex hotly. "And what about Gazza's little motto on his bonce? I suppose that just materialised out of thin air. Funny how it wasn't there at the beginning of the lesson. And what about the chewing gum? I suppose a wicked pixie shoved it up his hooter. Who do you think wrote that on the board? Keep the faith, Henry."

"Yeah, well…" said Henry, glaring gloomily out of the window to where Mr Jones was loading tents into a minibus. "I don't know any more. I'm all mixed up about this."

After lunch came PE. It was harder to daydream here; hard, but not impossible, as Alex had once spectacularly demonstrated by being lobbed from thirty yards when he was in goal for Livingstone house. A few pensive moments off his goal line had cost his house a place in the final and Alex a week of painful derision from his team mates. He was late arriving at PE because he had lost the key to his locker and had to get the caretaker to cut off the padlock before he could get at his PE kit. Consequently the changing room was deserted as Alex pulled on his cricket whites. It was a warm afternoon. The distant sound of play on the field outside came in through the open window. Alex yawned, taking in a lungful of air redolent with stale sweat, liniment and compacted earth. He picked up his bat and made a few practice swishes with it, imagining a machine (accessible only to himself) which could download into his brain all the skills of the world's leading sportsmen. Used to batting at number ten for the house team and seldom being called on to bowl, he considered what it would be like to score the winning runs in the House Cup, to pull a mighty six over the top of the sports hall whilst the assembled school gasped and cheered. "Hooray for Alex!" they shouted as he pulled off gloves and helmet to celebrate his fifty, raising his bat to all sides of the ground.

Alex was suddenly conscious that it was quiet. The breeze that had stirred the bit of brown cardboard in the broken window pane above his head had ceased. The distant voices of cricketers were stilled. Alex felt his pulse quicken as he stepped out onto the pitch. On the bench behind the sports hall a boy with a sick note from his mother was frozen in the act of doing his homework. Two girls were walking past with a wire basket of rounders equipment. Out on the cricket pitch a game was in full swing. There was something majestic about the arrangement of the field, caught in a moment, third slip leaping like a salmon to his left, arm outstretched for the ball. The batsman, recognisable beneath his helmet as Henry, had a look of anticipated horror as the ball found the edge of his bat. All other eyes were directed at the ball, which had paused within an inch of the fielder's fingertips. It was curious to see a speeding cricket ball hang motionless in the air, more curious still to touch it and feel some powerful force resist the pressure of his fingers. Despite all of his exertions he was unable to pluck it from the air. He was able, however, to move it a little way, so that its trajectory would carry it past the fielder's hand, thereby sparing Henry's wicket.

"There you go, Henry," he said. "Don't say I never do you a favour."

Gary, absent from school that day, was spared Alex's attentions. By all accounts he had been deeply shocked by yesterday's events and Alex wondered if the two circumstances weren't connected. He was probably still wondering how someone had written on his head without him noticing, how half the contents of the bin had found their way into his mouth, how he had managed to shove a piece of chewing gum halfway through his sinuses. The answers weren't coming any time soon.

So what to do? The girls' showers proved to be unoccupied so Alex went into the gym, where a group of Year 8 girls were playing badminton. Shuttlecocks proved easier to move than cricket balls, but the consequences of so doing seemed so slight it was hardly worth the effort. At the far end of the gym a group of boys and girls were using the trampoline. His

26

heart leapt within him when he saw that the boy at the peak of his trajectory, mid-somersault, was Macaulay Pitt. How sweet would it be to move the trampoline from beneath him? But how dangerous, too, he was forced to concede, and he didn't actually want to kill Macaulay. Humiliation would do nicely instead.

Alex fetched a pair of scissors from the first aid kit in the PE Staff Room and climbed up on to the trampoline. Standing close to its centre he was at the perfect height for cutting away Macaulay's shorts and underpants. As he had come to expect it was very hard to manipulate the fabric. It was necessary to hold this in his hands for some time before it softened sufficiently for him to apply the scissors. After what felt like twenty minutes or so, the shorts were removed safely into Alex's pocket. The prospect of severe revulsion came between Alex and removing Macaulay's pants, particularly since they were none too clean. He contented himself with making a couple of deep strategic cuts, leaving only a few connecting threads, so that they would certainly fall away the moment time re-started.

"Sweet," said Alex, surveying his handiwork with the pride of an artist.

It took some time to find his next target. Mason, whose bad feet disqualified him from PE, was loitering in the area of litter-strewn scrubland beyond the playing field, known euphemistically as the 'nature reserve'. Here, he was refreshing himself with a cigarette. Many of the shrubs hereabout were permanently stunted, such was the popularity of this place amongst the nicotine addicted. Alex approached Mason warily, leaning close to inspect the glowing red end of the cigarette. He found that although it appeared to be alight it gave off no heat, so he was quite able to hold it between thumb and forefinger to pull it free from Mason's fingers.

Having done this he reversed the cigarette and slid it back so that the glowing end was placed between Mason's lips. As an afterthought he tucked the remains of Macaulay's shorts into Mason's pocket, leaving a corner hanging out for easy recognition.

"Perfect," he said.

Having exacted full vengeance for his humiliation earlier in the week, Alex walked jauntily across to the main block to have a look in the staff room. This proved less stimulating than he had hoped because Mr Keane, whose bald pate he longed to inscribe with some witty motto, was nowhere to be found. Alex was reading with interest some of the confidential material on the staff notice board when a vague sense of disquiet in the pit of his stomach told him it was time to move on. And it was not a moment too soon. He had only just stepped out of the staff room when the world resumed its motion around him. He found himself suddenly face to face with Mr Davis, the Headmaster, whose presence in the corridor he had momentarily forgotten about. It was hard to say who was most shocked, since to the Headmaster it must have appeared that a boy had suddenly materialised in his path. Physical collision was only narrowly averted but nevertheless Alex was treated to a close encounter with the great man's famously lethal halitosis. For this reason Mr Davis was generally referred to as "Death Breath."

Mr Davis emitted a strangled yelp and grasped Alex's shoulder for support.

"Good God, boy! Can't you look out where you're going?!" he roared, it being quite out of the question that he himself might have been guilty of inattention.

"I wasn't in the staff room, sir," Alex heard himself blurt out before the initial panic had abated. His next action, placing a hand over his mouth, seemed equally unwise when considered dispassionately, but neither this nor the sudden pallor of his face seemed to register with the Headmaster, who merely glared at him fiercely before striding into his office. Alex took a couple of deep breaths and headed back to the sports hall. There was a great deal to think about. It seemed that Henry would be unable to join him in his adventures. Alex would have to get used to the idea of exploring the freeze frame world on his own. In purely practical terms stopping time seemed to have become much easier, but as for the mechanics of setting things going again, well, that remained as much a mystery as ever.

There had been something of a commotion in the gym, so Alex discovered when he made his way back through to the changing rooms. In the corridor outside, one of the more sensitive girls in Year 8 was being counselled, red-faced, by a couple of the female PE staff. A number of other girls stood about giggling gleefully amongst themselves. The PE staff room door was closed, but Alex could hear raised voices from behind it, one of which belonged to Macaulay, raised in plaintive denial.

"Shorts don't just vanish into thin air, lad!" asserted Mr Jones. "And whatever have you done to your pants? Were you *trying* to make a spectacle of yourself? Eh? Answer me, boy!"

Alex found it necessary to retreat into the boys' changing room before the effort of containing his mirth ruptured some internal organ. Once in there he leaned against a wall and laughed until the tears ran down his face. He was still laughing intermittently when he joined the others at cricket and was assigned to his usual place on the boundary, where it was thought he could do least harm. Henry, still batting after his narrow escape a few minutes ago, struck the ball a fierce blow which carried over the bowler's head and out towards the rounders pitch. This was sufficiently far from Alex for him to stand idly by with a clear conscience. The umpire, Mr Khan, signalled a four. Henry stamped his feet as the ball made its way back to the bowler. On the far side of the pitch a small figure, recognisable as Mason, emerged from the nature reserve, rubbing his mouth with the back of his hand. He was heading for the changing rooms where he would doubtless encounter Macaulay. Even from this distance Alex could see the white scrap of shorts hanging out of his blazer pocket. Alex's team had a spinner on now and Henry's batting partner put on a resolutely negative defensive display for the ensuing over. The change of field meant that Alex could cross to the side of the pitch closer to the gym and the sports hall. From here, closer to the open windows of the changing rooms, Alex could enjoy the sweet, sweet sounds of Macaulay discovering that Mason was in possession of his shorts. This had clearly placed a strain on their relationship. Mason, who was somewhat smaller than Macaulay, soon re-emerged from the changing room clutching a bloodied handkerchief to his nose. Henry, leaning on his bat, glanced across to see what was going on. Alex beamed across at his friend, licked his finger and made a long downward stroke in the air before him.

Chapter Three

The next day was Saturday. Alex awoke in a decidedly optimistic frame of mind. On Sunday his grandfather was taking him to an airshow at the local RAF base. He had been looking forward to it for weeks. But there was Saturday to get through first and Saturday afternoon meant going shopping with his mum. This was undoubtedly a hardship. Still, the golden anticipated glow of the following day reached even as far as Cardenbridge Mead, the rather seedy shopping precinct in the centre of the town, whilst he trailed with his mum from one shoe shop to another. There were only three shoe shops left in Cardenbridge, given that most of the smarter shops had migrated to the big new shopping centre at Collingwood, a few miles to the south. By this point, stopping time had become almost an obsession for Alex. He daydreamed extensively in all three shoe shops whilst his mum tried on what seemed like a significant proportion of their stock. It was in Wardworths, one of the bigger shops in the High Street, however, that Alex finally rediscovered his gift. He was queuing with his mum at the checkout, clutching a vacuum flask and a pack of batteries. It was stuffy. A pig-faced girl at the checkout cast her eyes upward in frustration over something and rang the bell for her supervisor. Alex shuffled his feet. He thought of the airshow and suddenly he was swooping upon the assembled crowds behind the control column of a Spitfire Mark IX. Hauling back on the stick, the throaty roar of the mighty Merlin engine loud in his ears, Alex pulled into a slow barrel roll. A moment later and he was over Normandy in 1944, a Messerschmitt 109 abruptly sliding before his gun sights. Instinctively, Alex squeezed the button on the grip and felt the fighter judder as his cannon spat deadly shells. Bits flew off his foe and the starboard wing disintegrated in a puff of black smoke. Alex pulled into a tight turn and watched as a tiny white parachute blossomed far below. So absorbed was Alex in the movement of this unfolding drama he hardly noticed that Wardworths, and everything in it, had ground to a halt. At length, with a start, he realised that all was still around him.

"Way to go," he said, with a slow nod.

Alex went for a joyful wander around the shop. One of the tills was open and he could have helped himself to a handful of bank notes had he wished to. It was the same with the pick 'n' mix. He eyed the confectionary hungrily for a few moments before moving on. Alex wasn't one of those boys who think a tiny theft is a thing of no consequence. After quite a short time Alex grew bored. He found, as expected, that everyone in the shop was completely rigid, hard as stone. As before, it was strangely difficult to move things, as though everything was held in place by powerful magnets. But once the force was broken, objects that had felt like stone became quite normal once more. He tugged at an improbably granite-like balloon until it came away from the grip of the toddler who had held it. Then it was suddenly feather-light in his hand. He carefully replaced it, and with a click it snapped into place, restored to stony rigidity. He swapped the contents of two of the hand-baskets carried by people queuing at the till but he had no particular grudge against anyone in Wardworths. The possibilities seemed limited here. It was simply much more fun at school. He pulled out his phone from the top pocket of his shirt and found it to be useless. It would have been surprising if there had even been a signal, but in fact the screen was quite dead. He shrugged. So, to get things going again…

Remembering previous experiences, Alex resumed his place in line, picked up his vacuum flask and batteries and gave his head a good shake. A minute or so later he was groggy from shaking his head and beginning to feel the first stirrings of panic.

"It's okay," he told himself. "This might take a little time. Patience is the thing."

And it might have been, but whereas yesterday Alex had been too busy to feel even the beginnings of anxiety, here there was nothing much to do and lots of time to dwell on the consequences of being stuck outside of time. He stamped his feet. He paced up and down the shop impatiently.

"Come on, come on," he said.

By what might have been an hour later, Alex was nearly sick with fear. His purchases were disregarded on the floor. For a short time he took to jumping up and down, clutching his head.

"Oh, no!" he said. "Don't panic. Don't panic. Stop saying everything twice, for God's sake… What on earth am I going to do now?"

His voice echoed hollow in the eerily silent shop. "What am I going to do? Oh Jesus, help! What am I going to do?"

He felt a catch in his throat and a tremor in his lower lip that he arrested only by biting it. A hot tear escaped from his right eye and trickled down his cheek, rapidly followed by one from his left. He blinked his vision clear for a moment and then surrendered himself to despair, head sunk on chest, his body racked by long gasping sobs. There is only so long a boy can realistically blubber for. Because his watch had stopped at 2.23 – and so had all the other clocks in Wardworths – it was impossible to tell how long Alex managed it. It seemed like a long time though. Much of it he spent clutching the column of rock that so closely resembled his mum, caught in the act of reaching into her bag for her purse. There was a disagreeably damp patch on her jacket by the time the tide of Alex's emotion had ebbed away. At length he wiped nose and eyes on a conveniently placed tea towel, glancing around glumly for inspiration. None came. Muttering anxiously to himself, he threaded his way out of Wardworths through an open door and into the High Street. A stationary traffic jam had formed behind a lorry unloading a pallet of fizzy drinks. A cyclist in skin-tight shorts balanced precariously atop his spindly machine as Alex hurried past. A Big Issue seller with a dog on a rope took an interminable swig from a brown plastic bottle. Walking fast, running at times, Alex made his way towards the police station on the ring road. He had great faith in the powers of the police. Perhaps amidst all this rigidity the servants of the law maintained a patient vigil. He was soon disappointed. The outer door was shut, and it took all Alex's strength and determination to force it open.

It was no use, of course. The fat desk sergeant was frozen in the act of opening a filing cabinet. A woman and child stood immobile by the counter, the child clutching a packet of crisps. Alex took in the situation at a glance and beat on his forehead with his clenched fists. He returned to the pavement outside, where he noticed for the first time that an accident was about to happen close by. A small fast car, pursued by a police car with flashing lights, was about to hit two girls crossing the ring road. Caught up in their own chatter, they were dashing out into a gap between cars. They had already crossed two lanes and were emerging into the third. They were never going to make it. The taller of the two girls was glancing up as the car hurtled towards them, an expression of horror frozen on her face. The other was still oblivious to the peril, her head turned away from the oncoming car.

Alex had problems of his own, but even so he stumbled to a halt, momentarily transfixed by this tableau. Not that there was anything he could do. Even if time sprang into action again he would never be able to warn them in time. Turning his back on this compelling spectacle with some difficulty, he set off back towards Wardworths. Bizarrely, as he threaded his way along a passage that led back to the High Street, the world stuttered briefly into action around him. Pedestrians resumed their paces, pigeons continued their flight and behind him on the ring road there was a screech and a sickening crunch, followed by the continuous sounding of a car horn. Then time froze once more, this time with a strange finality that filled Alex's heart with dread.

Nothing much had changed in Wardworths. Alex's mum had got as far as pulling her purse from her bag. The girl on the till had turned her head a little. That was all. Alex threw himself down at his mum's feet and wept a little more. Weeping bitter tears continued to achieve absolutely nothing, as Alex eventually had to concede. Time, as measured by conventional means, was completely frozen. Time, as measured by Alex's stomach hurried on. He was hungry and this organ was not one for keeping its needs to itself, even in times of crisis. His watch appeared, like all other visible clocks, to have stopped working, and this despite having had a new battery installed in it that same morning. Nevertheless, it was quite clear to Alex that it was around about tea time. In the circumstances he thought it would be acceptable to help himself to food. Surely most rational adults would concede that being stuck in time counted as an emergency. When he got back to reality he would pay for anything he had to take now.

Alex helped himself to a sandwich and a soft drink from

Boots. He sat outside to consume these in the open space with the little fountain that his father said brought eternal disgrace upon the town of his birth. Installed in the 1960s, it consisted of a number of stainless steel tubes from which were suspended what looked like a few glass light shades. A meagre trickle of motionless water splashed onto the concrete base. Alex regarded this with interest. Tiny droplets of water were suspended in the air like beads of glass. On the whole he was a resilient boy and already practical matters were starting to drive panic and despair out of his mind. Doubtless he would *eventually* get back into reality, so until that time he just had to bide his time and look after himself. He knew he shouldn't stray too far from his mum because questions were going to be asked if the world got moving again and he was suddenly found to be at home, or up at the park. He didn't suppose he would quickly starve, given the amount of readily available food in Cardenbridge, so once he had fetched himself an apple for his conscience's sake and a really large bar of chocolate for the rest of him, he began to recover some of his composure. He set off back towards the ring road to see what sort of accident had happened, feeling a twinge of apprehension as he returned along the passage past the pet shop and the cheap jeweller's. At the end of the passage several bystanders were caught in the act of swivelling to watch some sudden event. An elderly woman's jaw hung slackly, horror frozen in dull old eyes. Cautiously, Alex followed her gaze and stepped out into the road. The car that was being chased had smashed into a concrete lamp post. It was a mess, the front crumpled almost beyond recognition. Whoever was in it was going to be a mess, too. One of the two girls was sprawled in the road, her arms extended to break her fall. It was clear that she had narrowly avoided being hit. Presumably the car had swerved at the last moment, left the road and smashed into the lamp post. Of the other girl there was no sign. Alex felt a little queasy as he surveyed the scene. He approached the ruined car but hesitated to look inside. There was what might have been blood splashed on the windscreen. He backed away.

He resolved to go home. There were bound to be awkward questions asked if time sprang into motion again, but he couldn't hang about in the town centre indefinitely. At least at home he could make himself comfortable. The walk would take him no more than twenty minutes, if he maintained a brisk pace. Fortifying his resolve with chocolate, Alex set off through the eerily silent streets of his home town. At first the pavements were crowded with frozen shoppers and it was vaguely irksome to have to weave between them, but soon he was walking along the ring road where there were lots of stationary cars but only one pedestrian, at least in this section, a workman frozen in the act of unloading his van. When it was time to cross the ring road he used the pedestrian underpass. This stemmed partly from force of habit and partly from concern that he would be run over if time suddenly restarted when he was halfway across. As he emerged from the underpass a shadow passed over him. This was such an unexpected event that he flinched, twisted and craned his neck upwards.

"Whoa!" he said.

Although the world around him remained firmly immobile, a large dark object was passing above, silhouetted by the afternoon sun. Alex shielded his eyes. The object was moving smoothly but unhurriedly at a height of about twenty metres. Alex could perhaps have kept up with it at a sprint. Not that he did. He occupied himself by trying to reconcile in his mind the two notions of seals and flying in the air. Seals, he assured himself, were aquatic creatures and lacked the capacity for flight. So biologists believed. Nor were seals as large as this. The tail was the wrong shape, too, so was it a seal? It was almost impossible to tell now, as the rapidly diminishing object slid towards the gap between the spire of St John's and the multi-storey car park.

"No way," he said, as though this would somehow help to cast out illogicality. "No way," he said again, shaking his head for emphasis. He stepped up on a low wall for a moment and watched with interest as the object vanished behind the spire.

It occurred to Alex that his journey home would be enlivened by a little experimentation. In a world where seals (or things like seals) could get away with zooming about in the air, all the usual rules of behaviour were suspended. Simply because it pleased him to do so, he began clambering and walking over the bonnets, roofs and boots of the cars parked on Merrick Street. He whistled and sang as he did so, challenging the uncanny silence of the street. He found the effect satisfactory rather than otherwise and grinned at the thought of what Henry would make of it, or Nathan, or any of his other friends if they could see him now. But they couldn't, because they were trapped in 2.23pm and he was free as a bird, in a world where time was all his own. But what if he was trapped here forever? He stopped, slid down from the windscreen of a four-by-four and fought back tears once more.

"Oh my god, oh my god, oh my god," he said, like a mantra, running his hands through his hair. "What am I going to do?"

A part of Alex, a part somewhat distanced from the rest of him, recognised that he was subject to worrying mood swings just now.

He had to get home. Suddenly, his room, his bed, his duvet seemed like sanctuary in a world that had gone mad. He began to run, eyes dim with suppressed tears, nose suddenly streaming, through streets that were strange yet familiar. As a boy who took no particular pleasure in running and who had feigned illness on more than one occasion to avoid it at school, Alex found himself gasping, staggering, clutching at a searing stitch in his side, well before reaching home. Turning into Carlton Avenue he found himself suddenly face to face with another boy, a boy who had been stooping to gather up a sheaf of papers. This boy was very definitely not frozen. Alex lurched to a halt, panting, blinking, taking in a deep breath into his aching lungs and holding it, holding it. The boy let a few sheets slip from his grasp once more. They fluttered around his feet. The boy recovered first.

"What's the hurry?" he asked after a long moment in which they merely stared at each other.

"Hi," said Alex warily. He gestured vaguely. "I was er... running."

"Yes," agreed the boy, picking up some more sheets of paper but without taking his eyes off Alex. "I can see that."

He was a little shorter than Alex but carrying a lot more weight. A shock of curly hair topped off a head that tapered somewhat from neck to crown. He had a soft, round face and round glasses, too, which glinted as he straightened up.

Alex sniffed and wiped his nose on his sleeve in a manner that would have distressed his mum.

"How is it you're not... you know, like everyone else?" he finished lamely.

"You're new here, aren't you?" said the boy, approaching Alex. "I never saw you before. I thought I knew everyone here. That's weird. I never saw anyone new before. Where were you going?"

"Home."

"Uh, huh," the boy said as he blinked and pursed his lips, curiosity apparently satisfied. "Well, see you around then."

Holding the papers tight to his chest he set off briskly towards the town centre, with a backward glance of what might have been apology.

Alex stood for a moment and watched him go. Then the various thoughts that had been competing for prominence in his mind fell suddenly into order.

"Hey!" he shouted after the boy's retreating back. "What do you mean, *new?*"

The boy seemed not to have heard. Alex hurried after him and caught up just as he was crossing the bottom of Akeman Road.

"Wait a mo'," he said, catching at the boy's sleeve. There were a great many questions jostling for attention in his head, but the one that popped out sounded rather lame. "What's going on?"

The boy regarded him thoughtfully for a moment.

"That's a big question," he conceded, glancing first at Alex and then in the direction he had been walking. "I'm guessing things seem a bit odd to you. I suppose I'd better fill you in. Look, do you mind if we talk as we walk 'coz I'm in a bit of a hurry? My name's Will, by the way."

"Alex," said Alex, shaking the rather pudgy hand that was extended to him.

In the distance, beyond the flats by the ring road, another airborne seal could now be made out, gliding smoothly towards them.

"What is *that?*" he asked, nodding at the creature as it approached before disappearing behind the row of Victorian houses at the top of Hampden Hill.

The other boy turned, regarded it dispassionately and shrugged. "Dugong, I think. Could have been a manatee though. I didn't get a good look at it. I've not been keeping track today. Too much on, you see."

"Aren't they supposed to be water creatures?" asked Alex, reasonably enough.

"Ordinarily yes," agreed the boy. "But not here. They fly. Oh dear, it must all be a bit confusing for you."

"Well, yes, you could say that," said Alex. It was an enormous relief to find someone apparently normal in circumstances that were anything but.

"I was just going to the park to find Ganymede," said the boy. "He's the guy in charge around here. I guess you'd better check in with him if you've just arrived."

Together, they set off back along the ring road, retracing Alex's route past the stationary police car. Its rear was raised up as the officers inside slammed on the brakes. There was a cloud of dust. Two black lines of scuffed, skidded rubber extended behind its wheels.

"Nasty accident," commented Alex, nodding at the scene as they passed, moving in and out of the other motionless pedestrians.

"Yes. I suppose it is," agreed Will. "I hardly notice it any more. It's just… you know, part of the furniture."

"Right," said Alex, thoughtfully. "Have you been here long then? Isn't everything about to get going again any minute now?"

Will laughed. He pushed his glasses up his nose, which reminded Alex of Henry.

"I shouldn't think so. Once you're here, you're here. And as for time, well, 'Sticia is not *in* time, exactly."

"What's 'Sticia?" asked Alex.

"This is *Intersticia*," answered Will, waving vaguely at the frozen world around them. "Except mostly it's just called 'Sticia. What does Ganymede say? Oh yes, it's like an old-fashioned film. You know how a strip of film looks like a row of pictures with tiny black spaces in between? Yes? Each picture is a little snapshot of a moment in time. When we see a film at the cinema the pictures get shown to us so quickly it fools our eye into thinking we're seeing continuous movement. You know what I mean? Hmm?"

Alex nodded. "Yeah," he said cautiously.

"Well, Intersticia is like the space between instants, the world that exists in the little black strip between frames."

It sounded unlikely, but then Alex found himself in no position to argue. The little that he knew of physics, the simple certainties of existence, were suddenly called into question.

"There must be millions of them then," he observed. "Billions even."

"More than that," continued Will as they rounded the corner into Cheltenham Road. "There are an infinite number of them; as many as there are instants in time. They all have names, too. One of the angels told me what this one was called once. It took him ages to say it. The last tiny part of it sounded a bit like Hammersmith, so that's what we call it. 'The Hammersmith Intersticial,'" he finished, having a little chuckle to himself about this, while Alex considered the content of Will's last couple of sentences. There was a lot to go at.

"Who're *we*?" asked Alex, making a start.

"Oh, you know… There's about seventy of us. Mostly the whole crowd sucks. Lots of oldsters – some of them completely barking." He tapped his temple meaningfully.

"I haven't seen anyone except you yet," said Alex, glancing behind him as they passed the Red Lion.

"Yeah, well, 'Sticia isn't exactly Piccadilly Circus," acknowledged Will. "And most of us tend to stay out of the middle of town. Too many stiffs about." He smothered another giggle. "Sorry, I shouldn't say that. 'Staticons' we're supposed to call them, but Paulo calls them 'stiffs'. Quite funny actually, don't you think?"

Alex gathered Will was referring to the frozen people, one of whom Will slapped casually on the back as he walked past.

"Most of us hardly notice them anymore. They're just, you know…"

"Part of the furniture?" supplied Alex.

"Yeah, something like that. You see there are actually three states of existence, so Ganymede says. There's Reality. That's what we both dropped out of accidentally, like; there's Statica, that's the frozen moment of Reality that's all around us; and there's 'Sticia, that's us and everything else that doesn't belong to Statica. Weird I know. It still freaks me out when I think too hard about it. You'll get used to it though."

"I don't want to get used to it," said Alex, with feeling. "I just want to get out of it."

"Don't we all," said Will, with a hollow laugh. "I shouldn't hold your breath though. I've been here ages."

"Define *ages*," said Alex warily.

"I don't know," said Will, a little irritably, as though this were a foolish question. "Just ages and ages."

As they approached the park there were fewer pedestrians around. A large lorry was negotiating the roundabout in front of the imposing formal entrance with its marble pillars and its ornate wrought iron gates. Some moron had spray painted his name across one of the piers in large, ill-formed letters. The park was a popular haunt of morons after dark. Idiots, cretins and other losers went there, too. Will seemed to be anxious to get there quickly. He lengthened his stride as they approached the gates. Alex and Will passed through, hurrying down the parade, past the war memorial, past skateboarders, kids on bikes with stabilisers, mothers with buggies, the usual crowd on a Saturday afternoon, but immobile now and utterly silent.

"Odd isn't it?" said Will, noticing Alex's bemused expression. He pulled Alex aside to avoid his imminent collision with a pink Frisbee, paused in mid-air at head height, halfway across the parade.

"Yes, I think you could say that… what's that?" asked Alex, stopping suddenly. There was music, the first sound he had heard here, other than Will's voice. It might have been an accordion.

Will had carried on. "That'll be Ganymede," he said over his shoulder. "Come on, you'd better introduce yourself."

"Who's this Ganymede, then?" asked Alex, hurrying to catch up.

"He's the Main Man," said Will. "The Obergruppenführer. The Head Honcho. The Top Dog. Watch your step. He's on a bit of a short fuse, and well… he can do magic. Sort of. I don't really believe in magic myself, you understand, but I don't know how else you can explain it. This guy argued with him once and Ganymede struck him dumb. Completely mute. Never spoke again. I didn't see it myself but that's what they say. So, like I said, watch your step."

It was obvious enough that Will was genuinely scared of this Ganymede character, despite the light-hearted tone of his voice. Feeling a tiny thrill of apprehension, Alex moved up a little closer to his new friend. Will was pretty much all he had just now.

In the bandstand was an elderly vagrant of some kind, leaning against one of the pillars that supported the roof. He was playing the accordion that Alex had heard as they approached along the parade and he now looked up as they climbed the steps. The tramp was wearing fingerless gloves, a battered felt hat and at least three layers of coats. He had an enormously bushy beard and wild grey hair, so that he looked like a picture that Alex had once seen of Karl Marx, the founder of communism. The tramp continued to play the accordion as they entered the bandstand, seemingly unaware of their presence.

"So, where's this Ganymede then?" asked Alex, out of the side of his mouth, looking curiously at the tramp.

"Er, this *is* Ganymede," said Will, shuffling his feet awkwardly. There was a distinctly nervous edge to Will's voice. He stepped forward, dipping his head ever so slightly as though not sure whether he should be making a bow. "Ganymede, I, er…" he stuttered as he glanced apologetically at Alex. "I mean, what did you say your name was?"

"Alex."

"I found someone new," he finished lamely.

The tramp played a last few wheezing notes on his accordion and turned his gaze upon Alex. He had eyes like laser beams. Alex could see why Will was nervous. It felt like Ganymede was looking right through his eyes and into his head. Nor was he much liking what he found there.

"So," he said, stretching this word out more than was strictly necessary and injecting into it a disagreeably sarcastic tone. "A new recruit… Welcome to my little kingdom." A nod of his shaggy head and a wave of his free hand encompassed the park and presumably all that lay beyond it. Alex judged from Ganymede's tone that he wasn't going to be rolling out the red carpet any time soon. It had a rough, gravelly edge to it that fairly set Alex's teeth on edge. He didn't say anything at all for a while after that, merely considering Alex through narrowed eyes as though he thought he might be a dangerous criminal. Alex and Will stood awkwardly. Will fidgeted with his papers.

"I've done my quadratic equations," he said at last when speech of some kind began to seem absolutely essential. He offered them up in Ganymede's direction.

Ganymede didn't so much as spare them a glance. Alex

thought this rather rude, but kept his opinions to himself for now.

"Well," he said, addressing Alex. "You'd better know the rules. This is my sector and everyone in it answers to me. You will be given food and drink sufficient to sustain you, and bedding materials. In return you will perform any work task I consider appropriate. Without question – is that understood?"

Well, it wasn't, but Alex found himself nodding nevertheless. Ganymede approached Alex and loomed over him in a manner that he found most disconcerting.

"You will not interfere with the staticons in any way. Likewise, you will not interfere with any aspect of Statica. Do you understand?"

"Yes," said Alex, cautiously, as Ganymede continued to glare at him.

There was a long and rather awkward silence during which Alex had to work hard at not shuffling his feet and keeping his eyes cast down.

"Very well," said Ganymede at last, nodding his head slowly. "You will come back and see me tomorrow. Then I shall assess you properly. Goodbye."

There was such utter finality in the way Ganymede said this that Alex and Will immediately turned on their heels and withdrew, doing their best not to run.

"Hey!" roared Ganymede behind them. "William! Where do you think you're going?"

Will looked like he'd been shot in the back. He rushed back with his papers, pressing them into Ganymede's outstretched hand. Then they both ran.

They didn't stop running until they reached the park gates. Will, like Alex, was not a natural athlete but had the added disadvantage of carrying with him a rather prominent paunch.

He hunched panting, head bowed, hands braced against his knees.

"What's *his* problem?" asked Alex in outraged tones when he could get his own breath.

"He's always like that," said Will between gasps. "Everyone's scared to death of him. Well, maybe Paulo isn't, but Paulo's a bit different." He looked up. "Come on, I suppose you'd better stay with me tonight."

A large number of questions continued to suggest themselves to Alex's mind. One of them – "What does Will mean by *tonight* when time is meant to be frozen?" – was soon answered in an emphatically visible way. It was going dark. Although the clouds remained stationary in the sky, the heavens behind them began to darken. A moon, not quite the same moon that Alex was used to, began to edge itself up above the clock tower of the boys' school. It was a slender crescent moon, but the dips and hollows on its surface were subtly unfamiliar. Finding this somewhat unsettling, Alex did his best to ignore it as he followed Will back across Cardenbridge, to a small terraced house in Gladstone Street. Here, what Alex was already beginning to think of as a 'stiff', a young woman, was opening the door to what might have been a neighbour. There was room for Alex and Will to squeeze past and into the hall.

"I usually sleep in the back bedroom," said Will as they mounted the stairs, past a child clutching an electronic toy. "Some of us sleep outside, but it's too cold for me at night. Besides, there's plenty of houses like this that are easy enough to get into."

In the back bedroom there proved to be no bed, only a stack of boxes and an area of clear floor on which there was a large pile of blankets. It was dark in here, although the fake 'Stician moon shed a pale rectangle of light on one wall. Will produced something that looked like a candle and snapped the end off it, whereupon it began to glow, bright enough to cast sharp shadows around the room.

"Light stick," explained Will. "We get eight a week. I guess they last a couple of hours or so. And as for blankets, well, you can never have too many of them. And these are 'Stician ones, of course. Ganymede gets them for you. You can't sleep on any of the beds 'cause they're all hard as rock. Floor's as good a place as any. You'd better share some of my stuff tonight. Ganymede'll fix you up tomorrow, I guess."

Alex looked around him with interest as Will set about pulling the blankets into two roughly equal piles. It was impossible to tell without touching them which objects in the room were 'Stician and which Statical. Alex supposed the scatter of papers on the top of packing case must be 'Stician, likewise the biro and the glasses case.

"Are you keen on maths then?" asked Alex, indicating the scrawled figures on the paper.

"Not likely," said Will, with a hollow laugh. "That's the whole point of it, see. Quadratic equations! I ask you. I didn't even know where to begin. Dan Cutler up in Thurston had to show me how to do them. But that's the point – Ganymede won't give you anything to do you can easily do; he's a sadistic sod. He'll find out all about you tomorrow and then he'll make you do something you hate. Look at poor old Mrs Patterson. She's about a hundred and fifty years old and she has to shovel a big pile of sand from one end of her street to another. Next week she has to shovel it all back again. Best thing you can do is say you hate reading books or something. Maybe he'll give you a nice pile of paperbacks to work through."

Alex considered this, which on the face of it seemed just another example of the arbitrary power of the adult world to impose pointless labour on the child. The difference was that Ganymede could do it to other adults, too.

"What if I just refuse to do it? The stuff he tries to make me do, I mean."

"Then you'll get rather hungry, I'm afraid. Ganymede holds all the aces here. He doles out the rations, too, you see. If you don't come up to the mark you don't get the grub. You'll starve."

"I wouldn't have thought you could die here," said Alex warily. "How would that work then? This is crazy, all of it. I'm going to wake up and snap out of this… any… minute… now."

He said this with a lack of conviction so obvious, even to him, that his last sentence trailed off into a vague mutter.

"Don't go holding your breath on *that* one!" scoffed Will, a sadistic gleam in his eye. "Yeah, you can die alright. This old dude got fed up of the whole shebang and chucked himself off the top of the multi-storey. Nasty. He just lay there for ages and no one knew what was going to happen to him. Someone went and fetched Ganymede, of course, and then…" Will shuddered. "All of us who were there got this terribly scary feeling, like we ought to make a run for it. I wasn't there to see it myself, but they say, they say…" Will took off his glasses and polished them on his sleeve. He seemed unable to continue. Silence settled over the little room.

"What?" asked Alex cautiously, sensing sudden dread in Will. He felt a vaguely prickly feeling across his scalp at the same time.

"Nothing."

Alex did not pursue the issue for now. Besides, as though to break the spell, Will reached behind a vacuum cleaner box and came out with a bundle of cloth, which he carefully unwrapped. Inside were a few of what looked like bread rolls. He offered one to Alex.

"Here," he said. "Manna. It's good actually, but you do get

awfully bored of it after a while." He looked dreamily at the wall behind Alex's head. "Do you know, I actually dream of chocolate. Crisps would be nice, too, and maybe a big juicy burger with lots of ketchup. But you know what I miss most? Cake." He gazed, misty-eyed into the middle distance, pronouncing the word reverently, as though invoking some deity.

It was clear from looking at him that Will's relationship with cake had indeed been a passionate and enduring one.

The roll tasted lovely, like cheese and garlic with herbs, and Alex took big, jagged bites off it. The events of the last few hours had driven bodily needs out of his mind. Now though, his stomach reminded him how hungry he was. The roll was soon eaten. Alex was still hungry but there was only one roll left and he didn't feel that he should ask for it.

"Why don't you get some chocolate?" he asked. "There's loads of it around in the shops."

"Are you joking?" asked Will. "First of all, everything Statical is solid as a stone and can't be moved. Secondly, even if you could, it's like a capital offence to do so. Ganymede'd go ballistic. Didn't you hear what he said?"

Alex remembered the items he had helped himself to from Boots; the sandwich, the chocolate, the apple. He was about to say that he had found that he *could* move Statical things and turn them into 'Stician ones when a little voice of caution inside him told him to keep his trap shut. Besides, at that moment there was another voice.

"Paulo can," it said. "I've seen him do it."

A girl came into the room. She was small, with long dark, straight hair and large brown eyes. She might have been about Alex's age. Alex's relationships with the world of girls up to that point had been marked by mutual suspicion, if not downright hostility. This didn't mean, however, that he was incapable of noticing positive things about them. She was pretty, Alex thought. There was something elfin in the delicate line of her chin and nose.

"Oh, hi Kelly," said Will with a sigh that a sensitive person might have thought wasn't very welcoming. He nodded at Alex. "This is Alex. He's *new*," before continuing, "Anyway it was only a tiny little match Paulo picked up; hardly earth-shattering."

"More than you or me could do," said Kelly, having first greeted Alex. She came into the room and made herself comfortable on Will's pile of blankets, whilst their owner looked on in consternation. She looked him up and down with her dark eyes, a wry smile on her lips. "Come on, Will, break out the rations, there's a good chap. What kind of hospitality do you call this?"

"I'm afraid I haven't got a lot left," said Will, showing signs of anxiety.

"'Course you have," said Kelly confidently. Before Will could object or in any way physically intervene, she reached behind a stack of picture frames and came out with another bundle, which she began to unwrap.

"You've got to watch Will," she told Alex in a matter of fact voice, as though he wasn't even there. "He's basically okay, but he's not what you might call a big sharer."

She handed Alex another roll and took one herself. "Thanks, Will," she said. 'Can I tempt you?"

"You've got a cheek," grumbled Will, flushing about the cheeks somewhat but taking one anyway. "These have got to last until next Gathering."

"That's only two days away," said Kelly. "I don't suppose you're going to starve. I bet you were going to let Alex here have just the one and then sneak away and have a couple of private ones on your own."

"I was *not*!" protested Will, but blushing furiously in a way that tended to confirm this notion. "Anyway, what's it to you? I don't remember inviting you up here. You're always sticking your nose in things where it's not wanted. Why don't you p..."

"What's the Gathering?" Alex asked hurriedly, before things got nasty. He felt rather embarrassed for Will.

Kelly made no sign of leaving. She sat with her back against the wall and took a good long swig from the side of Will's water jug. She told Alex that the Gathering was a weekly meeting of the folks who lived in Intersticia. It took place in the park and everyone came from miles around. Ganymede gave them news, issued instructions, allocated new work tasks and gave out the manna that the 'Sticians would have to make last for the next seven days. Those whose work or attitude pleased Ganymede were rewarded with more manna, while those who fell from favour received barely enough to survive.

"You'll probably be introduced properly at the Gathering," said Kelly when Alex told her he'd already met Ganymede. "He'll want to size you up tomorrow and find out as much as he can about you. Don't tell him anything you don't have to. He wants to find out how you tick, what your weaknesses are; that kind of thing. He doesn't like surprises, Ganymede. He likes everything to run just so." She grinned at Alex, her long hair falling over her eyes. She flicked it away. "It's a pity he doesn't hand out new clothes. I'm sick of these ones. Look at this," she said, indicating the front of her top. Alex looked at her chest as briefly as was consistent with actually having done so. "I guess I must have spilled ice cream on me just before I got dropped into 'Sticia and now I'm stuck with it forever. You can't even take them off."

"Really? What about...?" began Alex, thinking of an obvious objection to this.

"You'll never need to," Kelly said, following his drift. "How long have you been here? Have you ever needed a wee?"

She was right. Nature had not called.

"I guess it's in case you get pulled back into Reality," said Will, moving things on. "You don't want to turn up back there in a completely different set of clothes. Questions would be asked, wouldn't they?"

"Weird," said Alex. "No baths in 'Sticia then."

"Not with your clothes off at any rate," chuckled Kelly. "It doesn't matter though. You don't sweat and you don't stink. You don't even get dirty."

"Jesus, you mean I've got to wear these clothes forever then?" Alex glanced down at his clothes, as if seeing them for the first time.

"You should worry," said Kelly, with a wry smile. "If I'd known I was here for keeps I'd never have worn these shoes. Still, poor old Roger Bradley is stuck in one of those funny green hospital gowns. You mustn't ever stand behind him, unless you want to, like, *really* freak him out. You can see his bum," she giggled, covering her mouth. "Really hairy, too."

"He reckons he must be in a coma or something in hospital," added Will, happy to join in with the mirth. "Like he's off to have an operation or something."

"What are the chances of getting sucked back in though?" asked Alex. "To Reality, I mean. I had the idea I was kind of stuck here."

"You absolutely are," said Kelly, "But sometimes people disappear. I guess they get sucked back into Reality eventually. Most of us here are daydreamers. We just kind of wandered into 'Sticia accidentally. But not all of us. I know for a fact Roger's in a coma in hospital. That's why he's all got up for an operation. And, well…" she was suddenly serious, glancing from face to face. "Some of us are… dead."

"Oh, for God's sake," said Will, turning away, an expression of genuine anxiety on his face. "Don't even talk about it."

There was an awkward silence. At last Will scrunched a sheet of paper into a ball and threw it at a picture of a stag on top of a hill.

"What? Like ghosts?" asked Alex at last, his mouth suddenly dry.

"Why don't you just leave it alone?" Will said, with a shudder. "It gives me the creeps."

"We don't know if we are or not," Kelly continued. "Dead, I mean. Can you remember how you got here? What you were doing the instant you fell into 'Sticia?"

"Of course he can't!" supplied Will, before Alex could open his mouth. "None of us can. I guess I was daydreaming, that's all. I can't remember though."

This was Alex's opportunity to say that it had been different for him, that he could remember every detail of the circumstances. He said nothing though.

"I woke up on the bowling green, down in the park," said Kelly, "With absolutely no idea how I got there."

"What about you?"

Alex gave her an edited version of his experiences. She nodded, picking at a loose thread in one of her shoes.

"But how do you know there are dead people?" asked Alex.

"Everyone knows," she said, with a tilt of her chin. "Everyone, but I think it's only a few of us. It's like as if this instant," she gestured around her at the frozen Statical world, "was their last one. Here they keep on going for a while. In Reality they're history. Ambulance turns up. Curtains. The End. Goodbye."

"Yes, and *goodbye*, Kelly," said Will emphatically. "I think you've officially worn out your welcome." He gestured at the door. "I'm sure you've got other stuff to do."

"Yeah, well, I guess I'll see you around," she said to Alex with a grin, getting to her feet.

Alex had found out a lot more about Intersticia by the time he went to bed, if you could call bed a pile of blankets in the corner of a room. It was hard to sleep. Will was curled up in the room next door. Alex had found that he was indeed unable to undress, as it was quite impossible to undo his jeans or pull his top over his head. Fortunately, despite having taken on board a considerable amount of food and drink, he felt no need to go to the toilet, just as Will had said. He had never felt more alone in the whole of his life, but strangely, although fear and self-pity competed for dominance within him, he proved incapable of tears. It was as though he had exhausted his supply of these earlier that day. He lay for what might have been hours, staring at the featureless expanse of the ceiling above him, whilst the day's events replayed themselves in his mind. Everything here was so utterly strange. Thoughts of his mum, caught interminably in Wardworths, and his father, wherever *he* was, passed before his mental vision over and over again. Light from the weird 'Stician moon painted a broad swath across the carpet. Alex reckoned that with a bit of effort he could close the curtains, but Ganymede's warning still rang in his ears. Besides, some instinct continued to warn him that he should keep his ability to do such things to himself. But the floor was hard. At length, Alex climbed onto the bed. This was hard too, but after a while, in contact with his body, it began to soften. The pillow softened, too, until Alex drifted into a shallow and uneasy sleep.

Chapter Four

Alex, who was awoken by the sounds of Will moving about in the next room, slipped quickly from the bed, all too conscious of the faint creaking of its springs. Will didn't seem to have noticed but Alex nevertheless felt a flush in his cheeks when his new friend came in with one of the manna rolls and a mug of water.

"Breakfast," he said. "If you can call it that. I'd offer you more but…"

Alex raised a hand. "Yes, that's fine. I know… Thanks, Will. I'll pay you back when I get some of my own."

"Oh, that's alright," said Will, in a tone of voice that managed to suggest otherwise despite his best efforts to the contrary. "I don't like to get too low, that's all. Kelly lives on the edge, see. She can't organise herself properly. She never lasts out all week and then she has to come scrounging off everybody else."

"She seems okay though," ventured Alex, brushing crumbs off his jeans. "How did she get here? Daydreamer do you think?"

Will shrugged. "How do I know? How do any of us know? All I know is we daydreamed ourselves into here. Most of us, anyway; that's what Ganymede says. I guess we have to believe him."

And that was the terror of it. Most of the people of Intersticia were, like he and Alex, caught in their daydreams, caught in a moment. There were exceptions; Roger Bradley, he of the hospital gown, amongst them. They couldn't remember. They had simply appeared in Intersticia, with no inkling of what they had last been doing in Reality. But some of them were dead. Such was the spectre that stalked Intersticia.

Outside, everything seemed pretty much as it had been the previous day. The clouds were exactly as he remembered them. Flying objects were amongst the stranger sights in Intersticia. A distant flock of birds hung motionless beyond the church tower. There was no one about as Alex set off for the park, unless you counted the stiffs, and there were plenty of those. You would have thought they'd have gathered dust, but there was no sign of it as Alex brushed experimentally at a young man's shoulder on Copeland Street. He journeyed via Wardworths, so that he could say hello to his mum, and have another go at getting himself back into Reality. Ten minutes of head shaking later he continued along the ring road past the accident, having accomplished nothing except a mild headache. There were moments, even now, when he still entertained the notion that this might be a dream of some sort, but with increasingly little conviction. It was with a slow pace and a heavy heart that he made his way down the parade to the bandstand. He was almost there when a 'Stician came running up behind him, startling him from one of a succession of gloomy thoughts. The newcomer was a balding middle-aged man, lean as a whippet and clad in tight black running bottoms and a red vest with two white bands across it.

"Morning!" he hailed Alex, passing him by without stopping.

By the time Alex had mounted the steps to the bandstand the runner was already halfway around the large pool that occupied the western end of the park, dodging briskly amongst the frozen strolling stiffs. He had, of course, been acquainted with the idea that he shared this world with others besides Will and Kelly. Nevertheless, the jogger's cheery greeting still sounded a discordant note in the silence of the park.

There was no sign of Ganymede. Alex waited in the bandstand for a time that he had no way of measuring but seemed a great deal more than was reasonable. The clouds remained perfectly immobile. The leaves on the trees were as still as though they were frozen in crystal. Only his pulse marked the passing of the seconds. Alex counted his heartbeats for a while. At last the dark shape of a dugong (or a manatee) came into view, crossing the park purposefully from north to south, finally disappearing behind the tall poplars by the football pitches. Its dark body undulated slightly as it swam through the quiet air. Bizarre. After this brief excitement drew to a close, Alex went for a little stroll around the park, always ensuring that he was in sight of the bandstand. He had a good look at all of the stiffs, wondering at the moist, glossy surface of their eyes, and at a little girl on a scooter, strands of blonde hair lifted in the non-existent breeze.

Nevertheless, when Alex next looked up, Ganymede was there, regarding him across the litter-strewn concrete shallows of the children's paddling pool. An involuntary spasm of alarm passed through him and he took a moment to compose himself, taking a deep breath, before making his way to the bandstand past a frozen toddler on a red tricycle. This time Ganymede had dispensed with the accordion. He looked Alex up and down in a manner that suggested no more than vague disapproval.

"So, Alex," he said at last. "And what have you got to tell me then?"

Strangely, Ganymede seemed less intimidating than yesterday.

Today he seemed no more than strangely unsettling. Alex was about to run through a list of personal details when Ganymede held up his hand.

"No. Not here I think. We shall go to my office."

He spoke each word slowly and with exaggerated precision, grinning through his tangle of beard in a way that was sinister rather than in any way reassuring. Beckoning to Alex, he led the way towards one of the big houses that backed onto the park. In a length of ancient wall, a green painted door stood open, giving access to a garden as unkempt as Ganymede.

"So what were the circumstances of your entry into Intersticia?" asked Ganymede when he had let them into a ground floor office. It looked just like a tramp's office should; piles of paper everywhere and a great many unwashed mugs that stood about amidst the chaos. On the top of a filing cabinet a kettle stood on a little primus stove next to a neglected pot plant. By this time Alex was actually delighted that the interrogation had begun. The long silence had been bearing down on him.

"Wardworths," said Alex. "I was in a queue."

"Really? You can remember that?" said Ganymede, studying him thoughtfully. "I had expected you to say you woke up and found yourself in the allotments, or some such place. Interesting."

He stroked his beard, dislodging an occasional crumb.

Alex told Ganymede an edited account of events, leaving out his minor interferences with Statica and his previous brief visitations there. Ganymede, who had put on small, half-moon glasses, sat at his crowded desk and made notes in a surprisingly neat hand.

"Hmm," he said when Alex had finished, and then, "Hmmmmmm." A more purposeful tug at his beard caused a little cascade of crumbs to fall into his scarf.

"Well," he said at last when the crumb supply was apparently exhausted, "The next Gathering is tomorrow. I shall see to it that you receive your material allowance. This will consist of three blankets, a tea cloth, a jug for fetching water and a cup. You will also receive a quantity of manna. You may fetch water from any watercourse. Interstician water flows there as well as Statical. The manna will sustain your body between Gatherings. In return for this you must work. To begin with I shall ask you to assist various 'Sticians in their tasks. This will enable you to grow to know the folk amongst whom you now dwell. In the meantime I shall consider your case and think of some work appropriate to your needs."

"How long do you think I'll be here?" asked Alex, bringing to utterance the most pressing question of the moment.

Ganymede shrugged, sighed deeply and put the cap back on his ballpoint pen with exaggerated care. It was as though Alex's question had wearied him deeply, had extinguished the last tiny spark of hope he had nourished for humanity.

"Who knows?" he said, shaking his great shaggy head slowly. "Who knows indeed? It is not in our power to decide. We *may* be called back to Reality. We may not. And time in Intersticia cannot be measured by traditional devices. There is no movement of the sun across the sky. Even the night here is no more than an artifice, created here for the convenience of mortals used to measuring the passage of time by nights and days. You will have noticed by now that the moon here is not the one you are used to in Reality."

Alex nodded.

"But how can time carry on here, for us, when it's stopped all around us?" he asked. "That's impossible isn't it?"

Ganymede laughed, a bitter laugh, Alex thought.

"Just because you don't understand it doesn't mean it isn't so," he said. "You mortals measure time in little arbitrary chunks which it pleases you to call seconds. And you maintain that there should be sixty to a minute, because some astronomers in Babylonia thousands of your years ago determined that it should be so. That's nonsense. Time is indeed broken into fragments, tiny particles of existence. The angels measure time in 'instants', four of them to a 'moment', thirty-seven moments to a 'while'. What do mortals know about time? What do mortals know about anything? Precious little."

If Ganymede had been trying to imply that he wasn't actually a mortal himself, he was doing a good job of it. He stared hard at Alex and steepled his fingers in front of him, leaning back in his chair to get a wider viewing angle.

"There's something odd about you," he said after a lengthy pause.

Alex thought this was a bit rich coming from someone as manifestly weird as Ganymede, pot calling kettle black and all that. It was, of course, impossible to bring this to utterance.

"Yes," continued the hairy old vagrant. "Decidedly odd, and I can't quite see what it is. That troubles me. You wouldn't be holding anything back, would you? Because I really wouldn't advise it."

Alex shook his head adamantly, feeling sure that his cheeks must be flushing in blatant contradiction of this denial, but if they did, it appeared to escape Ganymede's attention.

Alex had lots more questions for Ganymede, too, but on the other hand he had no wish to prolong the interview any longer than was absolutely necessary, so he was delighted when Ganymede waved him away and hunched down over his paperwork as though Alex no longer existed.

"I'll show myself out then, shall I?" he said hesitantly.

Since there was nothing but a grunt from his host, Alex made his way back to the park, pausing in Ganymede's garden to admire the splendid collection of gnomes, half buried amongst the rampant undergrowth. A shadow passed before him. He glanced up in time to see a dugong (or a manatee) pass majestically overhead. It was a strange world alright. He frowned. The dugong (or manatee) disappeared behind the row of poplars by the football pitches.

Kelly was waiting for him in the bandstand, sitting on the balustrade, swinging her bare legs. She was definitely pretty, Alex decided, confirming last night's first impressions. She gave him a warm smile as he approached.

"Ganymede not eaten you then?" she said.

"He wasn't too bad," conceded Alex, going on to give her an account of his interview.

"He must like you," said Kelly, with a low whistle when he had finished. "He was horrid to me."

"Who are the angels anyway?" asked Alex. "I thought Ganymede was the main man."

"He is, sort of…" agreed Kelly. "He's Head of Sector, but this sector is only a hundred square miles or so, and there must be thousands of sectors all over the world. Ganymede runs the sector, the angels run the world. They run Ganymede, in fact, although I don't think they always get on; I've heard him grumbling about their interference. I saw some once," she said. "Angels, I mean. I know it sounds mad, especially when you've just got here. There's lots of mad things about 'Sticia, you'll see. Doesn't make 'em not true though. I guess you've seen the manatees."

"Or dugongs," said Alex.

"Whatever. What've you got there?"

She nodded at the small bundle of manna rolls that Ganymede had given Alex to last him until tomorrow's Gathering.

"Manna," conceded Alex, reluctantly. "I've got to give three to Will, to pay him back for last night."

"How many does that leave?" asked Kelly, an acquisitive glint in her eye.

"Six," said Alex.

"Six. That's loads. You can spare *me* one then, can't you? I'm starving. *Please*."

She fixed him with a look of such concentrated pleading it would have shamed a spaniel. Alex's resolve crumbled.

"Alright," he said as he unwrapped his bundle and gave one of his manna rolls to Kelly, feeling surprisingly good about it. He took one himself, too, reckoning it must be around lunch time. They were walking towards the other end of the park by now, Alex tagging along after Kelly as she ambled towards the south gate.

"These angels then? Were they like, you know, proper angels: wings, haloes, the whole job?" asked Alex.

"Absolutely," laughed his companion. "Lovely wings, too. Like big white doves or something, and kind of semi-transparent. Dead impressive really. I guess they do it because they think we expect it of them. You know, like the false night they do for us. No, they turned up at the next Gathering after that dude chucked himself off the car park. I gather Ganymede really got it in the neck over that."

"Why? Was it Ganymede's fault?"

"Maybe, maybe not. I think the dude'd just had enough. You wait and see how you feel after a couple of weeks of living like this. If you can call it living, I mean," she said, with a laugh tinged with bitterness.

"What else would you call it?" said Alex.

"It's an existence," she answered, stopping suddenly to regard him thoughtfully. He had the impression she was weighing him up in the way Ganymede had been doing.

"There was something you said last night," said Alex. "It got me thinking. You said that some of the people are actually dead, they just don't know it."

Kelly pursed her lips and nodded slowly. "Yeah, that's about the size of it."

"Well, what did you mean, 'go on for a while'?" he asked. "I mean, I can see there'd be all kind of practical difficulties with dead folks getting back into reality. What if you'd actually died in hospital and ended up here in 'Sticia for now? It'd be a bit odd if you got sucked back into Reality and your corpse showed up suddenly in the bandstand, wouldn't it?"

Kelly grinned suddenly. "That, Alex, would be what we call a logical inconsistency and Intersticia doesn't much like stuff like that. No, I'll tell you how folks get back into Reality, if you really want to know." She glanced around conspiratorially as though she feared being overheard. "Will doesn't even like to think about it because he's chicken to his core, see?"

"Uh huh," said Alex encouragingly. "Go on."

She sat down on the edge of a bench next to a stiff holding a half-eaten baguette. There wasn't room for Alex to join her without budging her along a little, so he was obliged to remain standing.

"They say Cactus Jack comes for them," she said, flicking at a crumb of manna on her knee, and looking up at Alex with those big brown eyes. "Eventually, that is. You might be here for ages and ages first. I never saw it happen myself but I've heard others talk about it. Not that anyone really wants to, you know, talk about it or anything. It's almost like, what d'you call it? Taboo, that's it. You have to work on people a bit. They say this guy…"

"Cactus Jack," supplied Alex, trying to keep things moving on.

"… Comes and drags them back into Statica. Grabs hold of them, gives them some kind of death grip and sets them up as stiffs. He wanders about at night sometimes; gives everyone the creeps.

"Whoah!" breathed Alex. "Creepy. Do they know he's coming for them or anything?"

"Come on," she said, after a moment's reflection. "Let's go." It was clear that Kelly wasn't that keen to talk about Cactus Jack either.

"Let's go where?" was a question that suggested itself to Alex, but it was some time before he actually asked it. For the moment he was content to walk with his new companion as they threaded their way amongst stiffs at the south end of the big pool, where dozens of statical geese were being fed bread by a couple of stiff kids. Half a big white crust was caught in mid-air.

"Paulo's place," answered Kelly. "If he's there. He's supposed to be copying out King Lear. That's what Ganymede made him do this week. He really, really hates Paulo. And I mean really," she added, as though Alex might not have been following her drift. "I'm lucky; he just doesn't like me."

"Who *is* this Paulo anyway?" asked Alex. "What is he, the local "A List" celebrity? Everyone keeps talking about him."

"Paulo? He's seventeen. He's cool. I think so anyway. Other folks seem to think he's a bit of a bad lot. His face doesn't fit, you know, bit of a free spirit. He's always in trouble about one thing or another… Talks about vegetables a lot."

Kelly, who seemed to enjoy a private joke, smiled reflectively at this last disclosure, which caused Alex a twinge of irritation.

"What do you mean he talks about vegetables a lot?" he demanded peevishly, as they crossed the main road.

"He's kind of foul-mouthed," Kelly told him. "And that really hacks Ganymede off. He got so fed up with Paulo swearing he did some kind of weird magic thing to him. Now, whenever Paulo thinks he's swearing he's really just saying the names of veg. He doesn't know though. He still thinks he's bad-mouthing. Funny really. Don't laugh at Paulo though, will you? Not unless you want a kicking anyway. He really hates that. Being laughed at, I mean."

Alex made a mental note to himself not to jeer at Paulo. He was beginning to feel a little worried about Paulo, who sounded a lot like the kind of boy he spent much of his school career trying to avoid.

They came to a large detached house across from the park. Kelly led them along the side of it, through an open gate and into the rear garden. Here a patio door gave access to the house. Inside, a middle-aged woman was vacuuming the carpet.

"Paulo," called Kelly, her voice sounding hugely loud in the stillness of the house. There was no reply. Kelly frowned. They went upstairs. Here, in the master bedroom, were signs of occupation: manna crumbs, a jug, a few blankets. On the dressing table was a copy of the collected works of Shakespeare. Torn pages from it were scattered all over the room; scrunched up sheets of file paper lay everywhere.

"Jesus," said Kelly, with a low whistle. "I guess Paulo got fed up of it."

"Looks that way," said Alex, picking up one of half a dozen or so broken biros. "Not the studying type is he?"

"You could say that," agreed Kelly, looking at him with her head on one side. "I wonder if he left any manna. I'm starving."

"Fancy that," said Alex with a wry smile.

A brief search of the premises on Kelly's behalf revealed no manna, only a jug of water in the bathroom. Kelly was in the dining room and Alex was checking the kitchen cupboards when he became conscious of a small girl watching him from along the hall. She was perhaps nine years old. There was an expression of wonderment on her face.

"Hello," he said, looking up from his scrutiny of the cupboard under the sink.

"Kelly," said the girl in a shrill voice. Kelly appeared at her side.

"What?"

"Have you seen this?"

"Seen what?" The sprog whispered urgently in her ear for a moment. "Oh..."

Alex's first reaction upon spotting the unexpected brat had been to shut the cupboard door. Now he slowly stood up, wiping his hands on his jeans.

"What?" he asked into the heavy silence that had suddenly descended.

"You're not supposed to be able to do that," said Kelly at length.

"Do what?" asked Alex, knowing full well what she meant, and feeling suddenly intensely anxious about it.

"Move Statical stuff," said the younger girl, her small brow furrowed. "I should tell Ganymede. Then you'd be in trouble."

Alex, who had taken a fairly instant dislike to the undersized newcomer, found this dislike cranked up a gear or two.

"No, you shouldn't," Kelly told her, with mock severity. "Not unless you want your silly face pushed in. You never saw nothin', right?" She grinned and gave the girl a playful shove that bounced her off a wall. "Alex, this is Tanya. She's a pain sometimes but basically she's okay."

Tanya giggled and put her arms around Kelly. They hugged, Kelly picking up Tanya and jogging her up and down until she screamed.

"Paulo's gone," said Tanya, panting, when Kelly had set her down. "I don't think he's coming back."

67

"He's left his jug and his blankets," Kelly pointed out.

"He's got some more," retorted Tanya. "He stole some. I know he did."

"Where's he gone then, clever clogs?" asked Kelly.

"How should I know?" said Tanya with a shrug. "I saw him earlier. He was in a right strop."

"Mentioned a lot of vegetables did he?" suggested Alex.

"Yeah." Tanya chuckled. "Loads, I could'a made a casserole."

Kelly shrugged. "Oh well, I guess he'll show up tomorrow at the Gathering."

"Do you like having sticky-out ears?" asked Tanya, in that guileless way of the very young that makes it hard to object too much.

"All the better to hear you with," said Alex, making the best of it, after a moment in which he felt the blood rush to ears and cheeks.

"Wow! You must have hearing like a bat," she said with a frown.

Moving things on, Alex pointed out that Paulo didn't appear to have struck up much of a relationship with Shakespeare. Kelly seemed to consider this point.

"Well," she said, "It's never stopped him before."

Alex was beginning to think that the subject had moved safely on from his apparent ability to interfere with the forbidden world of Statica. No such luck. Kelly came into the kitchen and ran her fingers longingly over one of the glossy red apples in the fruit bowl on the table. It was like Snow White's apple.

"I can't tell you how often I've dreamed of apples," she said, regarding the fruit dreamily and then suddenly turning her eyes upon Alex. "Get it for me, Alex. Go on."

There was an intensity about her gaze that came perilously close to melting his resolve. At last Alex shook his head. "Can't," he said, feeling a hot flush in his cheeks.

"'Course you can," said Kelly, in an encouraging tone, taking Alex's hand in both of hers and pressing it to the apple. Alex flinched and withdrew his hand, although not before a delicious thrill had transfixed him. She licked her lips. "Come on, Tanya saw you close that cupboard door – so she tells me. An apple should be easy enough." There was something almost plaintive in her tone.

Tanya came up at her side. "Go on," she said. "I saw you do it, didn't I?"

But Alex was steadfast. He knew that he was looking at the thin end of a very fat wedge. Getting Kelly an apple was only the first step on a long and dangerous road that would involve the provision of sweets, chocolates, crisps and Heaven only knew what. He was far too scared of Ganymede to take so much as a humbug from Statica for now. He certainly wasn't about to start doling out treats to Kelly or anyone else.

"I can't," he said. "Tanya's wrong. I was trying to open it but I couldn't budge it. Honest. I can't." He felt bad about lying but the consequences of telling the truth struck him as infinitely worse.

"Can't or won't?" Kelly's mouth was set in a hard line now.

"Can't," insisted Alex, holding her gaze steadily. For the benefit of his little audience he made a passable pretence of trying to move the apple. He felt it stir under his fingers as he grunted and grimaced.

"See," he said, letting go. To his enormous relief it didn't roll out of the bowl.

"I saw him do it," said Tanya, stamping her foot and regarding Alex ruefully. "I know I did."

Alex slept at Will's house again that night. On the way back there from the park he was surprised to find a solemn procession of small creatures crossing the road. They were like nothing he had ever seen before. Each was about as tall as a large dog and covered in fine sleek hair, stumpy creatures with two short legs and no arms at all. Although they had no obvious necks, their heads were surprisingly human in appearance, except for the position of their ears, which were like terriers' ears, placed on top of their heads. Long tails swished behind them as they proceeded into a debris-strewn passage in stately single file. When they had gone, Alex stood for a while whilst his brain tried to assimilate what he had seen. Then he hurried onward, eager to ask Will if he knew what the creatures were.

Will was already there when Alex made his way up to the back bedroom. He was writing what he said was his diary.

"Not much of a diary really," he explained. "But there's not a lot else to do of an evening, unless someone comes round or you get invited somewhere."

"They're quite peculiar, aren't they?" said Will, rather understating the case, when Alex asked him about the strange little creatures.

"They're called 'snarks'. Ganymede's always going on about them. They're like his ideal creatures or somethin'. They don't speak; they don't even do anything much. All they do is think. They're supposed to be creatures that have evolved not to do stuff, like humans have, but to think."

At this point Will started doing a passable impersonation of Ganymede's voice, waving his arms around theatrically. "They are fine, noble creatures. They have beautiful minds. Do you hear me? *Bee-yoo-tee-ful* minds. Each one spends his days in contemplation of life, and the meaning of existence. Which is more than I can say for you 'orrible lot!" A snort of self-congratulatory laughter brought this to a close.

"They were going off towards Micklebury Hill when I saw them," said Alex, with a grin. "They hardly seemed to notice I was there."

"They wouldn't," said Will, tossing his biro up in the air and catching it. "They're too busy philosophising. Some nights they like to go up on Micklebury and stand about looking at the Moon. Ganymede says it fine-tunes their thought processes."

"Oh," said Alex evenly. "Does it?" He was becoming more and more accustomed to bizarre phenomena. "So what are we doing tonight then? Party, party, party, is it?"

"What do you think?" snorted Will. "I can do without Kelly coming round again and scoffing all my manna. She's like a manna hog. I never knew anything like it."

Will had an extended grumble about the austere regime in 'Sticia. Alex listened attentively enough, although he had the feeling he was listening to the first of many similar rants to come. Nobody ever had as much manna as they wanted. Ganymede doled out just enough to keep body and soul together. This meant that food was always a big issue with people, and kept everybody's minds focused on whatever work Ganymede had required of them. And then there was the boredom. There was so little to do, other than work. There was no television, no music, no cinema and hardly any books, except those that Ganymede saw fit to issue to them. And these were usually distributed only so that they could be copied out, translated or learned by heart. Ganymede had a passion for learning, particularly where others were concerned. He was even more passionately committed to it when those people were naturally averse to learning. Hence, Kelly was trying to learn by heart the poems of W.B. Yeats. Hence, Paulo's reluctant encounter with Shakespeare. On the other hand, those whose inclinations were cultured and bookish found themselves engaged in shovelling sand or carrying bricks. It seemed that Ganymede had an ironic sense of humour. Or possibly he was just a sadist, thought Alex.

Will was not one for staying up late. Having written his diary he went straight off to sleep. Alex wondered what on earth he found to confide to his journal. It was presumably little more than a bald record of manna lost, equations solved, empty streets wandered; it certainly seemed unlikely it would make racy reading. Alex decided his new companion was a bit dull. There must be more to life in 'Sticia than Will was making out. Instead of going to bed himself, he wrapped a blanket around his shoulders and made his way out into the street, past the stiff and her neighbour.

The faintest of breezes was stirring the cool air of 'Sticia and the flock of birds beyond the church was silhouetted against the peculiar false Moon. The familiar texture of seas and craters he was used to seeing on the genuine article was replaced here by something rather more regular, as though an artist had recreated it from a traveller's description. He took a deep breath of vaguely lavender-scented air and looked up and down the silent street, wondering where Kelly was now. His mind trawled uneasily over the day's events. Suddenly there was a faint sound and then movement, away beyond the cars at the end of the street. He could hear distant footsteps, firm and purposeful. Inexplicably, Alex was seized by a sense of dread so profound it was as though his heart had been gripped in a fist of ice. Gasping for breath, retracing his steps, he ducked behind the hedge that enclosed the tiny front garden. The footsteps came closer, and with every step the grasp of terror grew tighter and tighter. Alex found that he could hardly breathe. His labouring heart thudded in his throat. He hugged his knees to his chest and dared to peer sidelong through the gaps in the foliage as whoever it was passed briskly by. Alex had a brief impression of a tall male figure, dark jeans and a white T-shirt with a cactus on the front. And then he was gone, his footsteps receding along the street. Alex found that he was panting.

Chapter Five

The next day was the Gathering. This took place in the park, of course, which seemed to be pretty much the centre of things in 'Sticia. Alex made paper aeroplanes out of some of Will's less successful quadratic equations. These they threw and caught and chased, as they made their way across Cardenbridge to the park, until Will, chasing after Alex's plane, stubbed his toe with some violence against the kerb. He had to sit down for a while, grimacing and cursing whilst Alex jumped on and off the pavement, fidgeting with his aeroplane.

"I suppose there's not a lot of stuff to play with in 'Sticia," said Alex.

"Not really," grunted Will, massaging his toe. "The planes were a good idea Alex, but Ganymede keeps a pretty tight rein on the paper, too. You're supposed to hand any workings back in to him. And I look after mine. For my diary and stuff. We'd better hide these outside the park before we go in."

"How long have you been keeping a diary, Will?" asked Alex, as his companion put his shoe back on.

"Only a couple of weeks," said Will. "But life goes by so uneventfully here you tend to find it all blurs together after a while. I thought a diary would help me keep things in focus. I've been to lots of Gatherings, you see, but I've no idea how many."

"What do you mean, you've no idea how many?" asked Alex, wrinkling his nose.

Will was perhaps about to answer but at that moment there came the sound of a horn of some sort, a long clear blast that cut through the quiet air and echoed off the tall park buildings where the council had its offices.

"That's Ganymede blowing his horn to get things going," said Will. "We'd better get a move on."

They were passing through the park gates by now. From the top of the parade they could see that a few dozen people were gathered in the area around the bandstand, standing in small groups. Another small group was making its way up from the South Gate. Alex fancied he recognised Kelly amongst them. The horn blew again. Will broke into a lumbering run.

"Come on," he called over his shoulder. "We're going to be in trouble."

They were not the last to arrive. That distinction belonged to Kelly and Tanya, who were fixed by Ganymede's baleful glare during the last stage of their journey across the lawns. Most ages were represented in the crowd, from a doddery old woman of about ninety to a girl of about five, but there were no younger children or babies. The little girl had evidently been taken on by a middle-aged woman dressed for tennis. She clung to her side, the woman's long fingers half hidden in a mass of blond curls, as Ganymede surveyed his kingdom from the bandstand. As a newcomer, Alex found himself subjected to any number of curious glances as he joined the edge of the little crowd with Will. He recognised Roger Bradley, hospital gown revealing a strip of pale back, and next to him the runner he had encountered yesterday. Kelly soon found her way across to them, slapping Alex playfully on the back as she arrived and then pressing a finger to her lips as

Alex made to greet her. Ganymede was about to speak. He strode to the balustrade of the bandstand, picked up what looked like a post horn from an old stagecoach and blew one last tremendous blast on it, his hairy cheeks blowing up like purple veined balloons. The people of 'Sticia, who had been chatting amongst themselves in low voices, fell silent. All faces turned to Ganymede.

"Greetings, people of Intersticia," he bellowed, removing his hat and making a low, ironic bow. "Greetings. I trust the past week has gone well for you. I know that you have worked hard, in most cases…" Here he cast a disapproving eye here and there amongst the crowd. "And that effort will be rewarded in due course."

He paused for a moment, nodding grimly, as though the thought of parting with manna gave him indigestion.

"In addition we have two rare treats in store today. The first, to welcome a newcomer to our community. Always a pleasure." He nodded at Alex. "Step forward will you please, Mr Trueman."

Reluctantly, Alex made his way to the front of the little crowd and then up the steps to the bandstand. Ganymede, taking firm hold of his shoulders, turned him to face the people of Intersticia.

"This is Alex Trueman," came Ganymede's gravelly voice from behind him.

There was an awkward pause. Alex smiled sheepishly, feeling a little like an exhibit at an agricultural show. People shuffled their feet. An elderly woman began to clap her hands, and soon there was a ripple of polite applause. Alex wondered if he should make a bow.

"Good," said Ganymede, clearly satisfied with Alex's reception and nodding solemnly. "Some of you will get to know Alex well in the next few days, because he will be assisting you with your tasks."

The last part of this caused Alex some disquiet. What tasks exactly? And whom would he be assisting? A number of questions came to mind, but essentially it appeared that Alex was now a fully accepted member of this bizarre community within an instant, frozen in time. Despite these misgivings, he felt an agreeable warmth about the heart, a new confidence in his stride as he made his way back to his place between Will and Kelly, nodding and smiling at those who greeted him as he passed. Ganymede was already introducing the second item on his agenda. He announced a group outing to Micklebury Stanton, where someone called Sylvia DiStefano had a sculpture to show them. Many in the crowd seemed to regard this as a genuinely positive development, which confirmed in Alex's mind that opportunities for entertainment in 'Sticia were few and far between.

"Who's Sylvia DiStefano?" hissed Alex, to Kelly, whilst Ganymede got on to talking about the importance of everyone being kind to one another. It was a bit like being in school assembly.

"She's a famous sculptor," whispered Kelly, her breath warm on Alex's ear. "So she claims. Ganymede gave her some bits of wood to work with and she'd been making something out of it. Should be a laugh, anyway."

It seemed that Kelly didn't have high hopes of Sylvia's artistic potential. Will's appraisal of the situation was even less positive.

"Oh my god! We've got to traipse all the way up to Stanton, just to look at a bloody bunch o' sticks," he grumbled, at Alex's other side.

But first there was the main business of the day to be transacted. This consisted of the citizens of Intersticia being called up, one by one, and receiving their rations for the week. At the same time they were given new work tasks or required to continue with old ones. Some people came out of the bandstand with a light step and expressions of relief. They were the ones who had pleased Ganymede during the past week, or whose allocated tasks were less onerous than they might have anticipated. Others came out with furrowed brows or even tears in their eyes. There were raised voices, heated words, before an elderly man dressed as though for golf came stamping down the steps, his face a splendid crimson hue.

"That's Major Trubshaw," said Kelly, with a snigger. "He's always having rows with Ganymede."

Two girls of about Alex's age came over to talk to Kelly. One of them had features that appeared slightly too small for her face, the other had features that seemed slightly too large. The former was called Stacey, the latter Sarah. Alex soon found that he didn't much like either of them. Stacey, who was displaying a strip of flabby midriff between her jeans and her top, looked Alex up and down with a smirk before moving her attention on to Kelly.

"Is this your new boyfriend then?" she asked. "Given Paulo the push, have you?"

Alex found himself blushing at the first part of this; first, because he didn't care for being spoken about as though he wasn't even there, second, because the accusation was untrue, and third, because the notion was undeniably an intriguing one.

"His name is *Alex*," said Kelly, in aggrieved tones, "As you well know." She was blushing, too, Alex noted. "And as for Paulo, I haven't seen him since Wednesday. I thought he might be with you."

"Why would he?" sneered Stacey.

"Yeah, why would he?" added Sarah, with a broad and

insolent grin.

"He's such a total loser," continued Stacey, with a flick of her hair and a curl of her lip. "He's not *my* type."

"So where *is* Paulo anyway?" asked Sarah, looking around. "I don't see him. Ganymede'll blow his top if he turns up late again."

Kelly shrugged, affecting a sudden interest in her fingernails. "I don't know. I'm not, like, his keeper or anything."

"Yeah, well Paulo wants to watch his step," added Stacey, with a wag of her own finger. "He's going to get his self banged up in the House of Correction again."

"Yeah, well what's it to you anyway?" asked Kelly with sudden anger, eyes narrowed, small fists clenched at her side.

"Like I say," sneered Stacey. She was a skilled and prolific sneerer, Alex decided. "I'm surprised you have to ask *me* that."

She and Sarah both had a bit of a snigger about this before wandering off towards the playground, leaving Kelly swearing under her breath.

"Don't let her get to you," said Will supportively.

"Don't worry, I won't," snapped Kelly, but without conviction.

Alex's own interview with Ganymede was mercifully short, given that they had already spoken at length the previous day. He was handed a pile of blankets and a cloth bag containing manna. He also received a cup, an enamel jug and a handful of light sticks. Alex had been wondering about the nature of the work that would be set for him. This was settled when Ganymede grabbed his arm, rather roughly, and pointed him in the direction of a small group of people sitting on the lawn.

"There," he said. "See the skinny old beanpole with her hair in a bun? That's Mrs Patterson, go and introduce yourself. You'll be working with her for the next two days."

Alex nodded. "What about after that?"

"Let's just deal with the first couple of days, shall we? Come back to me then. Don't you worry, we'll sort you out." Ganymede managed to work a great deal of wholly unnecessary menace into this, which caused Alex to feel a little thrill of apprehension. There was definitely something creepy about the old tramp.

Alex slung his blankets over his shoulder, stuffed everything else into his jug and made his way across to Mrs Patterson's group. She struck Alex as the sort of elderly woman who would have been perfectly at home presiding over a church fête. She was dressed in a twinset with a double row of beads and had grey hair pulled back into a tight bun, giving her a rather severe look. She was talking to another elderly lady with enormous hips, but she looked up when Alex arrived. The face that turned to regard Alex curiously was a thin, unevenly powdered one, with several layers of bags under rheumy old eyes. It was a kindly face, Alex decided. Mrs Patterson took off her glasses, which made her eyes seem even weaker.

"Hello," she said. "It's Alex isn't it? And you must call me Gwyn. Mr Ganymede told me you were to be my apprentice. I don't know what I can have done to deserve such a favour from our benefactor. Still, we must not look gift horses in the mouth, must we?"

"Do you know what he makes poor Gwyn do?" asked broad hips in indignant tones. She had, Alex noticed, an irregular growth of black hairs on her upper lip, resembling a scatter of spiders' legs. "She makes her shovel sand. I ask you; shovelling sand, a woman of Gwyn's years. And her with her bad back and all. It's a disgrace, that's what I call it."

"Yes, well, we must grin and bear it," said Mrs Patterson with a brave smile. "I'm afraid Mr Ganymede's word is law around here."

"Mrs Ambrose was mauled by a bear," said a third lady,

rather surprisingly, in matter of fact tones. She was even thinner than Mrs Patterson and wore clothes of curiously antique appearance, as though gleaned from the costume department of the BBC to represent an Edwardian. Her eyes remained focused on the middle distance. "You see, now Mrs Gurney, she had a disagreement with her sister, and the outcome was most unsatisfactory... In every way," she added, with a significant nod in Alex's direction. Her eyes zeroed in on Alex, too, which made him feel uncomfortable, particularly since their point of focus seemed to be somewhere beyond the back of his head.

"Yes, dear," said what was evidently Mrs Gurney. "I'm quite sure that's the case." A twitch of her splendidly bushy eyebrows suggested mild irritation with a bit of resignation thrown in for good measure.

Alex formed the view that the Edwardian-looking lady was a bit mad.

"I live in Barnard Road," said Mrs Patterson, after sending her companion a sympathetic glance. "Number Twelve. Perhaps you'd like to come along around tenth."

Alex wondered what Mrs Patterson meant by tenth, but he wasn't able to ask because at that moment the red-faced Major arrived and began a heated discussion with Mrs Gurney. The discussion revolved around the injustice of Ganymede's regime – and it seemed that the Major was a prominent critic. Given that Alex had only just met Ganymede he didn't have very much to contribute to the conversation. Nevertheless, he listened with interest for a while before wandering back over to where Kelly was sprawled on the grass with Tanya. There were many apparent inconsistencies in 'Sticia, one of which was the grass. By rights it should have been a thickset mass of sharp green blades, impossible to walk on. Instead, it behaved exactly as ordinary grass, although the earth beneath it was hard as concrete.

Alex asked Kelly what Mrs Patterson had meant by 'tenth'. She could hardly have been talking about ten o'clock, given that no clocks worked in 'Sticia.

"She means tenth manatee," explained Tanya, before Kelly could open her mouth.

"Huh?" asked Alex.

"Tenth manatee," repeated Kelly. "They pass over at pretty much regular intervals during the day. It's not as good as clocks but it's all we've got. There are always twenty-two between dawn and dusk. You just have to count them every time you see one, and they're all slightly different if you look at them carefully. It gets to be automatic in the end. You hardly notice them but you still count them. It's twelfth now."

"Some are dugongs," added Tanya, nibbling at a manna roll and retrieving crumbs out of the grass. "Twelfth's a dugong. He's a big old fat one."

"Yeah," agreed Kelly. "Every other one's a dugong. They're the ones with the forky tails. Manatees' tails look sort of rounded."

"Why do they fly anyway?" asked Alex, feeling another surge of outrage about the state of things in 'Sticia. "They're supposed to live in water. It doesn't make sense."

Kelly snorted. "Well, if you're expecting things to make sense round here you're in for a big disappointment. What are you doing tomorrow anyway?"

"Shovelling sand by the looks of it," said Alex gloomily.

Ganymede, having transacted all his business, addressed the little crowd again. He blew another short blast on his horn to get everyone's attention and then placed both fingerless gloved hands on the rail, surveying the populace below with his mouth set in a grim line.

"Would anyone have seen Mr Potts?" he asked, managing to work lots of sincerely felt disapproval into the pronunciation of his name.

There was a low murmur through the crowd, but no reply. He glared suddenly in Alex's direction, causing Alex a moment of disquiet until he realised Ganymede's attention was directed at Kelly, standing at his side.

Kelly shook her head. Ganymede continued to stare until Kelly felt obliged to add to this. "Paulo? Not for a couple of days," she said.

"Hmmm," said Ganymede, stroking his beard and continuing to regard her stonily, as though she might have him secreted somewhere about her person. "Well, if he trolls in late today he can look forward to a thin old time this week, because he'll be lucky to get a single one of these."

He tossed a manna roll up in the air. When it bounced and skittered to a halt on the bandstand floor Ganymede ground it savagely underfoot.

"I will not tolerate rudeness, indolence or indiscipline," he barked, glaring around him so fiercely that the crowd instinctively drew back. "I hope that is understood by all of you."

Alex found himself nodding.

"Good," said Ganymede, rubbing his hands together. "Now, go and store your rations. We reassemble here at fourteenth."

And so they did. Will, Tanya and Alex left their rations at Kelly's lodgings, which was in a house conveniently close to the park and only a few doors down from Paulo's. Will, mindful of Kelly's appetite for manna, had some reservations about this.

"It's alright, Will," Kelly told him. "I'm not going to rush back here and scoff all your manna."

"You won't get the chance," said Will grimly. "I'm sticking to you like glue 'til we get back."

They arrived back at the bandstand, just as what Alex supposed had to be the day's fourteenth manatee drifted majestically overhead. A few stragglers were making their way down the parade but most of 'Sticia's folk were gathered around Ganymede, who was talking authoritatively about greed and indolence.

"That one's a manatee," said Tanya, following Alex's gaze. "See the tail. Sort of rounded like a big paddle."

"Rode one once," commented the lady that Alex now knew was generally called Mad Annie. "'cepting it were a dugong. I said to Mrs Worthington her sister has no right to be taking two o' them samplers. And her only paying tuppence halfpenny. A downright liberty I calls it. But would they listen? Oh, no!"

Mad Annie subsided into indignant muttering as the little crowd set off after Ganymede. Kelly nudged Alex in the ribs and made a face to show exactly how mad she thought Annie was. Ganymede was walking quickly up in front and by the time the last of the group was through the park gates they were already straggling out along the Micklebury Road. Alex, keen to get away from Annie, lengthened his stride, along with Kelly, Tanya and Will. Up in front, Stacey and Sarah were laughing and shoving each other hilariously whilst walking next to a tall, floppy-haired lad called Chad.

"He's all they think about, that Chad," Kelly told Alex. "And just because they think he fancies me instead of them, they hate my guts."

"Oh," said Alex in a tone of careful neutrality, mildly embarrassed by this frankness.

"And does he? Chad… you know, fancy you?"

Kelly shrugged. "Maybe. Not that it makes any difference to me. He's such a dork, anyway."

"You fancy Paulo though, don't you," piped up Tanya with a smirk.

"And you can shut up!" retorted Kelly, blushing furiously.

"See! She does! She does!" taunted Tanya, skipping triumphantly.

"Where is Paulo anyway?" asked Will.

Kelly stopped so suddenly that a balding little man behind nearly walked straight into her.

"Why does everyone keep asking *me*?" demanded Kelly, her brow clouded with rage. She stamped her foot. "How the hell should I know? I haven't *seen* him. Not for ages."

"Ooooh, touchy!" said Will and Tanya together.

Alex gathered the subject was closed.

Chapter Six

The Micklebury Road broadened into a dual carriageway after the primary school by the roundabout. Here, a group of stiff protesters bearing placards were demanding that the council should put in a new pedestrian crossing. "Speed kills," read one placard. "Slow down – Save lives," said another, a message which looked somewhat ironic in the present circumstances. The little procession wove in and out of the stationary lorries, buses and cars as the road curved its way around the base of Micklebury Hill. Witches were supposed to have met there once; ancient folks had fortified its top in a series of long-eroded earthworks called Micklebury Rings, and the last highwayman to have been hanged in the region went to the gallows in the lee of it. It was a local landmark in an area that history seemed largely to have ignored. A few hundred years ago, eccentric local landowners had embellished it by building on one outcrop a slender pinnacle of stone, called the Needle. On another shoulder, a passable imitation of a Greek temple had been constructed. These edifices, ill-maintained in recent years, were slowly crumbling, now the resort of winos and other unsavoury characters. The Needle came into view behind the looming mass of Micklebury as the 'Sticians left the dual carriageway and turned along a path that cut between fields and hedgerows. Here, brought into sharp relief by a stand of tall poplars, was a small white cottage,

Sylvia DiStefano's place of abode. Uniquely in 'Sticia she lived in her own home. The back door into her garden had been conveniently ajar when, in a moment of reflection during wood carving, she had dreamed her way into 'Sticia. Had it not been open she would have been trapped inside, a fate not unusual for those entering this realm.

"Ganymede gets to know somehow, and then goes and lets them out," said Kelly when Alex asked her about this. "He calls them 'cage birds'. I never saw anyone trapped myself but Mrs Patterson says she was banged up like that when she first came here. I guess quite a few of us must have been."

Stacey and Sarah were a little way in front of Kelly and Alex as they made their way along a steep track by the side of a field. They were talking loudly but not quite loudly enough to be overheard, laughing and occasionally directing humorous glances over their shoulders. It was quite clear who they were talking about, however. Abruptly, they stopped, and after a brief but earnest exchange, turned and came back towards them.

"Sarah's lost her ring," Stacey announced, as they halted. "You ain't seen it, 'ave yer?"

Whoever it was that made the rules for 'Sticia had decreed that although items of clothing were generally fixed permanently to the body of the wearer, smaller items like glasses, watches and rings could be removed and replaced.

"No," said Alex, shaking his head emphatically and resenting the accusative tinge in Stacey's tone. "What's it like?"

"Gold one," supplied Sarah. "Little heart on it, with a tiny diamond. I saw you was picking somethin' up when I looked back just now?"

Alex blushed.

"You've got a cheek," said Kelly, glowering at her. "What are you tryin' to say, exactly?"

"Yeah, why don't you push off," proposed Will, coming up behind them with Tanya.

"I was just bending down to have a look at a Statical stag beetle that was crossing the path," said Alex coldly. "That's all. Come down here and I'll show you if you like."

"What have you got in your pockets then?" insisted Stacey, with a steely glare, ignoring this suggestion.

"Oh, for God's sake," said Kelly, folding her arms and rolling her eyes in disgust. "What is this, the Spanish Inquisition?"

"Here, look," said Alex turning out his pockets. They were entirely empty except for a wad of crumpled tissues. "There, satisfied?"

Stacey sniffed. "Well, it must be round here somewhere."

Both of them pushed past and trudged on down the path in silence.

"An apology'd be nice," called Kelly after them, receiving only a rude gesture for reply.

Within a little while the population of 'Sticia was gathering in the orchard behind the cottage. Here, a white painted gate in a wall led through to the long green shoulder of Micklebury Hill. After a few words of encouragement from Ganymede, the 'Sticians passed through. They straggled along a steep path that presently emerged onto a grassy flat platform that offered splendid clear views back towards Cardenbridge. Here, there was a rickety wooden structure, perhaps twelve feet tall, made from the dry branches of trees that had been carefully woven together.

"It looks like an anorexic bonfire," said Kelly, with a snort of laughter.

Several of what might have been Sylvia's friends immediately turned upon Kelly and fixed her with withering stares. Kelly beamed back at them. "Well," she said unapologetically. "It does."

"Sylvia DiStefano made it," said the runner, who Alex had learned was called David Hemmings. He had run up and down the hill twice whilst everyone was walking up it, and thereby worked up a light sweat. He wiped his brow with the back of his hand. "It's a sculpture."

"If you say so," said Will dubiously.

"How come she can move Statical stuff?" asked Alex, spotting a logical inconsistency.

"It isn't Statical anymore," said Tanya, pleased to demonstrate insider information. "Ganymede made a whole pile of wood into 'Stician wood for her so's she could do her sculptin' with it." She sniffed, looking from sceptical face to face and concluded, "Waste of time, if you ask me."

Ganymede was preparing to speak. He clapped his hands and hush descended on the assembled populace. A tall bespectacled woman with sparse brown hair stood at Ganymede's side, wearing dungarees and an expression of smug self-satisfaction. This was presumably Sylvia DiStefano, a fact confirmed when Ganymede started speaking.

"Ladies and gentlemen of Intersticia," he began. "We are privileged to have amongst us an artist of national repute in the person of Sylvia here. Sylvia is best known for her installation works, one of which, some of you may know, was nominated for the Turner Prize shortlist last year. She is also celebrated as a sculptor, and her ephemeral works using natural materials in natural situations have won her international acclaim."

He indicated the anorexic bonfire. "What you see before you is her latest creation, Intersticia's first. I have been to some trouble to make the materials available to her and the results, as you can see, are extraordinary. Perhaps Miss DiStefano would be good enough to say a few words about it."

The only thing that Alex could see was extraordinary was

how anyone could think a slender pile of sticks was a work of art. There was a polite ripple of applause as Sylvia DiStefano took centre stage, a few of what must have been her friends giving her an enthusiastic hand.

Sylvia had lots to say about her work, much of it couched in language that left Alex feeling baffled and frustrated. It seemed that what Sylvia mainly wanted to convey was that she was a lot cleverer than everyone there.

"… challenges our preconceptions about the relationship between observer and observed," Alex picked out. "A synthesis of mind and matter through the medium of the natural environment," he heard. After a while he stopped listening. His eye, wandering from the edifying prospect of Sylvia DiStefano in full self-congratulatory flow, came to rest upon the edge of the forest behind her. Here, he detected movement in the shadows amongst the trees. He nudged Kelly.

"What's that?" he asked, under his breath.

"What's what?" hissed Kelly. Alex fancied he saw her blush a little.

"In the trees," he whispered helpfully.

"I didn't see anything," she said, before Sylvia's friends shushed them.

But Alex had an idea she was lying. So did Tanya.

"I bet that was Paulo," she hissed into Alex's ear as they made their slow way back into Cardenbridge.

"How long d'you reckon you've been here?" Alex asked Will that night as they sat finishing a manna roll in the yellow glow of a light stick. "In 'Sticia, I mean. You must have some idea."

Will shrugged. "I honestly don't know. That's another thing about 'Sticia. It does something to your memory. I don't know whether it's the boredom or the fact that nothing moves and the sky looks exactly the same all day; it just seems impossible to remember more than a couple of days. A few events kind of stick out in my memory but basically it's just a blur. That's why I've been trying to keep a diary."

"Well, it's an obvious way of keeping a track of things," said Alex reasonably. "A permanent record, I guess."

"You'd think so, wouldn't you," said Will, reaching for a sheaf of papers. "But take a look at that."

Alex found that he was looking at the pages of Will's diary. Traversed by Will's untidy handwriting the top sheets were crisp and white. As Alex leafed through the pile the sheets became increasingly yellowed and fragile. The bottom sheets crumbled into fine dust even as he handled them.

"Oops, sorry," he said, carefully laying them down.

"Don't worry," said Will. "That's what I mean. 'Stician paper crumbles after a couple of weeks."

"But there must be other ways of recording stuff," objected Alex.

"I'd like to know how," said Will. "Everything 'Stician wears out after a short while. I tried marking my jug once with a coin I had in my pocket when I got here. I couldn't make a mark on it. It's like 'Stician stuff has no effect on Statical." He shrugged, suddenly defeated. "Anyway, what's the point, huh? May as well just go with the flow."

There was something rather sad, rather weary in the set of Will's plump features as he gathered up his crumbling papers. Alex felt suddenly sorry for him.

"There's got to be an end to it," he said.

"Has there?" Will pushed his glasses up his nose and stared at him. "Maybe there is, but there's no way of telling when it's going to happen. You just get sucked back in, supposedly, when your number's up." He sniffed and crossed to the window, peering out into the dark street. "Unless you're dead, that is. And then, well then there's… Cactus Jack. I'd rather take care of it myself."

A strange prickle of dread crept across Alex's scalp at the mention of this name. He had seen Cactus Jack. He didn't say so though. Not now.

"What d'you mean? Like… topping yourself?" asked Alex hesitantly.

"Well, it isn't much of a life, is it?" said Will, with a bitter laugh. "'Limbo', that's what Margaret Owen calls it. She says we must endure it patiently, but sometimes I reckon my patience is pretty much used up."

"You don't have to die to get out of here," said Alex, making his mind up to tell Will what he had never told anyone in 'Sticia yet. "I've been in 'Sticia quite a few times."

"That's impossible!" Will eyed him warily.

"I promise you it's not," said Alex, eyes blazing with sincerity.

He told Will about the first time he had daydreamed himself into 'Sticia when he was at school (already, it seemed a lifetime ago). And then his subsequent, brief visitations before his final stranding here. Will listened in silence, polishing his glasses on his sleeve.

"There's something really, really odd about you," he said when Alex had finished. "I thought there was the first time I saw you. I never heard of anyone who could get in and out of 'Sticia. How did you say you did it?"

Alex told him. They both spent the next few minutes shaking their heads, gritting their teeth and scrunching up their eyes. It was no use, of course. Alex had almost given up hope that it ever would be.

The next day Alex was to help Mrs Patterson. He found her easily enough, in a quiet suburban street with blossom trees set at intervals along the grass verges of the pavement. The day's tenth manatee had already drifted overhead by the time Alex arrived. It had a little notch in its tail that Alex thought he might recognise in future, even had he not been counting.

There was a large pile of sand at one end of the street and by it stood Mrs Patterson, mopping her brow with a tiny lacy handkerchief. Next to her were a large galvanised bucket and a shovel, leaning against a wall. She set to with the shovel again, laboriously driving it into the sand and then emptying the contents carefully into the bucket, her thin arms quivering with the effort.

"Good morning, Mrs Patterson," called Alex as he approached.

Mrs Patterson laid aside the shovel once more and cautiously straightened her narrow back as she turned to greet him.

"Good morning, Alex," she said. "It is Alex, isn't it? Oh, yes. Of course. Hang on, let me get my breath." She laughed, a surprisingly shrill musical laugh. "You'd have thought I'd have got used to this by now. I've been doing it long enough. But today, at least it has pleased my good friend Mr Ganymede to lighten my burden."

Alex found himself wondering whether people could actually keel over through exhaustion here. Could you actually die here by ordinary means – heart attack, stroke, cancer and so on? Mrs Patterson indicated the other end of the street, where there was a smaller pile of sand.

"I have to move the rest of this sand up yonder, d'you see? Do you think you could help me with that? It would be nice to have a little break. I've been at it since seventh already."

Mrs Patterson looked so thin and pale and weary; it seemed certain that she must topple over at any moment. Alex was very glad when she was firmly established, sitting on a low wall, and he could get on with shifting the sand. The first few buckets were hardly any effort at all, but a dugong later he was beginning to ache around the shoulders and the palms of his hands were already red and raw. The pile of sand seemed hardly to have diminished. It was going to be a long day.

Around about twelfth Alex had had enough. His arms and shoulders were on fire and his knees felt like they would buckle at any instant. He sat on the wall next to Mrs Patterson, who poured him a drink of water from her jug. They had lunch, or at least each of them unwrapped their cloths and ate a couple of manna rolls, which was about as close to the experience of lunch as you were ever likely to get in 'Sticia.

"You've done very well," said Mrs Patterson, encouragingly. "And it's meant that I've been able to get on with a bit of knitting for Mrs Dubcek. She's absolutely hopeless at it, poor dear."

"Which would be why Ganymede makes her do it," observed Alex, around a mouthful of manna.

She nodded sadly. "Yes, I suppose so. Still, we must all make the best of it and help each other where we can."

"What's Ganymede's problem anyway?" asked Alex. "He's pretty odd isn't he? Is he, well, you know, like us?"

Mrs Patterson smiled vaguely. "Who can say? He certainly looks and talks like a human being. Supposedly, the angels chose him to run the sector at some point. It's as though he's Lord of the Manor, you see, master of all he surveys."

"Can't we get rid of him?" suggested Alex, looking gloomily at his bucket and shovel.

Mrs Patterson laughed a ripple of high, cheerful notes. "It sounds like you've been talking to that Major Trubshaw. He'd like to do just that. You wait 'til next Gathering, then we'll see some fireworks. I can't see anything coming of it myself, except a whole lot of trouble for the poor Major."

Mrs Patterson told Alex that the Major was circulating a petition around 'Sticia. Amongst other things the petition demanded that the people of 'Sticia should be allowed to assert their democratic rights to elect a leader for themselves. It also called for better living conditions and the chance to negotiate directly with the angels.

"Did you sign it?" asked Alex.

The old lady nodded. "I did. I think he deserves our support. At least he's trying to do something, although I doubt his motives are entirely altruistic. Still, I daresay nothing will come of it."

Alex looked up, his attention caught by movement on the periphery of his vision. What he saw almost caused him to fall backwards off the wall. Standing in the middle of the road was a creature nearly eight feet tall. Dressed all in black, like an undertaker, it had hugely long arms and legs and a small head thrust forward on a long, scrawny neck. There was a broad slash of a mouth beneath a huge beak of a nose, but where its eyes should have been there were only two tiny black specks, like the eyes of a sparrow. These were peering up and down the road, first at one pile of sand, then at the other.

"Good day, Mr Morlock," called Mrs Patterson, calmly. "I suppose we are allowed a break for luncheon."

Morlock turned to her and stroked a few lank black hairs across his shiny pate with a long and bony hand. He did not speak, although his mouth twitched into what might have been the faintest of smiles.

"And where is your companion, Mr Minion?" continued the old lady. "I trust he is well?"

Morlock made no reply. With a last glance at Alex, he wiped his nose with the back of his hand and strode off along the street, his long legs covering ground with impressive speed.

"Who was *that*?" Alex found to his surprise that he was whispering. "Or what?"

"Oh, that's just Mr Morlock, checking up on us for Mr

Ganymede," said Mrs Patterson matter-of-factly, getting on with her knitting. "Don't let it bother you. I know he's a bit odd to look at. He and Mr Minion keep an eye on things in 'Sticia for their master," she laughed once more. "Which is odd really, since the pair of them haven't what you or I would call a proper eye between them."

Mrs Paterson told Alex more about Morlock and Minion whilst Alex got on with shovelling sand. It appeared they were Ganymede's spies and police. Morlock was huge and gangling, Minion short and plump. Together they patrolled the streets of 'Sticia, making sure that Ganymede's will was enforced. Anyone who crossed Ganymede could find themselves dragged before him by the gruesome twosome, and anyone who Ganymede wished to punish would find themselves carted off to the House of Correction, a kind of 'Stician prison behind the aviary next to the park buildings.

"You've done very well," Mrs Patterson told him at the end of the day when they stood surveying the two piles of sand. "I never move half as much as that."

Alex reckoned he had shifted about two-thirds of the pile. He should easily finish it the following day; if he survived that long. His whole body was one big ache. His breaks for rest and water had become increasingly long and frequent as the day wore on. Mrs Patterson had taken a turn herself between nineteenth and twentieth whilst Alex went to fetch more water from the stream. Watching her feebly driving the shovel into the pile was painful to behold. Alex's existing dislike of Ganymede began to harden into something approaching detestation.

Aching from his day's exertions, Alex didn't feel particularly sociable that night. He groaned inwardly when Kelly came to visit, along with Tanya, of course, who seemed pretty much inseparable from her. Alex found that he very much wanted to roll himself in his blankets and go to sleep. With Kelly there he didn't feel that he could, although it was all he could do to stifle a succession of jaw-bending yawns. She was begging manna as usual and Alex soon found himself parting with two of his rolls.

"You should tell her to get lost," Will told him pointedly, having instructed her likewise himself.

"I'll bring some over tomorrow," said Kelly with an unapologetic smile. "Promise." She broke off a big piece of manna. "So how did you get on with old Mrs P?"

Alex told her, and about his encounter with Morlock, whilst Kelly munched appreciatively.

"That's funny," she said. "Because I saw his sidekick Minion twice today. He's the little fat chappy. I called him over to see if he wanted to listen to any Yeats but he just gave me that big cheesy grin of his and sidled away. I hadn't seen him for ages until today. If I didn't know any better I'd say Ganymede was keeping an eye on me."

"And why would he do that?" asked Will suspiciously. "Something to do with Paulo would it be?" A little light of realisation suddenly sparked in his eyes. "Hey! I know why you're always so hungry. I bet you're sharing your rations with Paulo."

Kelly made a disgusted face and cast her eyes upward. "That's typical of you, Will," she said. "You've got a nasty, suspicious little mind. I told you, I haven't even seen Paulo for days."

"Yeah, well," said Will, pointing at her with his pen. "Looks like I'm not the only one who doesn't believe you."

"So you think I'm a liar, do you?" Kelly was suddenly deadly serious, eyes narrowed, her lips a tight line.

"Well, I don't know what else to call it," he retorted. "If the cap fits…"

Suddenly Will and Kelly were shouting at each other, face to face, features contorted with anger. Alex and Tanya looked at each other helplessly.

"I saw Cactus Jack," said Alex on an impulse, before blows were exchanged. This had a most satisfactory calming effect.

"What?" Kelly and Will span round, differences suddenly set aside.

"Cactus Jack," said Alex slowly, surprised at the impact of what he had said. "I saw him, the other night."

"Where?" asked Kelly, absently twisting a strand of her glossy brown hair.

"Out on the front," said Alex. "He was coming along the street."

"Big chap, right?" asked Will.

"Cactus on a white T-shirt?" asked Kelly. Alex nodded. "Exactly when did you see him?" she continued.

"It was the night before the Gathering," said Alex. "I felt scared. I hid behind the hedge so I didn't see anything else."

Tanya, Kelly and Will all exchanged glances. Alex felt a bit of an outsider.

"It's not good, is it?" he ventured.

"It's not good news for whoever he's coming for," said Will slowly. "The game's up for them, alright."

"He could just be passing through the sector," said Tanya. "It's happened before and no one got taken. Chad told me."

"Everyone was okay at the Gathering the next morning," said Will. "He must have been… No, hang on." He stared suddenly at Kelly. "Paulo wasn't there."

"Maybe Cactus Jack came for Paulo," suggested Tanya in a small voice. She clung to Kelly's side.

Kelly bit her lip. Alex remembered the movement he had seen on Micklebury Hill when Sylvia DiStefano had been talking about her sculpture.

"I don't think so," she said. "They say he sometimes comes a few times before he zeroes in on somebody. It's like he sniffs them out or something."

"What exactly does he do?" asked Alex impatiently. "Does he shoot them or something? You'd expect something more like a big skull-faced guy with a scythe. Black robes. You know, that kind of thing."

"It's nothing like that," said Kelly, regarding Alex seriously, her manna roll forgotten now. "He just kind of tracks them down. He never runs, see… Jack. He just has this patient, steady kind of stride. There was this guy called Mitch. Seems his time here was up. Mitch sees him coming, of course, realises his number's up and legs it – as you would. Anyway, Jack just keeps on following until the dude's pretty much dead on his feet. I mean, where's he going to hide? He can't exactly barricade any doors, can he, what with them being Statical and all that? In the end Jack catches up with him. Jason Collingwood's got this place in Lower High Street. He was watching from an upstairs window. He saw Jack carrying this dude over his shoulder. Moaning and twitching he was. Jack just pushed open a door and carried him inside. No one ever saw him again. It's like he's never been in 'Sticia at all. I can show you the house, if you like. Anyway, after a bit Cactus Jack comes out, rubs his hands together and off he goes. Job done, end of story."

"End of Stavros," added Will grimly.

"Jesus," breathed Alex. "Why didn't anyone stop him? They could have helped the poor bloke, couldn't they?" He glanced from face to face but found no reassurance there.

"What do you think?" asked Will. "You saw him. How did you feel? Did you feel maybe you could step out and tell him to lay his lousy mitts off anyone?"

Alex remembered the sheer strength-sapping terror that had

seized him as Jack passed by.

"No," he admitted with a shrug. "I guess not."

Alex didn't sleep well that night. Cactus Jack haunted his dreams. Maybe he, Alex, had died. Maybe he had suffered a fatal heart attack or something. Perhaps that moment in Wardworths had been his last on Earth. More than ever he wanted to go back to Reality, but not like that, not as a corpse. He wanted it to be like stepping into a familiar room, just like it had been before. Now that world seemed oddly remote, despite its undeniable frozen existence all around him. It was as though he didn't belong there anymore. It was as though he was beginning to belong to 'Sticia instead.

By Alex's reckoning it was Wednesday the next day, although of course it remained 2.23pm Saturday in Reality. On his way to Mrs Patterson's, Alex stopped by in Wardworths to visit his mum. Once there he held Mum's stony hand and embraced her for a while, vaguely wondering if the effect he had on his mattress could be duplicated on stiffs if he held onto one long enough. Nothing happened. He had never really believed that it might. Despite this, Alex told her how things were going with him, keeping her up to date with events in his life. Not that it made any difference. His soft-spoken words sounded loud in the utter stillness of the shop. It made him feel a little better though. Just a little. Then, on an impulse, he crossed to the pick 'n' mix, casting a hungry eye across the toffees and the chocolate limes. Manna was all very well but it wasn't the same as real food. It was quite forbidden to interfere with Statica, he told himself. But then Ganymede wasn't there now, was he? And surely even Ganymede hadn't counted all the sherbet lemons. Who would ever know? For a while Alex conducted a lively inner debate. He licked his lips. He blew air into his cheeks. He glanced furtively about the shop. There was no-one there; no one 'Stician at any rate. At last, having carefully selected a target, Alex reached out and took a chocolate éclair. A brief tug against the strange magnetic force of Statica and it was free. He hurriedly unwrapped the sweet and popped into his mouth in case Ganymede, Morlock and Minion should suddenly burst into Wardworths like in a police 'sting'. It was delicious. Alex felt a thrill of wicked delight, leavened with guilt as the chocolate and toffee mingled in his mouth.

"Who's going to know, anyway?" he told himself. "I'll just have to be careful. Maybe I'll just have one every couple of days. No-one's going to miss them."

He set off for Mrs Patterson's house with the comfort of that rich taste in his mouth and a new spring in his step. No one else in 'Sticia could do what he had done. He was special. Alex whistled and slapped the back of the occasional stiff in comradely fashion as he headed for his appointment with Ganymede's pile of sand.

Chapter Seven

The next few days brought with them a variety of labours. There was more sand shovelling for Mrs Patterson, of course, and then a new interview with Ganymede in which he was allotted fresh tasks. One of them was cutting string for George Plaistow, who had arthritis in his hands, and the other was helping Stacey Lawler learn dates from British history. This last task was a particularly disagreeable assignment, not so much in the nature of the chore itself, but in the nature of the person he was obliged to assist.

"I don't know why I've got dates this week," Stacey told him plaintively. "I got colourin' in pictures last week, and that was okay." The tone of her voice suggested she held Alex personally responsible for this.

Stacey lived with Sarah in a terraced house in Bridle Street. Sarah was usually out with Margaret Owen, putting together a car engine they had been asked to reassemble, so Alex found himself alone with Stacey rather more than he could have wished for.

"And don't you go trying any moves," Stacey had warned him as they went upstairs together to her sleeping room to revise from her history book.

"Not so long as Hell doesn't freeze over," Alex told himself as he settled himself opposite her on a pile of blankets. Her lank bottle-blonde hair hung over her face as she pored over the book, her pig's eyes rimmed in clotted mascara.

"Here," she said, holding out a sheet of paper in a pudgy hand. There was chipped purple polish on her finger nails. "You'd better test me on these."

"Well, you'd better close the book then, hadn't you?" suggested Alex.

"Alright," said Stacey in aggrieved tones. "But I don't see what it's to you how I learns 'em."

Nevertheless, she closed the book. "Go on then, pick one from anywhere in the list."

"Battle of Trafalgar," read Alex, looking up in time to see an expression of pain traverse Stacey's face.

"I knew you'd have to go and pick that one," she grumbled.

Later they went out into the garden, which was fine by Alex, and sat on the lawn. He had suggested that a little fresh air might help her to think. Something had to, if she was going to learn her dates by the next Gathering. She was as thick as two planks. Worse, it was apparently Alex's fault that she was unable to learn.

"You're not givin' me a chance," she told him. "That's what I was goin' to say."

"We just did that one a few minutes ago," she grumbled when he had to remind her of the date of the Defenestration of Prague for the fifteenth time.

"Well, you still haven't learned it," Alex pointed out.

"You're still not givin' me a chance," she said bitterly, throwing herself onto her back. "Anyway, wossa 'defenestration'?"

"They chucked some dudes out of a window," Alex told her, thinking he'd like to chuck Stacey out of one. "In Prague, in 1618. Got that? Sixteen-eighteen. One-six-one-eight."

For additional emphasis he drew the numbers in the air in front of her.

Stacey groaned, rolled onto her side and lifted herself up on her elbow so that she could study Alex. A large expanse of flaccid white belly sagged between her top and her jeans. Her navel had a stud in it and part of a tattoo showed shyly under her top. Alex didn't like her looking at him, and he didn't much care for looking at her either.

"You've got sticky out ears," she pointed out.

"Yeah, and you're a fat minger," thought Alex. "But I'm keeping my personal observations to myself."

"Really? Are you sure?" he said, making an elaborate pretence of groping around the sides of his head. "Oh my god! They are quite big, aren't they?"

There was a silence in which Stacey appeared to study her nails.

"Do you fancy Kelly, then?" she asked, before Alex could get on with the Battle of Naseby.

"No!" he said, feeling as though he had been ambushed, and with the sensation of blood rushing hotly to every blood vessel in his face.

Stacey flopped onto her back again and laughed coarsely, which was the only way she had of laughing. "Yes, you do. You should see your face. Not that it'll do you any good. She's got a big thing goin' for Paulo, hasn't she? Think she's hot, do you?"

Alex wanted to tell her to shut up and mind her own business but somehow couldn't bring himself to do so. He found himself drawn reluctantly into a conversation he rather wanted to escape from.

"What's it to you?" he demanded peevishly.

"It's obviously somethin' to you, otherwise you wouldn't have gone all funny on me," she observed slyly. "No need to throw a wobbly, I only asked if you thought she was, you know, pretty or anythin'."

"Yeah… I guess so," he conceded, in what he hoped was an offhand kind of manner. "Not my type though," he added.

"Oh yeah? And what's *your* type then? Had a lot of girlfriends, have you?"

"I thought we were supposed to be learning dates," said Alex, blushing furiously.

"Yeah, and I bet you'd like one with Kelly – a date that is. Spend a lot of time with her, don't you? Well, don't trust her 'cos she's a devious little cow," said Stacey with feeling. "And anyway, I wouldn't go rating your chances. You break her in half and you'll find she's got Paulo written right through her like a stick o' rock."

As was becoming his habit, Alex stopped by at Wardworths on his way back to Gladstone Street, a place he was now beginning to regard as his permanent abode. He felt unaccountably depressed. Perhaps it was because he had spent nearly a whole week in 'Sticia now. As a result he disregarded his self-imposed rule that he should eat only a single chocolate éclair. Standing gloomily at the pic 'n' mix, Alex picked and mixed and helped himself until he'd had enough. This took a while. When he had finished, his mental state was somewhat improved but his physical condition had taken a definite turn for the worse. He felt sick and a little guilty. He went to apologise to his mum on his way out of the shop as darkness settled over 'Sticia and the big black shape of the twenty-second manatee passed overhead.

He spent what passed for the evening with Will, Kelly and Tanya, as had become routine by now. Chad joined them later on, with his friend Charles, a morose child of about twelve years who rarely left his side. Chad Beresford was a lanky eighteen-year-old with a mop of unkempt black hair and jeans so ill-fitting they could have accommodated someone twice his size. Talk soon turned to Paulo, he who seemed destined to hover for ever on the fringe of Alex's world. Chad was said to be a friend of Paulo's and Alex thought he detected a sly exchange of glances between he and Kelly when Paulo's name was first mentioned. Chad was, of course, the object of Stacey's affections but had little to say about his admirer that she might have regarded as encouragement.

"She's such a loser," was his considered view when Alex told the story of his day's labours. Alex could agree with him on this but he found himself in strong opposition to Chad's way of snuggling up to Kelly as they spoke, nudging her with his elbow whenever he thought he had something funny to say. This was often enough, given that Chad had himself down as something of a wit. He liked to hold forth on a variety of themes but the subject that really engaged his interest was himself. It seemed that he did lots of gigs as a DJ. It seemed that he had tried out for two Premiership football teams (before injuring his knee). It seemed that he was going to be a racing driver (if he ever got out of 'Sticia).

Alex found that he wanted to be elsewhere, a sensation that became increasingly acute as time passed by. He sighed. He looked at his watch, remembering too late that there was absolutely no point and pretending to study his wrist instead.

"I'm going out for a breath of fresh air," he said at length.

No-one tried to prevent his exit, so Alex made his way out and along Cardwell Avenue towards the centre of town. On an impulse he turned into Lower High Street where there were several big old houses divided into flats. It was into one of these that the unfortunate Mitch was said to have been dragged by Cactus Jack. 'Sticia's moon reflected eerily off the windows of number 112 as Alex stepped forward across the patch of weed-pocked gravel that served as its front garden.

This had to be the right building. Alex remembered the door described as a big black one and this was the only premises in sight that matched this description. He peered through the dust-streaked window at a living room partly stacked with cardboard boxes, as though the occupant had recently moved in and had yet to finish unpacking. A washing basket, overflowing with a variety of unfolded garments, occupied half of a small sofa. Alex had no clear idea what motivated him to explore here, now or indeed later, when he had time to reflect on his actions. Perhaps he was curious to see if Mitch was here at all, or whether he had simply vanished without trace. And then, of course, if Mitch genuinely was dead, his body might be here, a stiff in every sense. It was this thought that made Alex hesitate for a long time as he stood before the front door. It would be easy to simply turn and walk away but some unidentified yet powerful impulse kept him there. On the front door was an ancient brass door handle of majestic proportions. Alex regarded this anxiously, flexing his right hand and rocking backwards and forwards on the balls of his feet. At last, summoning up the necessary resolve, he tried the handle, which resisted, but Alex was used to this by now and something told him the door was not actually locked. He grimaced, using both hands now to heave against the handle. The resistance suddenly abated and the door creaked open. Alex looked over his shoulder at the motionless street. It was as though hidden eyes surveyed him from every dark, blank window. The hall ahead of him was empty except for a bicycle, leaning against the staircase. Taking a deep breath, Alex stepped over the threshold.

He ignored the front room and stepped cautiously past the bicycle into the kitchen at the rear of the house. Mum would strongly have disapproved of Mitch's housekeeping. A vast pile of correspondence had slithered sideways on the worktop next to the fridge, coming to rest on a plate of partly eaten toast. The sink was full of unwashed pots. Past a window sill full of neglected pot plants a view of an equally neglected garden opened up. Upstairs, the front bedroom had nothing in it, not even a bed. An expanse of dusty carpet showed where one had stood until quite recently. The door to the rear bedroom was closed. Alex felt a sense of gathering dread as he stood before it. "Jessica," said a colourful ceramic plaque, fixed at his eye level. It was absolutely silent. Alex could hear his own heart thudding in his chest. "Why don't I just get out of here?" he asked himself, reasonably enough, licking dry lips. "Come on, let's just go now." Failing to take his own advice, Alex closed his eyes and opened them again, clenching his hands into tight balls at his side. Then, swearing under his breath, he swallowed hard to dispel the sudden tightness in his throat and pushed against the door. There was resistance. Alex pushed harder, finally placing the whole of his weight against it and grunting with the strain. The door gave way suddenly and Alex stumbled forward, arms outstretched, fighting for balance. He collided with an ominous dark mass, a dark mass that swung heavily for a moment and then froze once more. Alex rebounded from the object and sprawled on the floor before it. The curtains had been drawn but a slither of moonlight picked out all he needed to see. He screamed, a shrill hoot of terror that felt as though it burst from the deepest recess of his being, and flung himself back, shuffling desperately away until his shoulders were pressed against a chest of drawers.

"Oh, my god," he gasped. "Oh my god, oh my god, oh my god!"

Mitch's body hung suspended from a length of electrical cable. The head tilted sideways, held there by the taught white line of flex. Eyes bulged sightlessly. Mitch's tongue lolled from his mouth. A child's red plastic chair lay overturned nearby. Alex knew beyond all doubt that this instant, this awful vision, was branded spitting and sizzling indelibly onto the naked surface of his brain. He scrambled to his feet and ran; gasping, panting, taking the stairs three at a time in his desperation to put distance between himself and Mitch's hideous dangling corpse. He stopped to gather his wits and his breath at the corner of Gladstone Street, holding his aching sides, taking a deep breath and holding it, holding it.

"Oh… my… god," he said one more time in a long exhalation.

So there *was* death in 'Sticia. He had seen it with his own eyes. And whenever he closed his eyes he could see it still. When he returned to Gladstone Street it was to find that their guests had left.

"Where've you been?" asked Will sleepily from his room, as Alex passed on the landing, but it was a question that carried with it little genuine curiosity.

"Just out," said Alex with a shrug. "Just out and about, you know. 'Night, Will."

Who could he tell? He had broken Ganymede's law by entering the house, using a power that he dared not admit he possessed. The burden of that dreadful encounter hung heavy on his mind, and it was a burden that could not be shared. Sleep remained a distant prospect, too. Curled in his blankets like some small frightened animal, Alex stared at the wallpaper, at the little flowers entwined around little columns almost lost in the darkness. He revisited memories of earliest childhood, of holidays, of relatives, of school, but always Mitch's dead face swam up through these insubstantial visions to haunt him, to deny him the respite of sleep.

Having hardly closed his eyes all night Alex turned up late and reluctant at Stacey's house, only to find Morlock standing outside, studying a big pocket watch. Likely enough it was the only functioning watch in 'Sticia. Having given Alex a meaningful stare, Morlock loped off towards the town centre.

"Damn!" said Alex, feeling like he'd just realised he'd forgotten his English homework. "Black mark for me then."

Another day in Stacey's company lay ahead, by the end of which Alex had added more to his portfolio of dislike for her. She was rude, impatient and self-centred. She was also painfully dense. But diversion was coming Alex's way. The tedium of the afternoon was broken by the arrival of Major Trubshaw with the petition that was already the talk of 'Sticia.

"I wonder if I may rely on your support?" said the Major, joining them on the lawn and brandishing a sheaf of papers. "I intend to present Ganymede with this petition tomorrow at the Gathering, outlining our grievances."

Major Trubshaw was a large man with a complexion that varied in hue from brick red to purple. He had a bristling white moustache and an air of barely restrained impatience.

"Not sure about that," said Stacey warily. "I ain't putting my name to anything I ain't read."

The Major thrust the petition at her, whereupon Stacey began to read, her lips silently forming some of the more challenging words. She stopped after a few lines.

"There's no way I'm signing that," she said, thrusting out a plump arm with the papers clenched in her fist at the end of it. "Ganymede'll go ballistic. You must be bloody mad!"

"I'll thank you to keep a civil tongue in your head," the Major told Stacey sharply. "I am merely articulating the legitimate demands of the citizens of Intersticia. Ganymede is bound to listen to us if we express our grievances together in this way. I urge you to sign. It is vital that we present a united front."

Stacey folded her arms and shook her lank blond head. The Major glared at her from beneath his bushy white eyebrows. It was a fascinating contest. Alex observed it with interest.

"I'll take that as a 'no' then," said the Major at length. "I must say, I find your refusal to support your friends and fellow citizens very disappointing." He turned to Alex.

"And you, you're that new boy, aren't you? Alex isn't it?" He stuck out a hand, which Alex cautiously shook, whilst Major Trubshaw beamed at him. "Could I ask you to read the petition?"

"Everyone else signed it, have they?" asked Stacey sourly.

"Almost everyone," said the Major crisply, whilst Alex cast an eye across the document.

The petition was pretty much as Mrs Patterson had said it was, consisting of a list of demands that seemed reasonable enough. Alex found himself entirely in agreement with them. On the other hand, he didn't want to get in trouble with Ganymede. He could see why Stacey was wary of signing. He cast his eye up and down the list of signatures, recognising several names, including those of Kelly, Tanya and Mrs Patterson. The Major reached into his jacket pocket and brought out a fountain pen, which he offered to Alex. Before Alex could reach for this, before he could decide whether to do anything with it at all, he had to deal with a sudden massive sneeze. He reached into his pocket and snatched out a grubby mass of tissues just in time to stem the worst of it. A number of chocolate éclair wrappers came out with the tissue and fluttered to the lawn. Stacey idly nudged one with her toe. Alex, wiping his nose and taking the pen, was suddenly conscious of Stacey fixing him with a thoughtful sort of look. He quickly signed his name at the bottom of the page and stooped to gather up the wrappers, almost oblivious to the Major's congratulations. He vaguely heard him say something about a forthcoming 'confrontation' and then the military man was away, with a cheery wave of his hand and a disapproving glare at Stacey. Stacey gave as good as she got. Alex slumped down heavily on the lawn, feeling oddly flustered.

"Right," he said. "Where had we got to?"

"You'll only go and get yourself in trouble, signing up to rubbish like that," Stacey told him, with an unconvincing grin. "Like trouble, do you?"

Alex shook his head.

"What about those chocolate éclairs?" she continued, her grin broadening. "Got any more of those, have you? I do like chocolate éclairs."

"No," said Alex hastily. "Those were just a few papers I had in my pocket when I came here."

"Oh," she said slowly, her mouth opening into an exaggerated pursed circle. "Would that be so?"

Alex could hardly get away quickly enough. Stacey showed no inclination to do any more date learning and lay on her back on the lawn, humming to herself. Alex made his excuses and headed for home, although the eighteenth manatee was only then gliding beneath the town hall clock. He felt unaccountably alarmed and confused, partly, he guessed, because he had signed up to the Major's polite rebellion, but partly because there had been something disconcerting in Stacey's attitude toward him. Had he given the matter more thought, and had Wardworths not lain directly on his route home, he might have avoided the place altogether. As it was, he made his customary visit to his mum and spent a few minutes browsing the pic 'n' mix whilst he tried to set his thoughts in order. He had helped himself to a Mars bar, too, before having restored a measure of calm to his mind. It was his imagination, he told himself, taking quick luxurious bites, his eyes darting furtively around the shop. He was simply panicked by the petition, that was it. Nevertheless, Alex still felt a little unsettled as he carefully disposed of the wrapper in a bin behind the till.

Whatever peace of mind he had regained by this didn't long survive walking outside into the precinct. There, sitting by the fountain, were Stacey and Sarah. Alex felt a little thrill of horror and guilt pass over his scalp.

"Are you alright?" Stacey asked him with a broad and insolent grin. "Look like you've seen a ghost."

"You do, you're all pale and sweaty," said Sarah, coming up to him. "I hope you're not coming down with anything."

"I'm fine," said Alex warily. He jerked a thumb over his shoulder. "I was just popping in to see my mum, see. She's one of the stiffs in there."

"Oh," said Stacey and Sarah together, nodding with mock solemnity. "Is she now?"

Alex wanted to knock their silly heads off.

"Here, what's that round your mouth?" asked Sarah, suddenly closing in on Alex with finger raised. "Looks like chocolate."

Alex reeled away from the advancing finger, wiping roughly at his mouth with the back of his hand. He was thoroughly alarmed now.

"But it can't be chocolate, Sarah," said Stacey in exaggerated matter of fact tones. "Because there is no chocolate in 'Sticia. Everyone knows that."

"That's right, Stacey," said Sarah, putting her finger to her lips. "How silly of me. I don't know what I could have been thinking of. But that little brown smudge did look so much like chocolate. It's all gone now. Perhaps it was just a figment of my imagination."

"Here, are you sure you're alright, Alex?" asked Stacey, all elaborately feigned concern. "You really do look peeky. There isn't anything troubling you, is there? We're all friends here, you know. And friends don't keep secrets from each other, do they?"

"No. Secrets are very bad things, aren't they Alex?" said Sarah. "They do weigh on the conscience so, don't they? You wouldn't be keepin' secrets now, would you Alex?"

All the time Stacey and Sarah had been advancing upon Alex until now he could feel Stacey's breath on his face, a very disagreeable sensation. She was bigger than him, too, and by a considerable margin. He wanted to push past them and run away as fast as his legs could carry him, but even in his reduced state he could see that this wouldn't do.

"No," he said. "I'm not. Look, I'm absolutely fine, honestly. I really don't know what you're getting at." He took a deep breath, composed himself and held Stacey's eye as steadily as he could. Seconds passed, and with it, perhaps, the immediate crisis. "Yeah, well," he said when it became clear that something else was expected of him. "I'd love to stand about talking to you ladies all night, but I'd better be off now. There's a couple of manna rolls with my name on them back home and I'm absolutely starving." He managed a bit of a laugh at this, but it sounded hollow even in his own ears. Nevertheless, Stacey and Sarah stepped aside to let him past. Trying to walk at a relaxed, measured pace, Alex set off along the stiff-cluttered High Street.

"'Bye, Alex," called the girls behind him with a mocking laugh. "Hope you've got a good appetite."

Alex could hardly bring himself to speak to Will that evening. All he wanted to do was retire to his bedroom, wrap himself up in a cocoon of blankets and go to sleep. But he couldn't sleep. The events of the afternoon continued to replay themselves in his mind. He was sure now that Stacey had rumbled him, that she knew that he had been helping himself to Statical sweets. Perhaps she and Sarah had spied on him in Wardworths. He had not noticed them, but that didn't rule it out. He could have missed them in the crowd, if they had remained very still. And if he had been spotted scoffing the chocs, what would Stacey do? Would she tell Ganymede? It was a terrible feeling. It was as though Stacey held him in the palm of her pudgy hand like some fragile little insect that she could crush whenever the fancy took her.

Much to Alex's relief it had been arranged that he should work with David Hemmings the following day. David proved to be the keen runner that Alex had seen on a number of occasions and lived on the lower floor of a large detached house in Crawford Drive. Alex was so used to seeing him at a brisk trot that it seemed odd he should be found leaning casually on the frame of the front door as Alex approached along the drive. A little way away the stiff that was presumably the owner of the house was frozen in the act of giving instructions to a couple of garden maintenance men who were unloading a lawnmower from a van.

"Hi, Alex," said David, with a laconic wave. "Welcome to my humble abode."

There was nothing humble about it, of course, and Alex found himself suitably impressed as David led him through a hall with a chandelier into a massive oak-panelled dining room. Here, a bay window offered views over a broad spread of immaculately manicured lawns. In the room, laid out on huge polished table, was the biggest jigsaw Alex had ever seen.

"It's a beauty, isn't it?" said David, as Alex tentatively lifted a few pieces and turned them over in his hand. "I'm meant to have it finished by tomorrow."

There must have been at least two thousand pieces from which a picture composed of various antique clocks was emerging. Perhaps two-thirds of it was complete.

"You'll have to get your skates on then," observed Alex.

"No worries," said David, apparently undaunted by this. "A job shared is a job halved, I say. Can I get you a manna roll?"

The corners and edges were largely in place so Alex began sifting through graded piles of colours and shapes in search of a number three that was clearly needed for one of the larger timepieces. David soon came back and placed a manna roll in front of Alex, whistling cheerfully as he got on with his work.

"So, settled in okay, have we now?" he asked, carefully setting a piece in place that showed part of a brass fitting. "You've been here a little while, haven't you?"

"Yeah, I guess so," conceded Alex. "I've met some nice people."

"And some pretty horrible ones, if I'm any judge," said David with a wink that engaged most of the muscles on one side of his face. "I heard you've been stuck up with that ghastly little trollop, Stacey Lawler, eh? Am I right?" A massive grin spread over his face. "Hard lines on you, I say."

"Yeah," said Alex, cracking a smile of his own. "Me, too. How come Ganymede's got you doin' jigsaws?"

"Well," said David, looking around as though he feared eavesdroppers and drawing closer to Alex. "I'll let you into a secret. I actually like doing jigsaws, but somehow Ganymede got the idea I didn't. Funny that, isn't it? It might have to do with something I once let slip to our Stacey. You know, unguarded moment and all that, confidences exchanged. I don't suppose she'd have passed it on though, would she? No, surely not."

David began to laugh, throwing a few pieces up in the air. He had a narrow, lined face and greying hair, a strip of which bridged a broad expanse of balding pate. There were deep laughter lines at the corners of his eyes. Alex judged he was in his mid to late fifties.

"You've got to know how to work the levers here, see Alex. Know how things tick. Things seem to have worked out okay, wouldn't you say?"

"You make it sound as though you like it here – in 'Sticia, I mean," said Alex, breaking a piece from his roll.

"It could be worse," agreed David, who was evidently the happiest person in 'Sticia. "Mrs Hemmings, if I'm to be quite frank with you, is a bit of a tartar and now I've got her exactly where I want her, which is frozen solid, razor tongue and all. I can run as much as I like, which is a lot, as you know. Rations are plain but wholesome. No, things aren't too bad on the whole. If I could just get myself a nice cup of tea I'd be happy as a sand boy."

Alex got on famously with David during the course of what proved to be a largely enjoyable day, since David had much to say about the various inhabitants of 'Sticia, much of it entertainingly scurrilous.

"Pompous old fool," was David's assessment of Major Trubshaw when Alex mentioned the petition. "But a decent enough stick at heart. He's setting himself up for a fall though, that's for sure. Could be fireworks tomorrow."

"How long have you been here?" asked Alex. "In 'Sticia, I mean. You seem to know everyone."

The subject matter of David's jigsaw had been turning Alex's thoughts to time, and the pleasing regularity of the design was almost complete now as daylight began to fade.

David shrugged. "Does it matter? A long time, I suppose."

"But how long *exactly*?" pressed Alex.

David smiled and studied his long, bony hands before fixing Alex with a steady, considering sort of look.

"Do you know, I honestly can't remember," he admitted. "The days and weeks just seem to blur together. Odd really. I

117

suppose it's because the clocks don't work."

But it was more than that. It had to be more than that, Alex told himself as he made his way back to Gladstone Street. It wasn't just that there were no functioning clocks. Hardly anyone seemed to be particularly curious about keeping track of weeks, days and months. And then there was Will's diary with the crumbling pages. It had been Saturday 7th May when Alex tumbled into 'Sticia, but what date was it now? He shook his head, paused and sat down on a garden wall whilst he considered the implications of this question. The moment he saw all around him – the woman with the dog, the ice cream van, the cat washing its paw on the wall next to him – all those were at 2.23pm on 7th May. But what date was it for Will, or Tanya, or Kelly or anyone else? Could everyone have their own date, their own place on the ever unrolling carpet of time? It made no sense.

It still made no sense the next day, which dawned exactly, precisely, tediously as it always did. Unlike his new friend, David Hemmings, Alex had begun to find this depressing. He longed to look along the garden from his bedroom window and find it shrouded in soft, dripping rain, or to see sharp morning shadows etched by slanting sunlight across the lawn. However, he was not looking forward to what the day held in prospect. There was the Gathering to be faced up to, the Major's promised showdown with Ganymede and the disagreeable thought of having to see Stacey and Sarah.

Will, nonetheless, was full of grim excitement. "I wonder what's going to happen?" he said, as they made their way towards the park. "I can't see Major Trubshaw doing any good with it. I bet he gets himself banged up in the House of Correction and we all get reduced rations for a week. I wish

I hadn't signed now. I should have known it was a bad idea. What made *you* sign?"

"It seemed like a good idea at the time," said Alex gloomily. "Anyway it looked like nearly everyone else had signed. I wish I could rub it out now though."

"Me, too." Will slapped his own head ironically as they passed through the park gates and hurried on down past the war memorial.

The Gathering began pretty much as it did last time, with Ganymede blowing his big horn and peering about him disapprovingly into the little crowd of 'Sticians. Alex squirmed when it seemed momentarily that Ganymede had singled him out for particular attention, but this attention was soon called elsewhere. The atmosphere was tense. There was an air of expectancy amongst the little knots of 'Sticians that had been entirely absent in previous meetings and the low murmur of conversation died away instantly with the fading note of the horn. A profound silence settled over 'Sticia as Ganymede surveyed the upturned faces of his subjects. Even he must have been aware that there was something amiss in this long, long pause, pregnant with anticipation. Suddenly, breaking the spell, there came the sound of someone clearing their throat and Major Trubshaw pushed through to the front of the crowd, the white sheets of his petition held high in front of him. There was a perceptible intake of breath from all around as the Major strode up the steps and thrust the petition at Ganymede. It was as though he were holding a loaded pistol at Ganymede's midriff, or brandishing a Samurai sword.

"On behalf of the people of Intersticia, I should like to present to you this petition," said the Major loudly, so that everyone could hear. Suddenly, it was absolutely silent in the park once more. All eyes were fixed on Ganymede and the Major. Unnoticed, a dugong moved evenly overhead. "*We* have compiled a list of *reasonable* requests," continued the Major, laying particular stress on the word "we." "They are requests that any *reasonable* person should deem acceptable in the difficult circumstances we all find ourselves in. These are extraordinary circumstances and *we* believe it is incumbent on *all* of us to behave in a responsible and humane manner. *All* of us," he added, looking hard at Ganymede in case his meaning should not be clear.

For a long moment nothing happened. It was as though Ganymede and the Major had joined the ranks of the stiffs in the park. Ganymede simply stared incredulously at the Major, and at the petition, as though he were indeed threatened by a loaded pistol or an unexploded bomb. Then he transferred his attention to the crowd, sweeping his laser beam glare across the assembled faces, so that everyone shuffled back a little.

"So, betray me, would you, you traitors?" his eyes seemed to say. At length, he snatched the petition from the Major's grasp and began to read it. His face remained an impassive mask as his eyes scanned the inflammatory document. At length he lowered the petition and fixed the Major with a stare of unheard of intensity. The Major's face took on a new richness and intensity of colour, but he did not flinch.

"So," said Ganymede, sweeping his gaze about the crowd now. "The people are unhappy, are they?" His tone was one of biting sarcasm. "They think that I am unfair." He singled out Roger Bradley in the crowd. "You, Mr Bradley. Do you think that I have dealt with you unreasonably? Do you?"

Roger looked as though he might faint at any moment. In contrast with the Major's, his own complexion had suddenly become deathly pale.

"Well, do you? Your signature appears on this… this… *document*." Ganymede spat out this last word with particular venom. "So I must assume you do. Unless the Major here has forged it. Has he? *Has* he forged your signature, Roger?"

Roger grimaced, his lips moved, but he made no sound. Ganymede laughed a bitter laugh and shook his head as though suddenly wearied by his subjects' ingratitude.

"Let me see," he said, glancing again at the offending petition. "You require more variety in your diet. You would like to be consulted when work tasks are allocated. Ha!" He turned on the author of the petition and abruptly snapped his grubby tramp's fingers right in front of the Major's nose. "I suppose you'd like the occasional gin and tonic."

To Alex's astonishment, a thought bubble, exactly like those he had seen in comic strips, sprang into being above the Major's head. Words, clearly legible, appeared in the middle of it.

"*Yes. A G and T would be very nice, since you mention it,*" said this message.

A little murmur and a shuffling of feet in the crowd showed that everyone else could read it, too.

"I see," said Ganymede, with a sly smile over the Major's shoulder. He took Major Trubshaw's arm and turned him to face the people of 'Sticia. "Is this some kind of coup? Do you wish to usurp my position and set yourself up in my place?"

"No, of course not," said the Major loudly and indignantly. "I merely wish to argue for an improvement in our living conditions."

But hardly anyone heard what he had said. They were too busy reading his thought bubble.

"*I'm damn sure I'd do a better job than you, you scruffy piece of garbage,*" they read.

"Aha," said Ganymede. "And these people, whom you claim to represent, whose signatures you have persuaded them to append to this document… let us consider them. What exactly are your thoughts regarding your supporters, supporters like, well, Roger Bradley for example?"

He turned the Major towards where Roger stood at the back of the crowd.

"I hardly see how this is relevant," protested Major Trubshaw.

"*Weakling, easy enough to twist his arm. That's why I started with him*," appeared in the Major's thought bubble.

There were gasps of horror in the crowd and a few sniggers. Faces turned towards Roger, who was suddenly looking hard at his feet.

"And what about my good friend Mrs Patterson?"

"*Senile old bat.*"

"Stacey Tucker?"

"*Hideous, fat little tart.*"

By now, the reactions of the crowd had alerted the Major to the fact that something was amiss. His face displayed a variety of emotions ranging from anger, through mystification to panic. This last emotion came to the forefront when Ganymede mentioned Margaret Owen's name. Margaret was in pretty good shape for her age, and must have been something of a 'looker' in her youth, as Alex had concluded as soon as he clapped eyes on her. What appeared in the Major's thought bubble showed that he thought so, too. More than that, it showed that the Major had a very particular interest in her, expressed in terms that caused a great hoot of scandalised shock and amusement to rise up from the crowd. Margaret buried her face in her hands.

The Major, aware now that something was seriously wrong, glanced upward and caught sight of his thought bubble."

"Oh my God!" he said.

"*Oh my God!*" it read.

More thoughts: panicky, terrified, regretful ones began to appear in his bubble, although the Major himself seemed incapable of coherent speech. He wagged his finger at

Ganymede. Murderous thoughts appeared. He shook his head, desperately. A stream of profanities appeared. With a last furious glare at his tormentor the Major plunged off the platform and hurried away towards the war memorial, the laughter of his fellows ringing in his ears.

Ganymede did not laugh. He only smiled a slow, wry smile and tore the petition into tiny pieces.

"Well, I don't think we'll be needing this again," he said. He crossed to the rail and leant on it thoughtfully, scanning the little crowd as though considering the future of an unwanted litter of kittens.

"Still," he said. "If anyone else feels like sharing their thoughts with us, let no one say that I don't encourage free speech."

Now he laughed, a deep ironic laugh, as the fragments of Major Trubshaw's petition fluttered to the hard 'Stician earth.

After all this turmoil, the ordinary business of the day, the allocation of tasks, the distribution of manna took place, and seemed dull indeed. To his surprise and consternation, Alex's name was not called until the very end. Kelly could see that Alex was worried by this.

"I wouldn't go panicking about it," she told him. "He calls people up in any old order. Don't go getting yourself all in a tizz."

But Alex read into it something very sinister indeed. Kelly, Tanya and Will had already had their audiences when Alex finally received his summons. They lounged on the grass, nibbling manna whilst Alex mounted the steps, troubled by a deep sense of foreboding.

"We'll wait for you," said Kelly. "Don't worry."

Ganymede looked somewhat tired. He had had a very busy day by now, of course, and his triumphant encounter with Major Trubshaw must have taken a toll of him. There was fatigue in the set of his shoulders as Alex cautiously approached him in the bandstand.

"Well, Mr Trueman," said Ganymede in an ominously soft voice. "We save the best 'til last, you see. And what have you got to tell me?" The quiet menace in this question had a marked destabilising effect on Alex's knees, which began to tremble uncontrollably. Ganymede had to know. Stacey must have dobbed him in about the sweets and chocolate. Suddenly dry in the mouth, Alex found himself incapable of speech. He was aware that guilt must be written in every line of his face and body.

Ganymede began to circle him, stroking his beard thoughtfully whilst subjecting his victim to the closest of scrutiny. It was as though he was being scanned by some incredible machine that could see inside every atom of his being. Alex could do nothing but wait, as the long, slow seconds trickled past. He tried to squeeze all thoughts from the forefront of his mind, to make of it a blank page. "Hmmm," said Ganymede after a while. "I had hoped that you would have made a clean breast of it, of your own volition." He stroked his beard pensively. "You are aware that it is absolutely forbidden to interfere with Statica?"

Alex nodded miserably.

"And yet I understand that you have done so. Occasionally we come across individuals who have the power to translate objects from Statica to Intersticia. It appears that you are one such individual. Intelligence has reached me that you have a sweet tooth, that you have interfered significantly with Statical objects in one of the shops in town." Ganymede pursed his lips and nodded grimly. "I have to say I am disappointed with you."

This came as something of a relief to Alex. Ganymede's

disappointment he felt he could live with; Ganymede incandescent with rage was a very different issue. There seemed no point in denying his crimes now.

"I'm sorry," he said, making a mental note to find some way of hitting back at Stacey at the earliest possible opportunity.

"You admit it then?" said Ganymede.

Alex nodded miserably.

"Then it remains only to punish you. You will be confined to the House of Correction for the coming week and placed on half rations, so that you will come to a better appreciation of the taste and quality of manna. During this time you will speak to no one. My servants will guard you." He turned his glare upon Alex now, restored to something of its normal intensity.

"I must warn you that there are very good reasons why we should not interfere with Statica. It is no eccentric foible of my own that causes me to impose this punishment upon you." He sniffed, looking outward suddenly over the park, which was almost empty by now. "Still, I doubt you have done serious harm on this occasion," and then, turning his terrifying gaze back upon Alex once more. "Nevertheless, be warned that any further offence will be dealt with very severely indeed. I hope I make myself entirely clear."

Alex found himself offering more apologies and pledges of future good behaviour, whilst Morlock and Minion appeared at his side. Behind Ganymede a procession of snarks began to emerge from a shrub and crossed the parade behind the war memorial. Ganymede turned, following Alex's gaze.

"Hmm, snarks," said Ganymede. "You would do well to admire them, to take them as your models. They are perfect beings, as old as the earth, as wise as the stars; perfect philosophical beings, whose only aim and purpose in life is to reflect upon the meaning of that existence. Noble creatures indeed. Each one of them is worth a hundred of us." He pursed his lips, seemingly affected by the immensity of the contrast between the snarks and the boy before him.

"Goodbye, Alex," said Ganymede. "Spend your week well. Consider the snark. Reflect upon your behaviour and rebuild your character."

Morlock raised a long and bony arm, indicating the distant aviary and the green shed behind it. With a heavy heart and eyes rimmed with unshed tears, Alex set off for the House of Correction.

"Where's Alex being taken?" he heard Kelly ask Ganymede behind him.

"I think you know," Ganymede told her. "But do you know nothing of his offences? Has he not confided in you? He is a thief. I take it he has not shared his ill-gotten gains with you then."

The rest of this exchange was lost to Alex as Morlock ushered him past the laurel hedges in front of the bowling green. He felt more miserable and ashamed than he had ever felt in his life.

Chapter Eight

The House of Correction was a large green painted shed. Conveniently, a council workman was in the act of cleaning it out. He was leaning on a broom outside, smoking a cigarette. Whilst doing this he was considering through narrowed eyes a huge arrangement of lawnmowers, plastic sacks, rolls of roofing material and other assorted equipment. The interior of the shed, having just been swept, was entirely empty, except for a length of hose coiled loosely on a hook and a few plastic pots and trays on the shelf beneath the dusty, spider-webbed window. There was no furniture of any description. Shutters at the windows made it gloomy within, but there were gaps between the planks here and there and thin strips of sunlight slanted through the darkness. A pile of 'Stician blankets lay in one dusty corner, all that could be considered furniture. Alex mounted the steps and glanced around his prison as Morlock closed the door behind him. He heard a key rattle in the lock and a bolt pushed across. Finally there were a few little clicks as a padlock was secured in place. Ganymede certainly wasn't taking any chances. Alex sat down on the blankets. It was growing dark outside. He lay for a long time and stared at the ceiling as the shadows lengthened and slender 'Stician moonlight crept into the House of Correction.

Ganymede would have been disappointed had he known that Alex's first preoccupation upon being locked up was not a consideration of the faults in his character but the likelihood of escape. The shed was a very old one and in many places the planks from which it was constructed had cracked or shrunk away from each other. On every side, by pressing his eye to the cracks, Alex could discern narrow strips of the shed's surroundings. In front he could see the bowling green, upon which various stiffs in white flannels were caught in the gentle movements of that game. Through a knot hole in the door Alex could admire the zebra finches in the aviary, a small child in a buggy pointing, her mother with tissue poised to wipe her nose. To the rear and on the other short side there was only the uneven foliage of laurels and rhododendrons. The walls and roof seemed sturdily enough constructed, but Alex soon discovered a weakness in the floor of his prison. In the corner furthest from the door and the windows was a loose board. And on the window sill, covered by a plastic seed tray, was a rusty screwdriver.

He told himself that he was uniquely qualified in 'Sticia to do this as he worked at levering up the loose board. The wood was old and splintered easily, breaking away from the one rusty nail that secured it to the joist. Alex's greatest problem was seeing what he was doing. The steady slivers of moonlight were hardly enough to challenge the darkness, and he worked partly by feel, at one point driving the screwdriver point painfully into his thumb.

"Damn!" he grumbled, holding the afflicted part up in a moonbeam to survey the damage, and then cautiously sucking the wound.

Nevertheless, after what felt like an hour or so, he had succeeded in working the board loose. At length, he worked both hands underneath it and a determined pull freed its further end from where it was held under the bottom plank of the wall. Exhausted but triumphant, Alex slumped against the wall, the precious board laid carefully aside. For a long while he concentrated hard on controlling his breathing and on listening. He had been making a lot of noise. Outside, 'Sticia by night remained as silent as it always was. Alex relaxed. After a while he peered down into the hole he had made in the floor. It was inky black down there and he could see nothing. He thrust down his arm and cautiously extended his fingertips until they found hard earth and a few dry twigs. There was a considerable space under the shed, enough for a person to crawl beneath it, he supposed. It must be raised on concrete piles. Still, it was small consolation that Alex's arm could escape from prison. Unless he could rip up another couple of boards the rest of him remained securely confined. And the other boards were rock solid. After a while he gave up. He was stuck there. He carefully replaced the loose board.

Curled up on the bare floor in his blankets Alex drifted into sleep. For the first time in nights he dreamed. He dreamed of his father, plying his international plumbing business in Bahrain, Qatar or somewhere out there in the Middle East. Alex was so used to his going out there on business that he scarcely took any notice of his exact destination. He pictured his tall, skinny father in a flannel suit, striding across the desert with a sink under his arm. He noticed Alex in his predicament and doffed his panama hat, mopping his brow with a big white handkerchief.

"A fine pickle you've got yourself into this time, lad" he told Alex. "I told you daydreaming would get you into a heap of trouble one day."

"I'm sorry, Dad," muttered Alex into his blankets.

And then his mum was there, got up for the gym in T-shirt and jogging bottoms. She gently pushed his father aside and knelt on the desert sand, a light breeze stirring the wisps of hair around her face.

"There's ineffable eye balm in solitude," she said softly. "Mordantly dangle the dewdrops of dalliance."

"You should listen to your mother," said his father, laying down his sink. "You never listen to a word I say, but you'll take it from her." There was bitterness in his voice.

"Endurance is steadfastly monitored," she continued, laying a hand on his cheek. "Take heed of the worm winds of Zanzibar."

Alex awoke with a start. His parents faded in wisps and strands of light before his mind's eye. All that was left was darkness and slanting slivers of moonlight. He pulled his blankets more tightly around him and slept once more, albeit dreamlessly.

Dawn came, and with it came Morlock, who unlocked the door and opened it just wide enough to stick his ugly head around the threshold. His sparrow's eyes glinted blackly in the sunlight as he turned to pick up something from the ground. Blinking in the sudden shaft of bright sunlight, Alex watched incuriously as Morlock placed a jug of water and three manna rolls just inside the door. Then Morlock withdrew, securing the various locks and bolts that imprisoned Alex.

"Not so much as a 'Good Morning'," grumbled Alex, surveying the food and drink bleakly. It seemed likely that three manna rolls were meant to last him all day. His stomach was making it abundantly clear this wasn't going to be enough.

He ate one of the manna rolls, savouring each mouthful and chewing the food until it dissolved to nothing in his mouth. Then he had a long drink from the jug, incidentally pouring a good deal of it refreshingly down his front. The day seemed to offer little prospect of entertainment, and there were seven of them to be endured until his release. Alex's spirits, raised somewhat by eating breakfast, sagged once more. He went around the shed, applying his eye to all of the cracks and knotholes for signs of activity outside. There were none. Not many people came to the park except on Gathering days. There were only the stiffs and beyond the door Morlock, standing almost as still, maintaining what would be a patient, day-long vigil. Alex tried talking to him.

"Hey, Morlock!" he said through the knothole. "What's the time?"

But Morlock showed no sign of having heard. He only raised a bony digit and scratched the back of his long neck.

"That must be a boring job for you," Alex said, in an attempt to engage his captor's sympathies. "I bet you get lots of rubbish jobs… I hope Ganymede pays you well."

Nor did this elicit any response.

"Oi! Morlock, you lanky, pig-faced old pillock!" he called, trying another tack.

Morlock only twitched and shifted his weight from one foot to the other. It seemed that neither insults nor pleading – nor indeed the voice of sweet reason – could persuade Ganymede's servant to engage in conversation with his captive. Alex abandoned the attempt. He slumped against the wall and buried his head in his hands.

Time passed. The rate at which it passed was impossible to discern, given that he could see no manatees (or dugongs). There were times when it seemed to Alex that he may as well kill himself. He considered the hosepipe on its hook and wondered if he could sling it from the rafters and hang himself like Mitch. Presumably his life in Reality would continue as before. For want of anything else to do he took a good wallow in the swamp of self-pity. A big lump rose up in his throat and his eyes filled with tears. He rocked to and fro on his haunches, giving himself up to black despair. After a period given over to this, anger began to take the place of self-absorption, and Alex wiped the tears roughly away with the back of his hands.

What right did Ganymede have to lock him up, anyway? Alex felt suddenly embittered and rebellious. He got to his feet and kicked and pummelled at the door, until his fists were raw and bruised. He shoulder-charged the back wall until the shed creaked and stirred on its foundations, but to no avail. Morlock remained unmoved. Alex cursed him and shouted until he was hoarse, using a vocabulary that would have scandalised his mum, had she been able to hear it. But she wasn't. She was stuck in Wardworths, a stiff like all the others frozen in this eternal instant.

Alex thought about school, about his first visit to 'Sticia, how much fun it had seemed then. If only he had known. His concentration during lessons would be like a laser beam if he ever got out of this lunatic world. He wondered about Henry. Where was he on this Saturday afternoon? Alex resolved to go and look for him at the end of his term of imprisonment. It felt about lunch time by now, but then it had felt about lunch time for a long time. Alex considered his remaining manna rolls. How small they were, but how wonderfully warm and succulent and tasty in the mouth. But if his stomach was already a yawning abyss of emptiness, Alex's spirit was filled with remorse for his weakness in face of the pic 'n' mix. If only he had been stronger. If only he had heeded Ganymede's warning he would not be here now. He had only himself to blame.

And so Alex, whose body had few options available to it, occupied his mind with wandering restlessly from one mental state to another, tarrying a while with guilt and self-loathing before returning to bitterness and so on.

He was interrupted in this state by a familiar, hateful voice that caused his scalp to prickle with pent up loathing.

"Hi Alex," shouted Stacey, from beyond the bowling green. "How are you doing? Would you like a nice chocolate?"

This was accompanied by sustained giggling from Sarah.

"I bet you'd like a nice chocolate éclair now," added Sarah, while Stacey whooped with laughter.

Alex applied his eye to a crack in the front of the shed and glared at them impotently. His shouted response only caused them more merriment as they sauntered across the bowling green.

"Ooh, language, language!" grinned Stacey. "Look how you're makin' poor Sarah here blush."

"What about your girlfriend?" demanded Sarah. "She hasn't deserted you, has she? Cruel, I call that."

Before Alex could put together an appropriately cutting reply, Morlock's long back cut across his narrow field of vision.

"Ganymede forbids this," he heard Morlock say in a voice like the creaking of rusty coffin hinges. "Go now."

There was the threat of future punishment implicit in this demand. Stacey and Sarah took the hint. With a last few jeers and catcalls they wandered off behind the tennis courts.

It was dark when Alex heard the next voice. Morlock had already gone. Alex assumed Ganymede saw no need to guard his prisoner during the hours of darkness when scarcely anyone ventured out. The voice belonged to Kelly, and Alex's heart leapt within him.

"Alex? Are you alright?" she called in a low voice from the other side of the door.

Alex, who had been curled up like a dog on his blankets, leapt to the door and pressed his eye to the knot hole. He could see the side of Kelly's head, her hair catching threads of moonlight.

"Here," he said, calling her to the knot hole. "I'm fine."

133

Well, he wasn't but he felt a great deal better for seeing Kelly.

"Chin up," she said, her face drifting into his view. "You must be bored stiff."

"A bit," Alex admitted. "My TV's only got terrestrial and my X-Box is on the blink."

He was very pleased with himself for having said this. It was, he thought, the sort of thing that Henry would have said. Kelly laughed, and then stifled it unsuccessfully. "What have you been doing then?"

"Not a lot. I've already formed an escape committee. Let me think. I'm working on a tunnel and I'm building a glider in the roof." A thought occurred to Alex. "Here, look. Can you crawl under the back of the shed?"

"I can try," said Kelly.

Alex rushed to pull up the loose plank, and after a few moments of grunting and cursing, Kelly's voice issued from the stygian darkness beneath the floor.

"Are you there, Alex? It's pitch black down here. I can't see a thing."

Alex reached down into the hole, his fingers brushing Kelly's face.

"Hey, steady on," she said. "You nearly put my eye out."

There was a rustle and then Kelly's warm hand found his own. For a few moments they held hands and said nothing. It was enough for Alex. He felt as happy as he had ever felt.

"This is good," said Kelly after a while. "I can bring you some stuff. I bet you'd appreciate a light stick. How much grub are you getting?"

Alex told her. Kelly made a low whistle. "No way! You must be starving. I'll see if I can wangle a few more for you. I know Will'll be keen to help out."

"Yeah?" Alex had his doubts about this.

"Well, perhaps not. I can be very persuasive though." Kelly

laughed. "It's true you can move 'Stician stuff then. Tanya was right. Why didn't you say?"

"Why do you think?" asked Alex, feeling uncomfortable.

There was a pause. "I guess you didn't feel you could trust anyone," she said at last. "You've only just arrived here. I don't blame you, I suppose. It's got all sorts of possibilities though, hasn't it? I wonder if Ganymede realises how special you are."

"What do you mean 'special'?" asked Alex. "You don't think I'm going to risk doing it again do you? I'd have to be mad. I don't want to get banged up in here for the rest of my life."

"I don't know," came Kelly's voice, sounding thoughtful. "I guess not... It isn't half uncomfortable down here. Do you want to throw me a blanket down?"

Kelly stayed for a long time, or so it seemed. They talked about the other folk of 'Sticia and about their lives in the real world.

"At least you've got one," she told him when he was grumbling about his absentee, globe-trotting father. "I never even met mine. He pushed off before I was even born and got himself killed in a diving accident on the rigs. The oil rigs, that is. You know, out in the North Sea. Very careless of him." She sighed. "So now it's just me and Mum. And Mum's got Parkinson's disease so I'm like nurse, cleaning lady, cook, shopper, companion and general dogsbody all rolled into one. Not that I'm complaining, mind. Still, that's one bright spot about 'Sticia. I don't have to do all that stuff. I get a lot more time to myself. And this week Ganymede has decreed that I have to spend it learning Latin. Isn't that great? I always wanted to learn Latin."

"I bet," said Alex, sensing irony.

The knowledge that Kelly was coming back made the next day almost bearable. Almost. There was an awful lot of it, of course, and having no means of measuring the passage of time was deeply frustrating. Alex spent some of it pacing up and down his prison and some of it making sculptures, in emulation of Sylvia DiStefano, out of the hosepipe and the plastic pots. Then he set up the pots like skittles and knocked them down by throwing dried up flower bulbs at them. He must have made a tremendous din but Morlock showed no sign of even having heard him. The strange creature continued to maintain his lonely vigil during the course of the long day. Alex felt relatively cheerful at times. No one else in 'Sticia, he told himself, would have been able to put the meagre contents of the House of Correction to such creative use.

He was hungry by nightfall, however, having earlier eaten all his daily rations in anticipation of Kelly's generosity later on. He was not disappointed, although it seemed like the night was already halfway through by the time she came knocking softly at the door. Alex lifted the loose floorboard and within moments there she was, beaming up at him seraphically in the yellow glow of a light stick. Alex could have kissed her. He would have tried, notwithstanding the obstacle of the floor, had he any confidence that she might have welcomed this.

"… And that's not all," she said, her eyes twinkling mischievously. "I got manna and…" She passed up a heavy rectangular object, "… reading material, if you can call it that."

Alex cast a doubtful eye over Paulo's copy of the Complete Works of Shakespeare.

"Well," he said. "Shakespeare's not really my style."

"It's got to be better than Collins's Latin Primer," said Kelly. "Proper books are hard to come by in 'Sticia. You know what Ganymede's like. If you're enjoying it, it can't be any good for you. That's his way of looking at things."

"Thanks for the manna, anyway," said Alex, looking greedily at two manna rolls nestling in a scrap of cloth. "I hope you're not going hungry yourself for this?"

"Not really," she grinned. "I cadged one off Tanya and one off Will. I'm the queen of the scroungers."

Alex ate. He gave some to Kelly, too. They munched contentedly.

"How's Major Trubshaw?" asked Alex after a while.

"No one's seen him," said Kelly, brushing crumbs out of her hair. "I guess he's keeping a low profile."

"He'll have to," laughed Alex. "Until he can learn to keep his thoughts in order."

"He's a funny old stick, Ganymede," said Kelly thoughtfully. "He's not exactly cruel in the rip your toenails out, boil you in oil sort of way. But he can still be quite a sadist."

"What is he exactly?" asked Alex. "Is he, you know, human like us? Or is he some kind of super being?" He shook his head slowly. "I can't believe I'm having this conversation."

"I know, it's weird, isn't it? It's like a dream but it isn't. It's all too real. For days when I first got here I kept on pinching myself to see if I could wake myself up. I can't even remember how I got here, not really. The last thing I remember is meeting my friend Jess by the town clock. After that it's all a blank. And then I'm here, wandering about like a lost soul until Tanya came upon me, up by the Hospital School."

"And what about Paulo?" asked Alex, after a while. "Has he come back?"

Kelly shook her head. "I don't think he is coming back," she said.

Kelly visited Alex every night afterward and made his term of imprisonment bearable. During the day he played with his good friends the hose and the flower pots. Sometimes he read Shakespeare, straining his eyes in the uneven light, and working his way gradually through Macbeth, Julius Caesar and

A Midsummer Night's Dream. At other times he merely sat and thought, which would certainly have pleased Ganymede. Alex doubted, however, that the nature of his thoughts would always have recommended themselves to his jailor. They were not self-critical thoughts. They were fierce and resentful thoughts of escape into the rough, high country beyond Micklebury. Let Ganymede catch him there. All the other 'Sticians were dependent on Ganymede for food, but not Alex. Oh no, Alex could look after himself. He entertained grim fantasies of survival in the wilds as the slow hours passed into days and his time in the House of Correction drew to an end.

Chapter Nine

Morlock released Alex on Sunday, the day before the Gathering, which was a welcome surprise. Time off for good behaviour, he supposed. So it was a good job Ganymede didn't know about the loose board, and the collected works of Shakespeare, and the extra rations he had enjoyed, thanks to Kelly. Alex emerged blinking into bright 'Stician daylight.

"Ganymede," creaked Morlock, pointing an arm as long as Alex's leg in the direction of the tyrant tramp's dwelling place.

Morlock was not one for idle chatter. He counted out words like a miser counts out coins. Perhaps he was worried he would deplete his stock. It was as though each word Morlock spoke was a word lost forever, spinning into the void. Alex mused on this as he made his way across a park more familiar to him now than it had ever been in Reality.

"I hope I have made my point," Ganymede told him when he was ushered into the tramp's presence. "You do understand now that interference with 'Sticia will not be tolerated."

Alex nodded, fighting back the urge to ask Ganymede what right he had to boss everybody about and strut about like some kind of mad dictator. But it really wasn't worth it. Despite his wild fantasies of living a lonely existence in the hills he had ultimately decided that he would keep on the right side of Ganymede from now on. This resolve had begun to weaken by the time Alex left. He had had to endure a lengthy lecture about morals, behaviour and the wickedness of youth. He had also been allocated his work task for the coming week, which involved an empty skip outside a factory unit on the Birmingham Road. His task was to fill it with water from the nearby River Rimble. Ganymede had given him a bucket to do this with. This in itself would have been conventional enough, had the bucket not had a big hole in the bottom of it. Ganymede had only laughed in a sardonic sort of way when Alex had pointed this out. Furthermore, he had not made it clear how far the skip was from the river. Alex soon found out. It was a good fifty metres from the river bank, beyond a sagging barbed wire fence and a patch of scrubby bush. By the time he had filled the bucket, scrambled up the bank and hurried across the yard to the skip, the bucket was almost empty. Two manatees and a dugong later and there was a meagre puddle of water around the child's broken bicycle that was all that the skip contained. Alex was already exhausted, his knees grazed from clambering up and down to the river and pushing past the bushes. The temptation to bung up the hole with a bit of Statical chewing gum was almost unbearable. Alex might have given in to it had it not been for the presence of Morlock, who stood by watching him all day with glum concentration. It seemed that Ganymede still didn't trust him. Ganymede had told him that for every centimetre of water in the skip at the end of the week he would receive a manna roll at the next Gathering. This had seemed straightforward enough at the time, but by the time three days of the new week had passed a future of starvation seemed to lie ahead for Alex. There was barely a hand's breadth of water in the skip and a broad damp trail led back across to the river. As he surveyed this bleakly at the end of what he thought of as Wednesday, Alex made the decision to cheat. He was not by nature a deceitful boy, so he assured himself, but Ganymede had forced him into it. By the time he was almost asleep in his bedroom that night he had summoned up the determination to take positive action.

"Where are you going?" asked Kelly, Tanya and Will that night when Alex picked up his jug and crossed to the door. As they often did, Tanya and Kelly were staying overnight. "Just out," said Alex, feeling defensive. "Can I borrow your jug, Will?" he added.

You *must* be thirsty," said Tanya sleepily.

"He's not thirsty, he's off down to his skip," muttered Will, propping himself up on one elbow. Will was no fool.

"Yeah, well. Maybe I am," conceded Alex. "I'll make a sight more progress when Morlock's not got his beady eye fixed on me, and with these instead of that leaky old bucket."

"What about Cactus Jack?" asked Tanya, her eyes wide in the darkness. "Aren't you frightened of seeing him again?"

"I'm not scared of going out in the dark," said Alex, with a glance at Kelly. He felt he owed it to her to say this, in view of the fact that she had ventured out every night to visit him in the House of Correction last week.

"I'll come with you," said Kelly, shaking out her hair and sitting up. "I don't feel sleepy anyway."

"You don't have to," Alex told her, but he was glad all the same.

"You both must be mad," snorted Will, pulling his blankets up over his head.

It felt like madness, hurrying though the still, shadowed streets, lit unevenly by the false 'Stician moon. Always in the back of Alex's mind was the stalking figure of Cactus Jack, patrolling the night like a peripatetic vampire. Mitch was there, too, of course, his dead face looming ominously in the darker recesses of skull. Alex knuckled his eyes and shook his head, as he always did when this memory swam up to haunt him. A little thrill of fear, like the aftershock of an earthquake, prickled across his scalp. Kelly didn't seem to sense it. She chattered happily enough as they found their way down through the industrial estate to Alex's skip.

"It's good that it doesn't bother you. Coming out at night, I mean," said Alex, as they set to work filling their jugs in the river. Its chuckling waters seemed louder still in the 'Stician night. "Some people won't go out at all. David was telling me."

"I'm pretty much used to it by now," said Kelly, stooping at his side. "You should know that."

"I bet you see Paulo," said Alex, straightening up, his heavy burden clenched wetly to his chest. "At night, I mean. You do, don't you? Come on, you can tell me."

"I might," conceded Kelly with a shy smile. She tapped the side of her nose. "But that's for me to know and you to wonder, isn't it."

"Yeah, well. I reckon I'm not the only one you've been offloading manna to," said Alex, carefully stepping over the strands of barbed wire and spilling a little of his load down his legs. "I bet Paulo's been feeling the pinch a bit last week, what with you feeding me too."

"Well, there's gratitude for you," said Kelly, sounding resentful, but grinning playfully. "What's it to you anyway?"

They had both sloshed their cargoes into the skip before Alex could work out any kind of reply to this.

"Just curious," he said lamely at last. "You have though, haven't you? I know you have. Where is Paulo anyway?"

They looked at each other for a long moment before Kelly shrugged and gestured towards Micklebury.

"Up there somewhere," she said. "Out in the sticks. He

comes down to see me up by the post office twice a week. You won't tell anybody, will you? Ganymede'll murder him if he ever catches him." Her eyes were wide and her pupils great dark wells of cautious trust. "Quite apart from what he'd do to me."

"*Would* I? You think I'd betray someone who introduced me to the delights of Hamlet and King Lear?"

"No, I guess not," she said, with a hesitant smile. She placed a hand on his arm and squeezed it in a way that made a delicious tingle pass along Alex's spine.

Kelly told Alex all about Paulo as they journeyed to and from the river. He was a 'free spirit', according to Kelly, if that's what you called someone who did exactly as they pleased all the time without bothering about laws or rules. Alex could think of another word to describe him, but kept it to himself for now. Kelly claimed he was good looking in a rugged sort of way. He had boundless self-confidence, she said. He had charisma; that was what it was, something you couldn't quite put your finger on but made him sort of fascinating. Regardless of this trait, Ganymede hated him – and Paulo hated him back. Alex was beginning to feel that he had known Paulo all his life by the time he and Kelly decided they had done enough. Alex had listened with mixed emotions. On the one hand it was interesting to find out more about an individual who continued to hover on the edge of Alex's world. On the other, the tone of voice with which Kelly talked about him gave rise to a strangely congested feeling in Alex's upper chest. He tried hard to convince himself it wasn't jealousy. By the time Kelly had finished telling him all there was to know about Paulo there was at least twice as much water in the skip as there had been before they started.

"Thanks a lot, Kelly," said Alex, with feeling, surveying their handiwork, his jug dangling loosely in his hand.

"That's okay," said Kelly, with a grin. "I'm like your fairy godmother, aren't I?" She mopped her forehead with her sleeve. "I'm sooo hot. It's a pity we can never get our clothes off. I could really fancy a dip in the river."

"Mmm, me too," nodded Alex, his mind working inwardly on this thought.

The next day, Alex laboured at a more relaxed pace, watched by Morlock, who had cast what might have been a suspicious eye over the level of water in the skip when he first turned up. Kelly confided to Alex that she had arranged to meet with Paulo that night. She promised to help him again though, before the next Gathering. On the way to what he now thought of as 'his' skip he usually met with David Hemmings, doing his morning run. He was in the habit, he explained, of running at least twice around the ring road morning, noon and night. Apart from when he was doing jigsaws David was rarely to be seen still for a moment. Even at Gatherings he jogged on the spot, shaking his hands from the wrist like some victim of the palsy.

On the day before the Gathering, however, Cactus Jack came for David. Alex knew he was somewhere in the vicinity the night before. On the way back home from his skip, he was assailed by a sudden sensation of dread, this as he turned the corner into Glanville Street. He dodged into a litter-strewn passage between two derelict houses, pressing his back hard against the wall, hardly daring to look out into the street. After a few moments the feeling faded and Alex found he was able to control his breathing once more. There was no doubt in his mind, though, that Cactus Jack had been near.

In the morning, he was methodically hauling his bucket out

of the river when David Hemmings staggered into the yard. He looked awful: ashen faced and trembling, his few strands of lank grey hair hanging loosely around his face.

"Alex! Help me!" he gasped, staring imploringly at Alex, and then at Morlock who had just that minute arrived for his day's scrutiny of Alex's work.

Morlock regarded David impassively, as though nothing out of the ordinary was going on.

"What?" said Alex, in confusion. "What's the matter?"

David glanced fearfully over his shoulder towards the entrance of the yard and then yelped. His whole body stiffened.

"That thing!" he gasped. "Cactus Jack! He's after *me*."

For a moment, he stared wide eyed with terror at Alex. There was pleading in his eyes too, as though he somehow imagined Alex could have a quiet word with Cactus Jack and call the whole thing off. Alex could do nothing except stare back, his mind paralysed with horror. And then David was off, splashing through the river and hauling himself up the far bank. Stumbling and lurching through the undergrowth on the far side, he disappeared amongst the rusting hulks in the scrap yard there. A moment later Alex's hair stood on end, every hair on his body. Cactus Jack appeared at the top of the track that led to the dual carriageway. At a leisurely, measured pace he trudged towards Alex, whilst Alex felt the blood drain from his face. Now it was too late to hide. He was rooted to the spot. His legs simply would not move.

Seen up close, Cactus Jack was a rather scruffy middle-aged man wearing torn jeans and the famous T-shirt by which he was known. He had close cropped hair and about a week's worth of greying stubble. Cactus Jack was nothing out of the ordinary to look at except in one respect. Morlock and Minion had eyes like sparrows. Cactus Jack had no eyes at all. Where there should have been eyes there were simply expanses of smooth skin. Morlock raised a hand in vague greeting as Cactus Jack strode past. There was no hesitation in his pace and he showed no sign of having even noticed Alex's existence. This was fine by Alex. He felt the iron grip on his heart relax as Jack splashed heedlessly through the river and followed David into the scrap yard. Alex had a feeling David would soon be coming back. The scrap yard was surrounded by a high, chain link fence on its further side, and the gate was locked. Sure enough, David tumbled out of bushes into the river a little way downstream. Moments later he was back with Alex, clutching his ribs, his legs torn by thorns and barbed wire. It was clear he was exhausted. Alex wondered how far David had already run with Cactus Jack in pursuit.

"Got... to... hide," he gasped, his eyes darting about madly until they fastened upon Alex's skip. This he clambered into, even as Jack reappeared between a stack of gas cylinders and a pile of broken wooden pallets. It was no use. David was doomed. Morlock stood by impassively as Cactus Jack approached the skip. Jack knew exactly where his quarry had taken refuge. He didn't even hesitate. He simply leant over the rim of the skip, seized David by his arm and hauled him out. There was no roughness or malice in this. It was as though he were simply pulling out a bag of coal. David's anguished shrieks and pleas made Alex throw up his hands to cover his ears.

"No, you can't!" he heard himself gasp, forcing himself to step towards Jack in a feeble gesture of interference.

It was altogether too late for David. Cactus Jack placed a hand on the back of his victim's neck and suddenly David went limp. Alex shivered as Jack slung the body easily over his shoulder. Had he just witnessed murder? Could it actually be described as murder if David was already dead in Reality? Was life in 'Sticia really life anyway? Jack would carry him off and set him up as one of the stiffs somewhere. Alex felt sick, confused, unsteady on his feet. Cactus Jack was already out of sight by the time he felt able to breathe normally.

He found himself meeting Morlock's sparrow gaze.

"Dead," he said, cracking his knuckles.

So David was dead. It seemed impossible. David was so full of life, more than anyone else appreciative of existence in this world. Perhaps it all made sense. Perhaps David had somehow sensed this was all the life he had left.

There was alarm in 'Sticia the next day. News had spread quickly about Cactus Jack's visitation and David Hemmings' removal to Statica. Well before the appointed hour for the Gathering, people were assembling to discuss the news. There was no sign anywhere of David's stiff. He could be anywhere in Cardenbridge, of course, so no one thought this out of the ordinary. In addition to this, there was rumour of a crime. Ganymede was reputed to be in a towering rage, although no one knew exactly why. Accordingly there was an unusual buzz of excitement amongst the little crowd as they waited for Ganymede to appear. Even Major Trubshaw was there, keeping a watchful eye on the thought bubble above his head.

"Is it true you saw Cactus Jack take David?" asked Tanya solemnly when she arrived with Kelly.

Alex nodded. He looked at Kelly, who seemed strangely troubled that morning. She smiled wanly at him. The smile soon faded when Will caught his elbow and asked him to recount the story of Jack's visitation for the tenth time. This was for the benefit of Chad, but soon attracted a small group of curious 'Sticians. Alex hardly had to concentrate on telling his story by now, and he glanced at Kelly over Chad's shoulder as he described David's last moments. Kelly, he thought, had seen the renegade Paulo again last night. This was confirmed when, after Chad had moved away, she beckoned to him and they both withdrew a little way from the crowd, under the shade of a large horse chestnut tree.

"Paulo wants to meet you," she whispered to him at length, although at this distance she could quite safely have spoken normally without fear of being overheard.

"Oh, does he?" Alex wasn't sure how to feel about this. On one level he supposed it was quite exciting to be summoned into the presence of 'Sticia's celebrated outlaw. On another he felt anxious about getting into more trouble with Ganymede. He was already worried enough on this score, given that his conscience was troubling him over his cheating with the skip. Kelly seemed to have mixed feelings about his meeting Paulo, too, although her motivations were less clear. She shrugged. She was about to say something else when Ganymede appeared in the bandstand and they moved forward to the edge of the small crowd. Tanya took Kelly's hand and fixed Alex with a wondering stare. Ganymede blew a long, clear note on his horn and the populace fell silent. Their attention was particularly focused today. One could have heard a petal drop from the blossom trees, had 'Sticia allowed such a thing.

"People of Intersticia," said Ganymede, sweeping his laser glare around the faces before him. "I regret to say that there has been an episode of criminal damage in recent days. As you know I seek to encourage a spirit of creative endeavour amongst you, and where I see a spark of invention in one of you I nourish that impulse, providing whatever materials I can, so that creativity may be expressed freely. Well…" he began, before swaying a little, as though groping for words grave enough to describe the crime he was about to recount. "Well, I see now how my generosity is abused, how at least one of you rewards artistic achievement. You will recall Miss DiStefano's sculptural work at Micklebury Stanton? You were all privileged to witness it a little while ago." He paused, nodding grimly. "That fine sculpture has been *destroyed!*" He paused once more to let the impact of this sink in. "All that remains is a pathetic scatter of sticks. Miss DiStefano cannot be amongst us today. She is too upset, as you may imagine." There was a low murmur amongst the crowd and then a tense silence even more profound than before as Ganymede looked from face to face. Alex couldn't meet his gaze. It was like that time at school when some idiot broke a sink in the boys' toilets and the whole school had to file past it whilst the headmaster scanned their faces one by one in search of a guilty countenance. Alex's had surely expressed plain and obvious guilt in every line and contour. So he had been aware. He had never felt so guilty in his life. A similar sensation gripped him now. Surely his face would betray him. He looked at his feet and then suddenly found that he wanted to laugh. It became almost unbearable. The thought of the pompous Sylvia DiStefano's ridiculous so-called sculpture being reduced to a scatter of sticks struck him as screamingly funny. Kelly evidently did, too. He nudged her elbow and they exchanged glances through eyes watery with suppressed mirth.

"I must tell you that I regard this as a very serious matter," continued Ganymede, before Alex and Kelly could demonstrate their disagreement by dissolving into helpless giggling. "The culprit, when I find them, will be very severely dealt with. If anyone has any information regarding this senseless act of vandalism I urge them to share it with me at once… I am particularly keen to speak to Mr Potts. If anyone has any information regarding his whereabouts I should be very interested to hear it." He looked hard at Kelly at this point. Two little red spots appeared on her cheeks but she held his gaze steadily.

Alex wanted to talk to Kelly about Paulo, but before he could do so Mrs Patterson stepped forward from the crowd.

"I'm sure we all deplore Miss DiStefano's loss," she said. "But there is another serious issue that merits discussion this morning. I wonder if you can confirm that David Hemmings has been taken from amongst us?"

It was Ganymede's turn to look uncomfortable for once. "Yes, I can confirm that," he said, after a lengthy pause for consideration. "It is not my practice to comment on such matters, but, as you say, Mr Hemming's time here has come to an end. He has been returned to Statica."

"The manner of his going, Mr Ganymede," continued Mrs Patterson doggedly, as Ganymede turned away. "Is it really necessary that he should be hounded down and then despatched in such patently distressing circumstances?"

"As I say," said Ganymede, glowering at her in a way which left no doubt about the consequences of further questioning. "I am not prepared to comment on such matters."

Just then Morlock came striding across the lawn. Alex realised uneasily that he was Morlock's target. The crowd parted to let the creature through and regarded Alex curiously.

"Ganymede. Now," he creaked to Alex a moment later, with his usual economy of speech.

"Huh?" Alex felt confused and alarmed by this unexpected summons. His mouth was dry and his stomach suddenly queasy as he followed Morlock to where Ganymede awaited him in the bandstand.

"Aah! Mr Trueman," said Ganymede heavily when Alex was ushered into his presence. "I have been wanting to have words with you." There was something in the cast of his features that boded ill, some tension in the set of his shoulders that caused Alex's spirits to droop still more.

"The little task I set you this week," he continued, wagging his finger in front of his beard. "My servant tells me you have done very well – very well indeed. So well, in fact, that we were wondering how you were able to achieve such splendid results. Perhaps you could enlighten us?" He raised a bushy eyebrow and studied Alex disapprovingly.

Alex, who had initially experienced a surge of relief from Ganymede's praise, now began to feel a sense of foreboding.

"I worked hard," he said cautiously into the expectant silence left by Ganymede. "Very hard," he added.

"You certainly did," said Ganymede. "And achieved remarkable things using a bucket with a hole in it."

He suddenly looked hard at Alex. "A hole in it Alex... a sizeable hole... so that the water leaked out. Hmmph! By my calculation, Alex, each journey from the river to the skip could have yielded only a litre or so of water. My servant, in his time observing you, counted each journey. There appears to be approximately twice as much water in the skip as there should be." He stabbed a sudden finger at Alex's chest. "How do you account for that discrepancy, Mr Trueman?"

"Morlock wasn't, er, there all the time," stammered Alex lamely.

"Not good enough, boy!" Those parts of Ganymede's face not concealed by hair or beard had turned a terrifying red now, and his voice likewise had acquired a hard edge of menace. "Tell me the truth!"

"You told me the amount of manna I was going to get depended on how much I filled the skip," said Alex bitterly. "It wasn't fair giving me a stupid bucket with a hole in it."

"So you cheated!" Ganymede roared at him.

"Maybe I did," conceded Alex. "But if you didn't give people such stupid things to do, maybe they wouldn't have to cheat." He felt a surge of anger. "I mean, look at poor Mrs Patterson having to shovel all that lousy sand. What was the point of that? Downright cruel that was. You're nothing but a big old sadist!"

The anger drained quickly away, taking with it the colour from his cheeks. He was conscious of having over-reached himself. Ganymede was staring at him, his eyes almost starting from their sockets with indignation.

"How dare you?" he demanded. "How dare you question my authority? I will not be spoken to in that way. You will be detained until you learn better. Morlock! Get this, this delinquent out of my sight!" This last injunction was made at such a volume and so close to Alex's face that he felt the heat of Ganymede's breath on him and a few flecks of spittle. "Take him back to the House of Correction at once. I shall deal with *him* later."

Various emotions jostled within Alex's breast as Morlock ushered him away towards the bowling green. He was terrified by the consequences of having defied Ganymede, but at the same time seething with rage at the injustice of the situation. This latter emotion gained the upper hand as they passed the aviary. Whilst Morlock was momentarily distracted by groping for the keys in his pocket, Alex made a run for it.

"Hey!" came Morlock's alarmed voice behind him as Alex pushed through the bushes in front of the park buildings, emerging on a sweep of lawn next to the boundary of the park. The wall was low here and Alex vaulted it in one swift movement. He landed awkwardly on the pavement of the Birchcombe Road, opposite the petrol station. A glance behind him revealed no sign of Morlock. Alex's first instinct was to simply leg it off along the road, but instead he darted aboard a double-decker bus that was unloading passengers at the bus stop. From the top deck of this vehicle, crouched amongst the stiffs, he had a good view of the park wall.

He was in time to see Morlock drop cautiously down from the wall, craning his neck slowly from side to side as he peered along the road in both directions. The creature walked a short way towards the bus, scratching his head pensively. Alex ducked behind a fat woman with a bag of shopping on her lap, peering out cautiously past her tightly permed head. Morlock stopped and gave the matter some thought. Then he turned on his heel and loped slowly back towards the park gates at the corner of the road. Alex realised he had been holding his breath. He breathed out noisily with relief now and slumped against the stony bulk of the fat woman.

Chapter Ten

A few minutes later and he was three streets away, running hard, his lungs aching with the effort. He didn't stop until he reached his own house in Tyndale Close, where he stood for a moment, bent over with fatigue, while he tried to bring his breathing under control. He had visited his own house on a few occasions since entering 'Sticia when feeling sad or lonely. But even in Reality he was locked out of it, and mindful of Ganymede's warnings he had never seriously considered trying to break in. Not until now, that is. Now Alex forced open the gate at the side of the house and made his way along the passage to the rear of the building. Here, with some difficulty, he picked up one of a pile of bricks by the side of the greenhouse. With this, heavy in his hand, he approached the kitchen window. It was here that he made a fateful decision. Until now his interferences with Statica had been of a relatively trivial kind. Now Alex resolved to use his unique ability freely and without restraint. There could be no going back.

"Sorry, Mum!" he muttered under his breath as he swung the brick at the glass.

The glass shattered with a crash that Alex feared must be heard from one end of 'Sticia to the other. After a minute or so it became clear that no one was running to investigate the noise. Mrs Dawson next door remained frozen in the act of hanging out her washing. A pigeon continued to hang in mid-air above the goal posts at the end of the garden. Alex carefully removed the jagged shards of glass left in the frame and brushed away those on the window sill inside. Then he clambered in.

Everything inside seemed utterly normal. It was as though none of the events of the last few weeks had ever taken place. Only the clock, stopped at 2.23pm, hinted at trouble. None of the lights worked. Nothing electrical functioned, but the taps, oddly enough, worked perfectly well. Rufus was standing frozen at the patio window, optimistically on the lookout for cats. Alex went and stroked the stiff fur of his back, tickling the back of his ears in the manner that usually made Rufus jump up to lick his face. It was all so strange. He went to his bedroom and lay on his bed. After a while its hardness softened to accommodate his weight, as he had expected it would. He gazed at his model aircraft hanging from the ceiling and felt as relaxed as he had felt for a long time. When he awoke he drifted gently into consciousness on a smooth wave of familiarity. The curtains, the books on his bedside cupboard, the clothes strewn on the floor; everything was exactly as it should be. Perhaps he had dreamed it all. But then his eye alighted on the clock radio. Two twenty-three pm, it read. Alex stared at it for a long time. He closed his eyes and sighed.

It was a wrench to leave his own home, but he concluded that he must. Sooner or later Ganymede would think of looking for him there. And he was determined that Ganymede's power over him should be broken for good. Alex found a rucksack in the garage and filled it with food. He also put in a big penknife, a picnic plate, a plastic mug, a tin opener and a box of matches, amongst other useful items. Then he left, first pausing to look wistfully at his parents' wedding photo on the big Welsh dresser in the lounge. The two young people smiled back at him, she looking mildly surprised by it all, he awkward and gawky, his arms held stiffly. He picked it up for a moment and then set it carefully back down, before leaving through the sliding patio door. He knew somehow he would never be coming back – not in this life at least.

It was growing dark outside and there was no one around except the inevitable stiffs, walking their dogs, driving their cars, riding bikes in the streets. Alex saw no 'Sticians as he hurried westwards, keeping to the backstreets as the contours of the land led gently upward towards Micklebury. As he emerged in fields next to the dual carriageway, the dark bulk of Micklebury Hill hove into view, the slender finger of the 'needle' beyond etched against the night sky. Soon Alex was trudging up steep slopes towards the black mass of the woods that clung to the shoulders of the hill, giving Miss DiStefano's cottage a wide berth.

He did not feel scared, and anyway there was no vestige of the dread that gripped him when Cactus Jack stalked the streets of 'Sticia. If anything he felt excited, and a grim sense of getting his own back on Ganymede made him flex his knuckles as he stepped cautiously into the outskirts of the wood. He was looking for Paulo, of course. Simple logic dictated that he should join the lonely outlaw in his exile. Alex had skills that would be of tremendous use to both of them. Surely they could survive indefinitely together on the wild fringes of Ganymede's world. With only Morlock and Minion to help him, and the whole of 'Sticia to run, he was never going to be able to find them. Alex consoled himself with these thoughts as he picked his way carefully through the darkness of the wood. There was only a little moonlight to guide him, painting dappled patterns on the brambles and the tree trunks, but presently another light came into view, a tiny spark of orange on the far side of a little valley. Alex's heart leapt. This had to be Paulo.

Nevertheless, he was cautious, stepping towards the light with all the woodcraft the boy scouts had taught him, setting down his feet gently amongst the dry undergrowth, lifting them again if there was any indication that a noise would be made. It was slow work and Alex's heart was in his mouth as he approached the orange glow. He saw now that the fire was a small one, in a clearing at the head of a little valley that held apart two low ridges on the north side of the hill. Soon, through a few last trees, he could see a seated figure silhouetted by firelight. He could smell cooking meat and hear Paulo humming to himself. Alex's mouth watered. He had smelt no other food but manna for so long. Unless you counted chocolate, that is, and chocolate was a different issue altogether. He felt well satisfied with his woodcraft; there was no sign that Paulo had detected his approach. This was the moment of truth. Abandoning caution, Alex stepped confidently into the clearing. It was a 'Doctor Livingstone, I presume' moment.

Paulo, for it was he, turned round and showed some evidence of surprise. He was a tall young man wearing jeans, a tracksuit top of some kind and a Burberry cap. Several chains glinted at his neck and there was a stud through his eyebrow. He grinned.

"*Sprout* me," he said, standing up. "*Peas*! You shouldn't go creepin' up on people like that. Nearly gave me a *potato* coronary."

Alex was reminded that Ganymede's disapproval of Paulo's foul language had resulted in such words being replaced by the names of vegetables. Still, nothing could have prepared him for the experience of hearing it in action. It struck him as enormously funny, but it would not do to make this obvious

157

to Paulo. He had to try hard to compose his features as he emerged into the circle of firelight. In one hand, Paulo held a leg of cooked meat. The other, marginally less greasy, he used to shake Alex's hand.

"You'd be Alex, then," surmised Paulo. "Kell' said she'd have a word with you. Quite a clever lad, I've heard." He winked at Alex and punched him moderately hard on the shoulder, causing Alex to wince. Paulo was half a head taller than Alex and powerfully built.

"What are you eating?" Alex asked him, regarding the blackened, spitted carcase amongst the flames of the fire. Here at last was the answer to the mystery of Sylvia DiStefano's missing sculpture.

"Snark," said Paulo, gesturing with the leg. "Want some?"

Alex felt suddenly queasy. His mind reeled with horror.

"What?" he gasped, looking aghast at the small carcase in the fire. Everything that Ganymede had said about the snarks came flooding back into his mind. "You can't…." He looked up at Paulo. "I mean, they're philosophers, the finest minds… ancient, noble creatures."

"Yeah, well," said Paulo with a shrug. "Taste like chicken."

However, with Alex to provide food for them, it seemed that Paulo's days of eating snark were over. This was welcome enough to Paulo and would presumably be a big relief to the snarks, whatever their philosophical take on death. Alex emptied out his rucksack and Paulo picked over the contents gleefully, making himself a snark sandwich using the loaf of bread Alex had brought.

"Drop o' brown sauce'd be good," observed Paulo, munching happily. "Pity you didn't think of it." He waved the sandwich at Alex, who was eating a packet of crisps. "*Turnip* genius you are! I tell you, you an' me are going to be like *that*."

Paulo made a gesture with two of his tattooed fingers, twisting them together to show how close he thought they were going to be. Alex, whose first thoughts upon seeing Paulo had been so joyous, felt reservations stealing up on him. It occurred to him that Paulo wasn't really his type, but what surprised and depressed him was that he was apparently Kelly's type.

"Here's to us," said Paulo, opening a can of coke. "And *cabbage* to Ganymede! I tell you what mate," he said with a leer. "Tomorrow, we're gonna' party!"

Why did this prospect not fill Alex with glee? He asked himself this question, and others, as they settled down to sleep, wrapped in blankets by the embers of the fire. Alex was beginning to wonder if he'd made a mistake.

The next morning he was sure of it. On Paulo's insistence they took up residence in Herborne Hall. This was the imposing Georgian mansion on the other side of the dual carriageway that swept past Micklebury on its way to Birmingham. It was the moneyed aristocrats whose stately pile this was, that had once adorned Micklebury with its 'needle' and its follies. Their descendants lived there still, and Viscount Lord Maynard, the fourteenth holder of his title, was famous locally for holding vintage car rallies in its grounds. There was no sign of any vintage cars now, or indeed of Lord Maynard, who spent much of his time up in London. The Hall was peopled only by the stiffs of the folks who worked there: a housekeeper, a grounds man, a cleaner at work in one of the bedrooms, and a pair of workmen mending part of the roof.

"We can live in style here, dude," observed Paulo, looking around him approvingly as they strolled through the public rooms together, admiring the splendid plaster work, the tapestries and the fine Louis Quinze furniture. "Hey!" came Paulo's gloating voice from the next room as Alex peered gloomily out of the window at a broad sweep of Capability Brown parkland. "Come and getta load o' this."

Alex found Paulo beaming at a magnificent four poster bed, draped with faded gold fabrics. It was easily as big as Alex's whole bedroom. "*Cauliflower* fantastic, 'aint it?" grinned Paulo. "I tell you what, mate." He jerked a thumb at the bed. "That's where I'm kippin' tonight. No more roughin' it out in the *potato* wilds for me."

He clapped a rough hand around Alex's shoulder. "My turnip salvation, you are pal. An angel must o' smiled on me in 'eaven."

Paulo was smoking a cigarette, having found a packet on Lord Maynard's desk during their tour of the ground floor. The way things were going, he was going to be needing another packet by nightfall. Alex wrinkled his nose as a curl of smoke came his way. His initial suspicion of Paulo was gradually solidifying into profound and genuine dislike, as Paulo was exactly the kind of youth he spent so much time trying to avoid in school. Now it was beginning to look as though he was stuck with this one indefinitely.

Alex was feeling no more warmly towards his new companion by the time they met Kelly, later that night. They walked back along the dual carriageway towards Cardenbridge, and there she was, waiting outside the post office. Kelly was pleased to see them, giving them both an enthusiastic hug. Alex approved of this, at least so far as his own hug was concerned.

"You really set the cat amongst the pigeons," Kelly told him, "Leggin' it like that. You should've seen Ganymede's face when old Morlock came and gave him the news. I thought his head was going to explode. And of course I then got the third degree, didn't I? And Will. He wasn't best pleased about that. We're both on reduced manna now, just because Ganymede thinks we know something we're not tellin' him. Everyone's talking about it. Ganymede didn't even set new work tasks. Can you believe it?"

"Wow," said Alex, impressed and a little scared by the impact his escape had made.

"And guess what he's asked everyone to do instead?" she continued, looking grave. "Look for you two," she said when Paulo and Alex shook their heads. "Basketfuls of manna and no work ever again for anyone who tracks you down."

"*Peas!*" cried Paulo loudly, slapping his thigh in glee. He grabbed Kelly by the arms and swung her around in an impromptu jig. "I don't *runner bean* believe it. We're like Robin *turnip* Hood or something."

Alex found it hard to envisage Paulo stealing from the rich to give to the poor; he didn't come across as the altruistic type. He demonstrated this soon enough in the post office, where he prevailed upon Alex to pick up a few essentials for their evening's entertainment. This started off with chewing gum and moved on to include cans of lager, cider and a bottle of wine. Paulo had to have more cigarettes, of course, and greed got the better of him here. Alex found himself having to lug about a whole carrier bag for him.

"Hey, Alex, I don't suppose you could get a car going, could you?" asked Paulo, looking at the beer and the cigarette shelves. Alex shook his head vehemently, his mind recoiling at the horror of that prospect. And then there was the till, which stood conveniently open whilst the young Asian girl behind the checkout reached in for change.

"We may as well have some dosh whilst we're at it," said Paulo, eyeing the notes greedily. "It's only standin' around doing nothing."

"What the hell are you going to do with cash?" Kelly asked him, reasonably enough, loading cans into Alex's rucksack.

"There's nowhere you can spend it."

"Well, you never know," said Paulo, looking from face to face. "What if we get dumped back in *courgette* Reality. Be a bit *carrot* handy then, wouldn't it? Go on big ears, break out the cash."

Alex, the size of whose ears had been remarked upon too many times since entering 'Sticia, felt a fresh pang of resentment.

"Uh, uh," he said, shaking his head decisively. "I draw the line at cash."

"You'll draw the cauliflower line where I *turnip* say you will," said Paulo, his mood swinging abruptly from cheerfulness to menace. He loomed over Alex in a way Alex found reminded him all too vividly of Ganymede.

"Better humour him," said Kelly with a nervous smile. "He's like a little boy really. He has to have his own way."

Paulo's eyes continued to bore into Alex's, who reluctantly reached into the till and broke free a handful of ten pound notes.

"And the rest," said Paulo, holding out a big grimy hand.

Alex felt sick and bitter as the three of them made their way back towards the Hall. The Paulo situation had turned sour with alarming rapidity. Paulo struck him as being all too similar to the appalling Gary Payne, but whereas he and Gary were parted at the end of each school day, Alex's connection with Paulo had a worrying feel of permanence to it. Up until this point he had told himself that he would replace any minor thefts from Statica, if he ever got back into Reality. Now though he was a genuine, actual thief of the sort you read about in the court pages of the Cardenbridge Chronicle. Paulo, who fell very clearly into the category of the minor criminals and ne'er do wells mentioned in those pages, had made him into a criminal. The shame of it, what would his mum say? The experience of reaching into the till and feeling the solid mass of notes nestle into his palm was seared into his consciousness like physical trauma. This was serious stuff. He could go to prison or something. And it was all Paulo's fault. A poison gout of hatred leapt within his breast as Paulo nuzzled his face into Kelly's neck. They were up in front, arm in arm, lurching about and laughing and giggling as they walked amongst the Statical traffic on the road. Alex, burdened by two carrier bags, glared resentfully at Paulo's back.

"We're made," he overheard Paulo say to Kelly. "We're *potato* made. Now we've got Big Ears back there the whole of this *onion* place is ours. *Peas!* We don't even need *cabbage* Ganymede any more. He can stuff his *broccoli* manna up his *aubergine!*"

They paused whilst Paulo gave Kelly a cigarette. Alex, who had strong feelings about smoking, felt his throat tighten with annoyance. He felt the irrational urge to rush up and knock it out of her mouth, stub it out in Paulo's eye. His body, recognising the futility of this imagined act, advised caution – that way lay a certain thumping. Choking down a sudden tide of bitterness in his throat, he trudged after them. *He* was Paulo's dream come true. That was the worst of it. He was Paulo's meal ticket for evermore by the look of things. And Alex wasn't going to stand for it because if Paulo needed Alex, well, Alex certainly didn't need Paulo.

He might have put up with it for Kelly's sake, but she was clearly besotted with the big oaf, and as they sat around in Lord Maynard's green drawing room, eating sandwiches and drinking beer, Alex felt like the world's biggest gooseberry. At last they slept, wrapped in sleeping bags that Alex had found for them in an outhouse, Kelly nestled against Paulo, his hand entwined in her hair. Alex surveyed this scene miserably from the other side of the room, across a carpet strewn with beer cans and packaging. The realisation came to him that he wasn't going to be able to stand it. He was going to have to get out of there. At last, having made this decision, he crawled from his sleeping bag and made stealthily for the door. He wasn't stealthy enough though. Paulo opened one eye and then was suddenly awake, glaring suspiciously at Alex.

"Oi! Where you going?" he demanded.

"Er, nowhere," said Alex awkwardly.

There was a moment, as Paulo freed himself from his sleeping bag and came towards him, when Alex could have fled. After all, the door was Statical. As soon as Alex closed the door behind him, Paulo would be securely imprisoned. But so would Kelly, and it was this thought that made him hesitate. It was as though Paulo read his mind. He slipped between Alex and the door.

"That's right, mate," said Paulo firmly. "You ain't goin' nowhere."

"What's goin' on Paulo?" asked Kelly sleepily.

"Nothin'," said Paulo, his pale eyes holding Alex's. "I think our pal here was thinkin' of takin' a walk. Is that right, Alex?" He seized the front of Alex's sweatshirt and pulled him close so that Alex could feel his breath on his face in a manner that again reminded him disagreeably of Ganymede.

"Only you might get lost, my friend. And I can't risk that appenin', coz you are my *courgette* meal ticket." He nodded to Kelly. "Kell', get the rucksack! There's some tie wraps in there. Bring 'em over 'ere, will ya!"

Alex had wondered why Paulo had wanted tie wraps from the Hall's workshop. Now he knew. Suddenly, a blade glinted before him as Paulo pulled a flick knife from his pocket. He found himself forced to kneel on the floor and bend forward, his arms held behind him whilst Paulo secured his wrists together with the narrow plastic strips. His ankles received the same treatment. Alex was soon completely helpless, cursing and wriggling, whilst Paulo looked on dispassionately. Kelly had protested almost as much as Alex had. Not that it made any difference.

"We can't take any risks," Paulo told her. "It breaks me up havin' to do this, yeah? But we'll be *chives* if he does a runner, won't we? You don't think I'd do it unless I 'ad to?"

"Sorry, mate," he said, stooping down next to Alex. "You left me with no choice."

There was apparently genuine regret in Paulo's voice. Alex told him what he thought of him, mentioning no vegetables.

"Yeah, well," said Paulo. "I guess you owe me that. Ordinarily I'd break your scrawny little neck, but, you know, ladies present, an' all." He laughed.

"We'll have those off you first thing tomorrow," Kelly told Alex softly. "I'm sorry about this but he gets desperate. You don't know what it's been like for him."

Alex didn't care what it had been like for Paulo. He only cared about getting free of the tie wraps, which were digging into his flesh painfully by the time Wednesday morning dawned. Paulo snipped them off for him with a pair of pliers, and Alex rubbed his wrists ruefully. Still, Paulo was taking no chances by day either. He tied a length of rope around Alex's middle and made it clear that he, Paulo, was always going to be on the other end of it. Paulo's regrets and apologies made not a jot of difference to Alex, as there was no getting away from the fact that he was now a prisoner. Alex could not meet Kelly's eyes. She tried to be pleasant to him but he felt bitter and humiliated. It was as much as he could do to speak to her. She squeezed his hand sympathetically when Paulo wasn't looking.

"I'm not having this," Alex muttered to her.

"I know," she said. "It's not right. We'll sort something out."

Paulo had in mind a visit to the Fountain Inn, up at Dorston. There was a skittle alley there. By tenth manatee Alex found himself obliged to play skittles with Kelly and Paulo. This was a little awkward at first. Statical objects, brought by Alex into 'Sticia when he picked them up, had a habit of becoming Statical again if they were set down in their original places. Alex got round this by marking them with chalk so that they were never stood back in their original Statical places. Feeling gloomy about things in general, he didn't get much out of the game. The same could not be said of Paulo and Kelly, who were whooping with delight at the unaccustomed entertainment. Skittles leapt and span as the heavy wooden balls cracked amongst them. Alex had a few goes for the look of the thing, but all the time he was thinking of escape.

"Tonight," Kelly whispered to him, as Paulo set up the skittles ready for her turn.

She was as good as her word. Whilst Paulo snored contentedly, full of cider and nicotine, Kelly slipped across to where Alex lay, with Paulo's pliers in her hand. She nudged Alex gently awake and then inexpertly snipped at the tie wraps securing his wrists and ankles. Alex winced at the pain as she accidentally nipped his flesh, but the loud snap of the bonds breaking bothered him more. They both remained stock still for a moment, Alex lying on his side, Kelly crouched behind him. Paulo continued to sleep.

"I'm really sorry about this," she whispered. "He's not a bad lad, honest he isn't, but you'd better make a dash for it. Leave the doors open will you, so's we can get out and… I tell you what, could you break out a load of food at the post office and put it where we can get at it?"

"What are you going to do?" he asked her, turning so he could meet her eyes through a curtain of dark hair.

"I don't know," she said with a shrug. "Stay with Paulo, I guess."

Alex had views on that, but he kept them to himself for now. He struggled to his feet, stiff limbs protesting. For a moment they stood close. There was an awkward pause during which various impulses competed for control of his bodily movements. Before any of these could get anything done, she kissed him briefly on the lips and then put her finger there, taking it away to point at the door. Alex left, the soft pressure of her lips on his own still vivid in his memory.

Chapter Eleven

By dawn he was miles away, heading for Henry's house on the outskirts of Scourton. Mindful of the risk of pursuit, he kept to the fields wherever possible and crossed roads cautiously, having first observed them carefully from behind walls or hedges. He had done as Kelly asked at the post office, and now all he wanted to do was put as much distance as possible between himself and the horrible Paulo.

"Tough on the snarks though," he thought. Still, he'd left enough food, beer and cigarettes to keep Paulo going for at least a week. With a bit of luck he'd smoke or drink himself to death.

Alex had come to the grim realisation that he was truly alone at last. He could never return to the bosom of the 'Stician community and he would more than likely never see any of his friends again. He would be obliged to live as a lonely fugitive, a hermit, until Reality reclaimed him once more. And God only knew how long that would be. Nor did it seem likely he would ever see Kelly again. He felt thoroughly miserable as he picked his way across a field parallel to the Ambersley Road. In the distance, as he descended Ridge Hill, he could see the blue-grey bulk of Winderley Edge. He was close to Henry's house now, in the dip by Scourton Mill.

Bizarrely, Winderley Edge shimmered as he strode onward. He felt a sudden dizziness and a shortness of breath. Gasping, he realised that the Edge had vanished, even as he continued to pace. In its place was another hill, clad in trees, a white painted pub close to the summit. Alex's momentary disorientation abated as he realised he was looking at the hill he had just walked down. Disorientation was replaced by confusion. He stopped, gathering his breath. Then he turned slowly to face Winderley Edge once more.

"Okay, so I must have come to the edge of the sector," he told himself. "Guess I can't go any further."

He tried nevertheless, stepping out cautiously towards the Edge. Once more the air shimmered, his stomach lurched and he found himself walking in the opposite direction.

"So that's where my world ends," he said, shaking his head.

By this time he was very much in need of somewhere to sleep. Retracing his steps he satisfied this need by breaking into a house in Ardingshall and slept until well into the new day. When he awoke, he judged that the day was already far advanced, although of course he had no way of telling for sure. One of the more slender dugongs passed overhead, which he thought might be the fifteenth, but he couldn't be certain. Alex had no scruples about interfering with Statica now. He helped himself from what proved to be a disappointingly stocked fridge and picked at a chicken drumstick, whilst looking cautiously out of the front window. A faint tremor beneath his feet made him pause mid-mouthful and cross to look up and down the street. It was as though there had been a minor earthquake. He had a good view of the village's high street from here, and net curtains shielded him from detection. It was likely, he supposed, that the good citizens of 'Sticia would be out looking for him. However, since there were less than a hundred of them, with something like a hundred square miles to cover, the chances were he would be able to evade capture. Hence, he was surprised to see a stranger, a man apparently busily engaged in doing something to the ground in the garden of the house opposite. He was wearing a sober grey business suit and had ill-cut dark hair. From this distance Alex could see no more. He was strangely fascinated by the man. He thought he knew everyone in 'Sticia by now, at least by sight, and this man was definitely someone he had never seen before. Alex finished the drumstick and disposed of it tidily in the pedal bin under the kitchen sink. Then he opened a packet of chocolate biscuits and returned to the front window. The stranger was still there.

After a while, responding more to blind instinct than to sound reasoning, Alex stepped out into the street and approached the stranger. There was no one else around. 'Sticia, as usual, was eerily silent, so Alex could clearly hear the man mutter to himself as he thrust a long stick into a hole in the ground, occasionally pulling it out again and studying it carefully. He was so absorbed in this task that Alex was able to approach quite close to him.

"Hello," said Alex at last.

The man swivelled in alarm. He fumbled in his pocket and drew out an object which he appeared to manipulate with his fingers. Instantly the man was transformed into an angel. He was a good head taller, dressed in what Alex supposed might be described as 'shimmering raiment', with a brilliant halo and magnificent, dove-soft wings half folded behind him. The angel's glow bathed the lawn around him.

"Hail, mortal," the angel said in a deep, mellow voice.

Before Alex could more than make a start on feeling awestruck, there was what looked very much like interference on the television and the angel disappeared once more. The man in the suit remained, stabbing frantically at the object in his hand. The angel reappeared briefly once more, sparked, distorted itself into a humorously short squat angel and then shrank to a bright dot. This too vanished.

"Bother," said the man, throwing the object on the lawn in front of it. "I just can't get the hang of this." He kicked at it ineffectually. "I don't know why I couldn't have held on to the Mark Fourteen."

"It's alright," said Alex. "You don't have to do that for me."

"Well, thanks," said the man ruefully. "I suppose the cat's out of the bag anyway."

"Who are you anyway?" asked Alex, who was pretty certain he wasn't looking at an ordinary 'Stician by now.

"Oh, I'm sorry. The name's Malcolm," said the stranger, stepping towards Alex with hand outstretched. "I suppose you'd call me an angel, despite the embarrassingly dodgy special effects." He laughed rather nervously as they shook hands. Had he been an ordinary mortal Alex would have said he was in his early twenties. His face was angelic enough, even without special effects, but it sat beneath a haircut straight from Hell. His suit looked slightly too big for him, too.

"I never shook hands with an angel before," said Alex, feeling pleased at how well he was taking things. It was as though he had lost the capacity to be shocked. "What's that?"

This question referred to the object that Malcolm was retrieving from the ground. It looked like a polished stone in the shape of a more than usually stylish TV remote. But there were no buttons, or any other features for that matter, on its smooth grey surface.

"This? Oh, it's a molecular transponder," said Malcolm, giving it a rub. "Piece of junk, too."

"What's it do?" asked Alex.

"Lots of things," said the angel. "I was using it to locate anomalies."

"Ah," said Alex, nodding sagely, and then, "To locate what?"

"Anomalies. Faults and disturbances in the fabric of this sector of Intersticia. There are lots around here, caused by folks messing about with Statica, usually. Sometimes we call them 'spikes'. You know, they're like sudden spikes in a waveform."

Alex felt a twinge of anxiety.

"I can't seem to get a steady reading," explained Malcolm, showing Alex the long rod he had been pushing into the ground. "There's a minor anomaly near here but it keeps fluctuating. I shall have to try a few other places and see if I can triangulate on it."

Alex, mindful of the drumstick and the chocolate biscuits, had an idea about the source of the anomalies. He was suddenly conscious of the half-eaten biscuit in his left hand. As though reading his thoughts, Malcolm noticed it at the same time.

"Oh," he said, looking at Alex's hand.

"Yes," said Alex, taking a bite off it. "It's me, I'm afraid. Is it a problem?"

"It could be," said Malcolm, slipping his transponder into an inside pocket of his suit. "That's what we're here to investigate. You see, if there are too many spikes in a sector, you get instabilities, and if you get too many instabilities, well… you know…" he made an ominous cutting movement with his fingers under his chin. "We could lose the interstice."

"Huh?" Alex took another bite.

"The interstice," repeated Malcolm patiently, gesturing vaguely with his hand. "All this – the place where we are. There's talk of folding it."

"What, like destroying it?"

"Uh, huh."

Now Alex began to see why Ganymede was so keen to

keep folks from interfering with Statica. His jaw dropped, his mouthful of biscuit half chewed.

"But what about everyone here?" he asked incredulously.

"Discontinued," said Malcolm with a shrug. "Sorry."

"Discontinued? You mean, like, *dead* don't you? Why don't you just say so?"

"Yeah, I guess so," admitted the angel. "Tough. I know, but there you go..."

"It's easy for you to say that," said Alex indignantly. "In fact, I'd say it's a bit more than tough."

"I get it," said Malcolm. "Now look, don't jump the gun. Nothing's been decided yet. We may be able to get a clean-up team in. I guess you'd better come with me to see Tony – he's my boss – particularly if it's you that's been sticking a spanner in the works. He'll want to have a word with you."

"Oh, right." A thought occurred to Alex. "Look, you can't get me back into Reality, can you? Things are a bit awkward for me here."

Alex explained why things were a bit awkward for him; his running afoul of Ganymede, his difficulty with Paulo. Malcolm, sitting on the garden wall, listened patiently to him, running his finger pensively along the edge of the rod. He didn't look like an angel, Alex had to conclude. And he was wearing odd socks.

"Sounds like a mess," said Malcolm when Alex had finished. "I was never in this sector before, but it sounds like this Ganymede character's sailing close to the wind. I heard Tony talk about him and he wasn't complimentary, I can tell you. He's with Ganymede now. As for getting back to Reality, well I'm afraid that one's not really our remit. You're on your own there, pal. It happens when it happens."

Malcolm had his transponder in his hand again.

"Anyway, we'd better go see Tony," he said, studying its

surface carefully.

"Right," said Alex. "Everyone's out looking for me by the sounds of things."

"Well, there's no way they're going to spot you en route," said Malcolm pensively, tapping the wider end of the transponder.

Before Alex could respond, the air shimmered, much as it had at the end of the sector, earlier that day. He had a brief sensation of weightlessness. The world shattered and quickly recomposed itself into the form of Ganymede's office. With a lurch, and a sensation in the pit of his stomach that reminded him of being on a roller coaster, Alex's feet re-established themselves on solid ground. He gasped.

"I know," said Malcolm apologetically. "Always a bit odd, the first time. You never quite get used to it either. I still get the shivers."

What had to be presumed to be angelic light shone from under the door of the room next door. Raised voices could be heard, including, from time to time, that of Ganymede. The discussion sounded ill-tempered, although Alex could make out little of what was being said.

"Tony," mouthed Malcolm, putting a finger to his lips. He crossed to the door and knocked softly. The voices carried on. Malcolm knocked more sharply. This time the voices ceased.

"Is that you, Malcolm?" said someone from within. "Get yourself in here."

With an apologetic glance at Alex, Malcolm opened the door just wide enough to admit himself, closing it gently behind him.

"And what kind of manifestation do you call this?" he heard an unfamiliar voice ask, before the door clicked shut. Alex found himself alone.

Ganymede's office was much as he remembered it – the

familiar clutter of mugs, pot plants and piles of paperwork. Alex's eye was drawn to a printed document on Ganymede's desk, a fountain pen lying lidless beside it.

'Census Return' was the title of the document, next to a row of figures that might have denoted a date. Alex edged nearer, keeping an eye on the door. There was a long string of digits in a box next to the word 'Sector' and Ganymede's name next to another one.

'Daniel Beddowes', read Alex, with a frown. Perhaps this was Ganymede's real name.

Underneath was a list of other names, some of them familiar. Next to the names, in a column labelled Origin, various descriptions were written. Most of them said simply Disassociation. One said Coma. The name Roger Bradley stood next to this. Alex frowned. Interesting. His eye scanned quickly down the list of names and then stopped.

Deceased, read one description at the foot of the page. Next to it was a familiar name. David Hemmings. Alex felt his throat tighten.

"Jesus," he said, under his breath.

There was no sign of his own name on the page, or those of Paulo or Kelly. Alex flipped over the page. More names. There was his own – Disassociation. And Paulo – Coma: now there was a surprise. And Kelly. Alex gasped, stepping back involuntarily from the desk. He stared at the entry, but the letters remained stubbornly clear and focused. There could be no mistake.

"Deceased," he breathed. "Deceased." He glanced around wildly. "Christ, Kelly's dead!"

He had hardly recovered from this shock when the door opened and Malcolm put his head round it.

"Can we have a word?" he asked.

His mind still reeling, feeling a deep sense of foreboding, Alex stepped into the room. A table with two chairs was laid with a meal, disturbed and half-eaten; manna rolls and a glass jug of water. At least Ganymede didn't apply double standards. He wasn't tucking into a five course meal with a nice claret. This forced Alex to concede a little grudging respect to him. Ganymede was there, leaning against a sideboard, staring at him with undisguised hostility. With him was another angel, this one authentically winged and white-robed, filling the room with light. Clear radiance streamed out of his face, which looked significantly older and more careworn than Malcolm's. In addition to this he looked in a thoroughly bad mood. This had to be Tony.

"Hi," said Alex in a small voice.

"Hello, Alex," said Ganymede in a voice that strained itself to be polite. "This is Tony, he's in charge of Intersticia."

"Indeed," said Tony, inclining his head towards Alex. "And it looks like you've been making a bit of a mess of this interstice."

"Sorry," said Alex meekly, glancing from face to face. "I didn't know."

"Well, I don't know why you didn't know!" snapped Ganymede. "I thought I made it abundantly plain to you."

Tony raised his hand, before Ganymede could launch himself into a new bout of criticism.

"Do you understand the consequences of interference with Statica?" he asked.

"No," said Alex. "Not really." He got the feeling that if Tony wasn't exactly on his side, then Ganymede was in big trouble, too. It wouldn't do any harm to drag Ganymede further into the mire. "It wasn't explained to me."

Tony shot Ganymede a very satisfactory wounding glance, which made Ganymede cast his eyes upwards to the ceiling and clench his fists.

"Well perhaps someone *should* explain to you," said Tony, who had an undeniable air of authority about him. "I wouldn't normally think this necessary, but then you are evidently very far from being an ordinary Interstician. It is very rare to come across someone with such marked ability to translate material objects from Statica to Intersticia. Most inhabitants of Intersticia find it impossible, and so the two worlds exist side by side harmoniously. You need to understand the relationship between them."

Stepping forward he used a slender, luminous finger to trace a red line on the table top. The line had an arrowhead at one end of it.

"Imagine this line represents what you think of as Reality," he said. "The world you dropped out of. Time advances like so, and you are always at the leading edge of it, at the very tip of the arrow, with the past reaching out behind you."

He lifted the red line so that it hovered in the air before Alex's eyes. Then he traced another arrow line, this time a shorter blue one. Its own arrow head met that of the red one, but it hung downwards and at right angles to it.

"This blue line represents Intersticia," said Tony. "You can think of time here as advancing at right angles to that of time in 'Reality'. Observe."

The blue line began to lengthen, but the two arrows remained head to head.

"Which is why time in Intersticia moves onward while time in Reality appears to be frozen."

Alex nodded. This did indeed make sense, providing that one was prepared to cast away all that three hundred years of scientific discovery had set in place.

"But the relationship is delicately balanced," continued Tony. "It relies upon logical consistency. Consider this from the viewpoint of Reality. If things inexplicably alter from one instant to another, inconsistency is established. If you used your unusual powers here to move a table from one point in a crowded room to another, people in that room in Reality would see an inexplicable and doubtless startling event take place from one instant to another. That is what we call an 'anomaly'. Anomalies lead to logical inconsistency, and logical inconsistency leads to the breakdown of physical relationships and deterioration in the fabric of space-time. The Universe has an infinite capacity to heal itself, but it can do so in rather undesirable ways. Catastrophic ways, I may say," he said with a grim smile. "It is best to intervene before this becomes inevitable. We in the angelic community are tasked with the preservation of balance. I have to tell you that balance is in grave jeopardy in this sector. There are numerous anomalies here, some of them severe."

He looked hard at Ganymede, and then at Alex. He had a very long chin, Alex decided. An uncomfortable silence ensued and Alex began to feel that something was expected of him.

"Oops," he said, which quickly struck him as inadequate, and then, "What are we going to do, then?"

"We haven't decided yet," said the angel, nodding gravely. "It may be possible to bring in a clean-up team. Resources would have to be made available. I don't know, it's a mess," he said as he glanced meaningfully at Ganymede again at this point. "We shall be having a meeting of all interested parties in the near future to decide what should be done. In the meantime, Malcolm here needs to continue to assess the damage. I can trust you to do that, Malcolm?" he said sharply.

Malcolm, who had been studying his fingernails, suddenly jerked upright.

"Hmm? Oh yes," he said.

"You are aware that your position as Head of Sector will need to be reviewed," said Tony to Ganymede, after a moment of staring critically at Malcolm. "I shall be sending a report to Mike on the matter. I have to say that I am disappointed in you, Ganymede. I acted contrary to the advice of others when I appointed you. Since that time I have begun to wonder if they were right and I have made a mistake. Your imprudent use of scarce resources and your cavalier attitude to security only confirm me in that view."

Alex could hardly keep himself from smirking. The corners of his mouth strained outwards, held in place only by pursing his lips firmly together. Oh joy! The sight of Ganymede getting it in the neck made him feel that little bubbles of warm air were being inflated in his chest. Ganymede, for his part, scowled and shuffled his feet.

"I was acting on good authority," he growled. "When I made those modifications… I had a clear understanding with Gordon."

"What you may or may not have agreed with my predecessor is no concern of mine," snapped Tony. "You certainly have no written authority of any kind from me. How you think giving a citizen visible thought bubbles constitutes responsible use of delegated angelic prerogative I really can't imagine. And what was the other one?" He tapped his head and grimaced in a parody of thinking hard. "Let me see. Oh, yes. Psycho-auditory modifications to some youth's speech to correct his use of profane language. A marvellous use of constrained resources that was. I suppose you think that's funny? I suppose that appealed to your sense of irony?"

Ganymede flushed deep red under his facial hair, but seemed incapable of reply.

"Fine. Well, I'll bid you good day," said Tony stiffly. "I shall monitor the position here with interest, and I daresay a meeting of Council will need to be convened. You will both be required to testify. In the meantime, I will thank you not to further abuse your authority with regard to Alex here. You will answer for it if you do." He beckoned to Malcolm. "Come on, we must try to see Raphael before he goes to dinner."

With this, both angels disappeared, shrinking into tiny bright dots that blinked out of existence, leaving a vaguely electric smell. For a moment there was silence, and then Ganymede erupted. Had he been Paulo he would have named every vegetable under the sun. When he had finished ranting and waving his arms around he stood glaring at Alex, his chest heaving. Once, not long ago, Alex would have felt intimidated. Now, he only felt vaguely amused.

"Get out of my sight!" roared Ganymede at last.

Alex got out of his sight, as directed, with a wry smile and at a leisurely pace. He heard the door slam behind him and laughed until his sides ached as he strolled out into the 'Stician dusk.

Before he had gone far he came upon Stacey and Sarah, sitting on a low wall outside the White Horse, kicking their legs. They stood up quickly enough when Alex hove in view.

"Look who it isn't," crowed Stacey. "I know a man who'd be pleased to see you." She nudged Sarah. "What do you reckon? Do you think we should have a little word? Ganymede said he might be puttin' some extra manna our way."

"Have as many words as you like, for all I care," said Alex airily. He favoured Stacey with a tight little smile, and looked pointedly up and down her considerable paunch. "Looks like you could do with a few extra rations. You don't want to go wasting away, do you?"

The resulting expression on Stacey's face was highly satisfactory, but Alex only allowed himself a glimpse of it as he turned on his heel and walked away. A stream of abuse followed him up the road, but he cared not a jot. He felt that he had done something to even the score so far as Stacey was concerned. He was still dwelling happily on this thought when he reached Will's house.

"Hi, Will," he said cheerfully, walking in as Will and Tanya ate their supper by the glow of a single light stick.

"Alex!" they said together, leaping to their feet.

"All hail the conquering hero!" he said with a broad grin, spreading his arms wide. "Your idol returns."

"Where have you been?" asked Will, while Tanya hugged Alex. "Everyone's been out looking for you."

"So I hear," said Alex. "I've been roughing it with Paulo and Kelly up at the Hall."

"Yes, well Ganymede went, like, totally ballistic when you legged it. He'll crucify you if he gets his hands on you. I never saw him so pumped."

"He hasn't even given us any work," added Tanya. "Everyone's just, you know, milling around doing nothing."

"What on earth have you done?" demanded Will. "I know you cheated with your task because Kelly told me, but it must be something more serious than that."

"And where is Kelly?" asked Tanya, craning her neck to look past Alex, as though she thought Kelly might be lurking in the hall.

Alex told them all about the events of the last few days, whilst Will and Tanya listened wide-eyed.

"I knew I saw you move Statical stuff," said Tanya triumphantly, when Alex confessed to his interference with Statica.

"What, so you can just go and help yourself to anything you please? Chocolate? Doughnuts? Cakes and stuff?" asked Will enviously.

Alex nodded.

"Well, come on then," said Will, brushing crumbs off his sleeve. "What are we waiting for? Let's get down to the cake shop right away."

"Haven't you been listening to a word I said?" Alex asked him. "I really can't. Ganymede had good reason to tell me not to mess about with Statica. He just didn't bother telling me why. Me doing stuff like that destabilises 'Sticia. If things get any worse here the angels are going to pull the plug on our bit of it."

"Oh," said Will. "And what happens to us then?"

"I don't know. I guess we sort of 'die' here. We'd carry on in Reality, of course."

There was a pause as Will and Tanya considered this point.

"Do you know," mused Will. "For a king-sized bar of Fruit and Nut, I almost reckon it'd be worth it."

"And another thing…" said Alex, ignoring this notion.

He told them about the census return he had seen in Ganymede's office. And about Kelly. So much had happened since that furtive glance across the page, the horror of it had receded from the forefront of his mind, but now that consciousness came flooding back. He had felt confident, triumphant even, after witnessing Ganymede's humiliation. Now he felt suddenly deflated. A pensive silence settled over the room. The light stick reached the end of its life, too, and darkness gathered around them.

"You mustn't say anything," said Alex into the gloom. "She doesn't know. What good would it do telling her, anyway? There's nothing to be done about it. She's just, well, dead."

"So Kelly's a ghost?" quivered Tanya's small voice.

"No," said Will. "Course she's not. It's just that she only exists here now in 'Sticia. It's all over for her in Reality."

"But what happens if the angels close us down?" persisted Tanya. "What happens to Kelly then?"

Alex hadn't considered this. He did now.

"It's alright for the rest of us," said Will. "We go on living our lives in Reality. I guess it'd be curtains for Kelly though."

"Isn't there anything we can do?" asked Tanya plaintively. "Kelly *can't* die."

"And what about Cactus Jack?" asked Will. "Do you think he'll be coming for Kelly next?"

"I don't know," admitted Alex. "I only got a quick glance at the list. I was looking for names I know. There might have been other names with deceased next to them."

He swallowed hard. David Hemmings' name had been above Kelly's. And he hadn't noticed any more occurrences of that sinister word between them in the list.

Chapter Twelve

The next morning they had visitors, who proved to be Morlock and his sidekick Minion. Minion, who was as short as Morlock was tall, made Morlock seem a chatterbox by comparison. He said nothing at all. Perhaps he was incapable of speech. He had the same tiny sparrow's eyes as his partner and simply stood grinning at Morlock's side whilst Morlock summoned Alex into Ganymede's presence. The grin had a look of permanence about it.

"I'll be along later," Alex told Ganymede's envoy. "When I've had breakfast."

Morlock and Minion looked at each other uncertainly. They were evidently not used to being fobbed off. Minion's grin faded a little.

"Come *now*," creaked Morlock, insistently, stepping forward.

"I'll come when I'm ready," said Alex sharply, thinking that angelic protection made him pretty much bulletproof. The balance of power between him and Ganymede had shifted very satisfactorily in his favour.

"And I wouldn't go thinking about laying your bony hands on me," he added as Morlock flexed his knuckles so that they clicked. "I think your boss would take a dim view of that."

"Very well," said Morlock after a moment's consideration. He turned to leave.

"Just a moment," called Alex after Morlock's retreating back.

A thought had occurred to him. "What happens to you and your little pal if this bit of 'Sticia goes belly up?"

Morlock turned. His long face stretched itself into an even more mournful expression.

"Dead," he said, before stomping off down the stairs.

Hardly had Morlock and Minion departed than a new visitor arrived. This was Malcolm, who materialised suddenly in the middle of Will's room as Will was folding his blankets. Will yelped and sat down hard on a pile of books. He blinked and gaped at the newcomer as the blankets fell disregarded to the floor.

"I'm sorry, did I startle you?" said the angel to Will, as Alex emerged from his own room. "Oh, there you are, Alex. Tony wants you to help itemise all the spikes; you know, the anomalies."

"Fine," said Alex, "Although I've got to see Ganymede at some point. He sent his pals to get me. This is Malcolm," he explained for Will and Tanya's benefit. Tanya was almost as still as a stiff, her hand frozen in the act of carrying a glass of water to her open mouth. "He's an angel," he added. "Kind of in plain clothes."

"I'm sorry about the halo and wings and so on," said Malcolm apologetically. "I've got a problem with that at the moment. You'll just have to take me as you find me."

"Fine," said Will weakly. "Don't go to any special effort for me."

Being able to materialise and dematerialise at will was a great aid to getting about. By the time Alex had done it half a dozen times it was almost second nature to him. They went to Wardworths first, where Alex introduced Malcolm to his mum and where they spent some time studying the pick 'n' mix. Malcolm wanted to know exactly where the sweets had come from and then spent a long time doing what he described as 'triangulation'. This involved taking readings from his transponder in various places around the stall.

"That's given me a good three-dimensional picture of the anomalies," he said at last, pocketing the shiny stone. "Quite trivial those. Hardly a spike at all: more a ripple really. I shouldn't think they're causing much of a problem. I daresay a couple of chocolate éclairs going missing wouldn't create much of a stir in Reality."

It was likewise with the Mars bar and with the minor items Alex had 'borrowed' from Boots. Malcolm wrinkled his nose, studied his transponder and told Alex 'Sticia could probably survive them. He was less sure about Stanton Post Office though.

"Uh, uh," he said, holding the transponder up for Alex to see. "We have a major problem here. Look, the reading's off the scale. See? Hell of a spike."

Alex could see nothing of the sort. He could only see smooth grey stone. He nodded though, to show willing.

"Yep. This is the big one. I'd better triangulate on it."

Alex stood about glumly whilst Malcolm got on with his job. He felt uncomfortable. He and Paulo had made serious inroads into the drinks chiller, and various boxes and packets were scattered on the floor between the aisles in the grocery part of the shop. This could be replaced, he supposed, but lots of stuff was gone. He imagined Paulo and Kelly were busily working their way through it, wherever they were. Alex mused unhappily on this thought whilst Malcolm homed in on the till. He made a low whistle.

"Wahay! This one's a doozey."

"Paulo made me raid the till," said Alex guiltily, moving up alongside Malcolm. "I don't know how much he got."

186

"Yes. Well, he got a pig of a spike along with it." Malcolm stroked the transponder thoughtfully and held it up to the light. "Do you know, there's something odd about this sector. I'm picking up a really strange reading. It's not exactly an anomaly, not in the sense of creating disturbance anyway. It's just a strange kind of constant background thing. Makes it quite hard to calibrate for the usual stuff." He frowned. "Never mind, it could be this lousy transponder, I suppose. Anyway, where're we off to next?"

"The Hall, I guess," said Alex glumly.

At the Hall there was no sign of Paulo and Kelly, although there was plenty of evidence of their occupancy. Cigarette stubs, sandwich packaging, milk bottles, cereal packets and beer cans lay strewn around Lord Maynard's elegant apartments. Paulo, armed with a spray can, had humorously spray painted the housekeeper's face green. He had also sprayed uncomplimentary comments about Ganymede on various walls.

"*Sprout* Ganymede," was written in large letters across a mirror and an adjacent section of wall in the green drawing room. "Ganymede is a *runner bean*," appeared amongst the mounted heads of stags in the billiard room. There were many others.

"Oh dear," said Malcolm, with a wry smile. "He is a bit of scallywag, this Paulo."

"What a mess!" said Alex with alarm, running his hands through his hair.

"It's a problem alright," agreed Malcolm. "This place's got more spikes than a porcupine. Come on, we'd better make a start. You'll have to do something about getting hold of this Paulo sometime soon. He's single-handedly screwing up the sector now you've taken a break from it yourself."

By the time they were finished at the Hall, Malcolm was ready to go. There was an urgent meeting he had to attend, he said. And he had to write up all his findings. Besides, he had done enough for one day. He gave Alex a smooth grey pebble, the size of a fifty pence piece.

"If anything urgent comes up, or you think of anywhere else you tore a great hole in the fabric of 'Sticia, you might want to summon me with that," he said. "It's like a pager. Give it a firm squeeze and picture me in your head. Otherwise, I'll be in touch again if I need you."

Alex weighed the stone in his palm. He was about to ask Malcolm if he couldn't spirit him back to Gladstone Street, but before he could do so Malcolm had vanished.

"Never mind," said Alex glumly, pocketing the pebble. He frowned. It was a long walk home from the Hall.

It was after dark by the time Alex made it to Ganymede's. He would have rather have gone back to Will and Tanya, but he supposed he had better keep his promise to Morlock. The creature was there at the door, waiting. He said nothing as Alex passed, merely hissing bleakly, his lips drawn back over big yellow teeth. Alex had half expected Ganymede to be in one of the towering rages he was famous for, but instead he found him sitting at his desk, making notes in a small black book.

"Ah, Alex," he said, taking off a pair of glasses Alex had never seen him wear before. "Never mind, better late than never. I've been thinking it's time the two of us had a proper man to man discussion."

He drew back a chair and indicated it with a big hand. "Here, sit down." He poured Alex a glass of water and slid it in front of him. For a moment he seemed to consider Alex, nodding thoughtfully.

"You and I got off to a bad start," he conceded. "Looking back, there are some things I regret about the way I dealt with you."

There was a mildness in his voice and manner that filled Alex with suspicion. As a celebrated wolf, sheep's clothing fitted him badly.

"I want you to understand me," he continued. "And there are aspects of life in Intersticia I want you to understand, too. Things aren't always as they seem. I daresay the others think I'm a crusty old so and so. I don't doubt that some of them hate my guts. Do you think I enjoy that?" He shook his head sadly. "Of course I don't, but they don't understand what I'm up against. They haven't got the first idea." He shook his head in sadness at the ignorance of his subjects. "Still, the angels charged me with running this sector and that's what I'm going to do. I've done it longer than you can possibly imagine and I'm not about to give up on it now. One thing I'm not, Alex, and that's a quitter," he said, wagging a finger resolutely.

"Establish a work/leisure balance, they say. Give them meaningful tasks with a measurable outcome, they say. But what resources do I get? I can barely feed everyone as it is. I don't think you have any idea how hard I work. I don't think anyone does." He smiled grimly. "Come with me, will you please, Alex."

Pushing back his chair and setting down his glasses on the desk, Ganymede crossed to another door. Feeling curious, despite his severe reservations about Ganymede's sincerity, Alex followed. Ganymede opened the door. On the other side was a plain hall, with other doors leading off it.

"After you," said Ganymede, with a polite gesture.

Instead of walking into a hall, Alex found himself falling. At least it felt like falling. Had he not been so used to strange experiences in recent days, he might have been seriously alarmed. As it was, he soon landed on some spongy surface on all fours and scrambled into a sitting position, dusting off his hands and staring around him curiously. It was dark, but the ground beneath him was like thick moss, luminously blue, as though lit by countless millions of fibre-optic filaments. The black air around him swarmed with sparks of light. These varied in size and colour, some gliding majestically past, some darting unpredictably here and there. It was rather beautiful. Alex wasn't exactly frightened. After all, he was under Tony's protection, but the thought did cross his mind that Ganymede might have decided to murder him in an act of heedless spite. This thought was coming to the forefront of his mind when Ganymede appeared beside him. He was carrying two nets of the sort used to catch butterflies and a large jar with a lid.

"Pretty, isn't it?" he said, gesturing at the bizarre environment in which they found themselves. "It's called Yer-bishnic-az-kesh, or something like that in angel-speak, but I just call it TheOtherPlace. These little sparky jobs, they're what I like to think of as sub-atomic particles. I know a bit about particle physics, you see, from the days when I used to be able to hold down a job in Reality. Those little blue ones – I think of those as tachyons. See that large orange one, slow moving – that's a meson. Watch out for the spiky purple ones. Quarks they are. Hurts like hell if you get one in the face."

"Okay," said Alex, glancing at Ganymede wonderingly. "And the point of all this?"

"The point of all this," said Ganymede with a grim smile, "Is that we have to catch some of the little suckers." He handed Alex a net. "Off you go."

They were surprisingly hard to catch. Even the slower ones seemed able to put on a spurt when Alex crept up on them with his net. Still, after a breathless chase, he caught himself a meson.

"Is that all?" said Ganymede disparagingly when Alex presented it to him, fizzing and sparking spasmodically in the mesh of the net.

He held up his jar, with a grin, to reveal half a dozen whirling, coloured sparks. "You'll have to do better than that." He suddenly stiffened, staring over Alex's shoulder. "Look! A Higgs Boson. Those are rare as hell."

Without further explanation he was off, bounding across the blue moss in pursuit of a bobbing red blob the size of a hen's egg. After a moment's hesitation Alex set off after him. It was easily the oddest experience of his life, and in recent weeks he had had some pretty strange ones. It was exhausting work, too. Somehow he seemed a lot heavier than usual, so that it was an effort to move, and the soft moss underfoot only made things worse. According to Ganymede they had to gather fifteen quarks, eight mesons, seven tachyons and a Higgs Boson. By the time Ganymede had a jar full of writhing light, Alex was fit to drop. Ganymede, who seemed only mildly winded, considered the jar.

"I think that'll do for now," he said.

"What now then?" asked Alex, trying to control his breathing. "And what, actually, is the point of all this?"

"Home," said Ganymede with an enigmatic grin. "And then a little cookery."

Alex had no idea where they were in this featureless landscape, but Ganymede led them towards a slender line of light which soon resolved itself into the outline shape of the door they had entered through.

"Excellent," said Ganymede, leading Alex back through into his house. Another door opened into a small kitchen, where a woman was frozen in the act of washing the floor. Edging past her, Ganymede set the jar down on the kitchen table and switched on the oven.

"Hang on, I thought electricity didn't work in 'Sticia," objected Alex.

"It does here," said Ganymede, getting bowls and various utensils out of cupboards and drawers. "Angelic prerogative. That's what it's called. They make a sort of exception for me, if you like. If they didn't I wouldn't be able to provide you all with manna, and everyone would starve then, wouldn't they?"

He brought down a big brown bag of flour-like substance from one of the higher cupboards and set it next to the bowl. Soon, using scales, he was carefully measuring out a quantity of this and adding water to it from a blue striped jug. He gave the muddy mixture a vigorous stir with a wooden spoon.

"And now the vital ingredient," he said with a grim smile.

He unscrewed the lid from the jar and carefully poured in the various coloured sparks of light. One of the quarks shot across the kitchen and collided with a lampshade with a loud 'ping'. With some difficulty Alex recaptured it with his net. Ganymede stirred the mixture with his spoon and wiped his hands on the front of his outermost coat. The state of his fingernails did nothing to inspire confidence in him as a chef.

"And that's manna?" said Alex.

"It will be when it's cooked," agreed Ganymede, putting out dollops of it onto a baking tray. There were six dollops when he had finished.

"But that's not even one person's daily manna allowance," said Alex incredulously. "And you must hand out hundreds every week."

"Nearly two thousand," said Ganymede evenly, putting the tray into the oven.

"But how can you? There can't be time," protested Alex.

"Time is a relative concept," said Ganymede straightening up. "As you should know by now. The room we are in now, and TheOtherPlace, are outside of 'Stician time, just as 'Stician time is outside Statical."

"This is all totally mad!" said Alex, shaking his head. "Too much!"

"Au contraire," said Ganymede patiently, adjusting the controls on the oven. "In an infinite universe everything is possible. More than that, it's inevitable. Open up your mind."

Alex's mind was blown wide open. He sat down heavily on one of the chairs, forced once more to reassess his opinion of Ganymede.

"You must be exhausted. How much time must you spend chasing those funny sparks in there?"

"Lots," said Ganymede simply. "But the love and gratitude of my people makes it all worthwhile."

There was such bitterness condensed into this one statement, you could have dissolved diamonds in it. Alex felt a pang of regret, and for a moment he almost felt sorry for Ganymede.

"But they hate me, don't they?" said the big tramp, as though he could read Alex's thoughts.

"Well, you haven't got much of a fan base out there," conceded Alex.

"I'm tired," said Ganymede, pulling up another chair and using the woman's back as a foot stool. "Sometimes I'm really tired, but I don't want to lose this sector."

"I'd have thought you'd have been glad to be rid of it," said Alex. "It's a whole lot of work, that's for sure."

Ganymede stroked his beard thoughtfully and leant back in his chair.

"Problem is, I haven't got a lot to go back to in Reality," he said in a voice tinged with sadness. "Things didn't really work out for me there. Here I'm something a bit special, see. There I was just the sweepings of the gutter. People looked through me, like I wasn't even there, and when they did look at me it was with that special look of disgust. Pity, from time to time, but mostly disgust." He sighed, looking at his hands. "And then I dropped into Intersticia and suddenly everything was different. I'd been getting by in a kind of fog of cider and cheap British sherry. It was like walking out into clear daylight. And suddenly I was special. Like you, I found I could translate objects from one world to another. The woman who was running the sector when I showed up was making a dog's breakfast of the whole show and she pretty soon got pulled back into Reality. The angels gave *me* the sector… Best day of my life," he said with no trace of irony or exaggeration. "Best day of my bloody life."

Suddenly he was looking at Alex. There was no hostility in his gaze, no humour, only a blank neutrality that Alex had never seen before.

"Will you help me?" asked Ganymede simply.

"What? Help you to do what?" asked Alex, although he knew very well. He just wanted to hear Ganymede say it.

"Help me keep the sector," said Ganymede. "I think we can save it; iron out the spikes, you know… the anomalies. You heard Tony, they're having a meeting in a few days. If we can cut down on the damage by then, I may be able to tough it out. If not, there's only one obvious candidate to replace me."

"Oh?" said Alex carefully.

"You," said Ganymede gravely, tilting his head to one side and continuing to regard Alex steadily.

Alex laughed nervously. "What? You think I could take over from you?"

Ganymede nodded. "It isn't what I think that cuts the mustard. You heard what Tony said. You have very rare qualities for Intersticia. It could be you, Alex, unless we lose the whole interstice, that is, and it could yet come to that. But if we hold on to the interstice it really could be you."

Alex swallowed hard. "Not me," he said. "You can keep it, so far as I'm concerned. And best of luck to you."

It was Ganymede's turn to laugh now, throwing his head back, a slow, sardonic laugh. "So you'll help me then?" he asked.

"Yes, I'll help you," agreed Alex, shaking the horny hand that Ganymede thrust out towards him.

"But not for you mate," thought Alex, as he held Ganymede's hand. "For Kelly, because 'Sticia's all she's got."

When Alex arrived home there was a note for him from Malcolm. As Will mentioned this to Alex, the notion of a glittering golden scroll came momentarily into his mind. Instead there was a handwritten note on a scrap of lined paper torn from a jotter.

"Don't use the 'pager' thing I gave you," Alex read. "It's Tony's. I must have picked it up by mistake. Be in touch tomorrow. Malcolm."

"He was in a hurry," said Will. "I said you might have gone to Ganymede's but he didn't want to go there after you. Said he had an appointment he was running late for."

"Right," said Alex, absently feeling for the 'pager' stone in his pocket.

"And where have you been all day, anyway?" asked Will. "There have been loads of people tooling about up at the park wanting to know what's going on. Chad had a punch up with Jason Collingwood about something he said about Gill Lenkowicz. Mad Annie's going about with a blanket over her head saying the world's going to end…"

"You didn't say anything to anyone about, you know, the angel?" asked Alex, anxiously. "Or Kelly, or anything like that?"

Will shook his head. "No, but I tell you what. Margaret Owen saw Paulo down by the golf course. And he was asking after you."

"Oh great!" said Alex, slapping his forehead. "That's all I need. I bet he's run out of fags. He'll be back to grilling snarks unless he can get me to break out some more rations for him. I'd better tell Ganymede."

"Ganymede?" Will looked at him curiously. "What's with you and Ganymede all of a sudden? I thought you were sworn enemies."

Alex told him all about his surprising interview with Ganymede, the making of the manna, the extraordinary request he had made. Will sat with his back against the wall and listened incredulously, the glow of a light stick reflecting off his glasses. Tanya came in just as Alex was finishing, having spent most of her day at Margaret Owen's.

"You mustn't say anything about this to anyone," Will told her. "Top secret."

"So you're working with Ganymede?" she said. "Doesn't that make you a traitor?"

"I've got to," said Alex. "We've got to try to save the interstice. It's mostly my fault it's all messed up. Kelly's definitely had it if the angels close it down."

Tanya nodded, her small eyes filling with tears. "Will you tell her?" she asked, her voice trembling.

Alex shook his head. He put his arm around Tanya's narrow shoulders. "No, Tan. There's no point, is there? I wish I'd never told you now."

"Don't you think we've a duty to tell her?" said Will, frowning.

"What good will it do?" asked Alex. "There's nothing we can do about it. It'd only freak her out."

"We don't even know where she is," observed Will.

"Not now we don't," said Alex. "But when she and Paulo get to hear that Ganymede's got other stuff to worry about other than rounding up Paulo, I think they'll be coming to find *me*."

Chapter Thirteen

The next day was theoretically Saturday, so Alex told himself – the third Saturday since his entry into 'Sticia. Ganymede came to call for him and they set to work repairing the worst of the damage that he and Paulo had caused. They began at Alex's own house, where Ganymede stripped out the shards of broken glass from the kitchen window and replaced it with a new pane. Morlock and Minion served as errand boys, hurrying off to find tools and materials from wherever their absence would be least disruptive to the fabric of 'Sticia. The glass was carefully removed from a derelict factory unit on the industrial estate. Putty was taken, a little from each pot on the shelves in B&Q. When the work was done and even the tiniest fragment of broken glass removed, Ganymede stood back to admire his handiwork.

"Well, it's a start," he said. "Although God knows there's a whole lot more to do. We could do with your friend Malcolm here to tell us how we're doing."

"I could have paged him," said Alex regretfully. "But he gave me the wrong pager."

"Yeah, well," said Ganymede dryly. "Angels aren't all they're cracked up to be."

They made their way to Stanton Post Office next, their journey taking them past the park, where knots of idle 'Sticians had gathered to talk and to speculate on the strange

197

goings on in their world. Mrs Patterson and her friend Mrs Gurney accosted them in the street outside. Mrs Gurney, whose pelvis you could surely have driven a horse and cart through, was anxious to be reassured that manna supplies would be available as usual at the end of the week.

"There have been thefts," Mrs Patterson told him. "A number of the younger people are behaving in a very immature fashion. I suspect they are bored, Mr Ganymede. I assume you will take matters in hand in due course. All sorts of rumours are flying about."

"You may be assured that I shall deal with it," said Ganymede, with more courtesy than might have been expected. "Think of this week as a holiday. Make the most of it, as next week I shall set more than usually exacting tasks."

He raised his hat to her politely and they resumed their journey, Alex almost jogging to keep up as Ganymede strode out along Love Lane.

"See what happens," said Ganymede, "When everyone's got nothing better to do than mill about aimlessly. You'd think they'd appreciate it, wouldn't you, a little extra leisure? But how do they reward you, except by fighting, falling out with each other and generally getting themselves into a tizz? Can you see now why I try to keep everyone busy?"

"I'm beginning to see," admitted Alex, "But there's more than that to it, isn't there?"

"Maybe," said Ganymede, giving him a sidelong glance. "If you mean that I have to work like a damned slave to keep everyone alive, so I don't see why everyone else shouldn't have a piece of it, too. Yes, there's that, too."

"And is that why you set everyone tasks that are guaranteed to wind them up?" asked Alex. "Like making Will do quadratic equations and such like."

"There might be a strand of truth in that," conceded

Ganymede. "But that's not all. A little bit of perceived injustice and suffering brings people together, you see. Do you think Will did all those equations himself? No. He got someone to help him, didn't he? Likewise poor old Mrs Patterson always has someone take pity on her and help her shift her sand. It's part of the glue that holds our little society together. And if hating my guts gives everyone a shared interest, then so be it."

At the post office, Malcolm was waiting for them, which pleased Ganymede no end. The angel explained that he needed Alex to help him triangulate on a new spike he had detected. This was in the freezer. Alex had forgotten that Paulo had made him fetch out a couple of ice creams.

"That's one angel we could do with on the team," said Ganymede out of the side of his mouth as they approached. "Being able to teleport us about would be more than a bit useful, given the time pressure we're under."

"We're not asking you to do anything that would get you into trouble," Ganymede told Malcolm after this had been outlined for him. "We're only asking you to monitor anomalies, which is exactly what Tony wants you to do. I don't suppose there's anything in your brief that says you can't keep on checking up on them as we try to correct them."

"No, I guess not," said Malcolm frowning. "But I can tell you, Tony's really gunning for you, Ganymede. Anything that comes between Tony and Tony chucking you out on your ear's going to yank his chain big time." He grinned and rubbed his hands together. "Which is all the more reason for bringing it about. Come on then, where do we start?"

They began replacing as much as possible on the shelves, sending Morlock and Minion back into Cardenbridge to fetch replacement cans and packets from the supermarkets there. There was still doubt as to where they should be placed though. They experimented with various arrangements of cans in the chiller, whilst Malcolm stood by, taking readings off his transponder.

"A bit more to the left," he said, whilst Alex made minor adjustments to a four pack of lager. "That's better. No. Stop, too far. Back the other way. Hang it. This is going to take all day."

The three of them stood back, regarding each other glumly.

"Well, it's a bit better," said Malcolm. "But there has to be a better way." He scratched his chin, where a puny goatee beard looked as though it was trying to establish itself. "Got it! I could pop back to the previous interstice and have a look at things there. Wait a mo."

With this Malcolm disappeared, shrinking rapidly into a tiny white dot, and then nothing. The vaguely electric smell was all that remained of him.

"Angels can travel in time?" said Alex, looking hard at Ganymede.

Ganymede shrugged. "So it would appear."

A few moments later and Malcolm was back, bearing with him a glossy A4 sheet with pictures of the chiller on it, all taken from slightly different angles. Using this they were able to position the cans with pinpoint accuracy. Malcolm took a new reading after this and punched the air in glee.

"Look at that!" he said, brandishing his transponder in their direction entirely pointlessly. "Trace! Spike squashed flat. It's hardly more than a blip now, no bigger than those down at the supermarket your pals filched those cans from."

The money in the till proved to be more problematic. Even a close look at a photo taken in the previous interstice failed to make clear exactly how many notes had been taken.

"I can't interfere with Statica," said Malcolm, when Alex

suggested he should go back in time again, take out the notes and count them. "They'd be down on me like a ton of bricks if I got caught doing that. Like I said, I only monitor and report. That's my job."

"We're going to need Paulo for this then," said Ganymede. "Or more to the point, we're going to need his pockets. I mean, I don't suppose he'll have been able to spend it."

"I just hope he hasn't been lighting up with tenners," said Alex gloomily. "Can't *you* find him for us Malcolm? You are a super-being with wondrous powers after all."

"Kind of you to say so," said Malcolm modestly. "But sadly I haven't got the right kit. There's a mate of mine works in Location but he's off sick this week." He frowned. "I could put in a request I guess, but that has to go through Moira and she'll probably tip Tony off. She knows he's got his eye on this interstice."

"Well, we'll just have to find him ourselves," said Ganymede grimly.

"He might find us," said Alex, going on to explain that Paulo was likely enough to come looking for him when his lager stocks ran low.

"It'd better be soon," grunted Ganymede. "We've got that lousy review meeting to look forward to in a few days. Any news on that, Malcolm?"

"Not yet," said the angel. "He's trying to get hold of Glenda, but she's tied up with another review, somewhere back down in the eighteenth century."

"Weird," said Alex, shaking his head, "Truly weird."

It struck him that the daydreams that had been so much a part of his life before his entry into 'Sticia had hardly been more bizarre or inventive than the reality he faced here. And yet daydreams seemed to have quite slipped from his mental agenda. It was as though there was no need for them.

Whichever part of his psyche had once demanded them found itself more than satisfied with the prevailing level of oddness.

The following day, what Alex thought of as Sunday, Ganymede left him and Malcolm to get on with the job. Things were going seriously awry with the folk of 'Sticia and Ganymede needed to get on top of the situation. An elderly friend of Mrs Gurney was refusing to come down from some scaffolding she had climbed up. In addition, Major Trubshaw's unguarded thoughts had got him punched in the mouth by Will Evans, the rather boring little Welshman with the big nose. Ganymede had to start interviewing his subjects once more and get on with keeping them all usefully occupied for the following week. And of course there was manna to be prepared for the next day's Gathering. Alex now had an idea how much effort this involved.

Will and Tanya helped, too, as they all did their best to repair the damage at the Hall. There were all sorts of objects to be set back in their proper places and a great deal of graffiti to remove. Fortunately, the spray can Paulo had used was of the sort used for colouring hair at parties and washed off without difficulty. Even so, Lord Maynard's housekeeper was going to glance at herself in the mirror later that day and wonder if she was sickening for something. Some of the walls needed a thorough scrubbing, but silk emulsion proved resilient enough and by the end of the day only a very sharp-eyed observer would have noticed anything amiss. Malcolm studied his transponder and pronounced himself satisfied. Alex, Will and Tanya set down their buckets and sponges and slumped on the floor in attitudes of exhaustion and relief.

That night Alex and Malcolm reported on their progress to Ganymede. Ganymede looked tired, too, and the delicious smell of freshly baked manna permeated the rooms of his house. He told them he had also managed to interview thirty-two 'Sticians, coax Mrs Gurney's friend down from her perch and give the Major a large plastic bin liner to go over his thought bubble. He had a look at Malcolm's transponder and slapped the angel cheerfully on the back when Malcolm told him the anomaly count was reduced by more than half.

"Excellent," he said, stretching for a yawn. "If we can get hold of Mr Potts in the next few days, I'm thinking we may just get away with it."

"Maybe," conceded Malcolm with a grin. "I'll be off then."

He began to move his hands in the way he did before dematerialising, but then paused. "Oh, by the way," he said. "Did you know that Atropos is back in this interstice? Someone in Personnel told me earlier. Nothing significant is it?"

"Who's Atropos?" asked Alex.

"Atropos... oh, he's the Cutter of Threads," said Malcolm in a dramatically spooky voice. "You probably know him as Cactus Jack. What's the matter?"

The colour had drained from Alex's face. He sat down heavily on one of Ganymede's office chairs. Ganymede looked at him curiously for a moment and then realisation sparked in his eyes.

"He knows," he said. "Damn it, he knows!"

"Hmm? What?" asked the angel, his eyebrows creeping up his forehead.

"I must have left the census returns out on my desk the other night when he was here." He turned on Alex, his eyes blazing. "How much did you see, lad? The truth now!"

Ganymede had fallen back into cross old hectoring Ganymede mode. It was as if the last few days of sweet reasonableness had fallen away. His face was vivid red with rage.

"Enough," admitted Alex, momentarily frightened by

Ganymede's sudden fury. "I didn't have time to get a proper look. I saw who was dead though. And it's Kelly next, isn't it?" Alex's fear ebbed away to be replaced by cold indignation. "She's for the chop isn't she? Cactus Jack's coming to get her."

"You've got no right to know that," roared Ganymede.

"But I do know," Alex shouted back at him. "You shouldn't have left it lying around if you didn't want people looking. Anyway, what on earth do you think I'm going to do about it? Knowing isn't a fat lot of use, is it?"

"You'd better not have told anyone else," warned Ganymede, wagging his finger.

"I told Will and Tanya. That's all," said Alex, resentfully.

"You damn fool," snapped Ganymede. "And I daresay they've blabbed it about to everyone else. That was confidential information."

"Well, you should have kept it locked up," Alex told him, feeling more and more confident, "Shouldn't you?"

"Hey!" said Malcolm, raising his hands in a placatory gesture. "Simmer down, both of you. There's a problem here?"

"You could say that," said Alex bitterly. "Kelly's my friend."

"Oh," said the angel, looking awkwardly at Ganymede. "I see."

"Can't you do something to stop him? What's his name… Atropos?"

"I think you overestimate my authority, friend," said Malcolm. "Atropos is Death's delegate in Intersticia. Death claims his own and there's absolutely nothing we can do about it. When your number's up, it's up. End of story." He drew a finger meaningfully across his throat. "It's like it takes a while for Death to realise some folks keep on going in Intersticia, even when they popped their clogs in Reality. It may take time, but he catches up with them in the end. Doesn't like loose ends, Death. Atropos snips them off, see… Sorry about your friend, Alex." Malcolm put a hand on Alex's shoulder, which made Alex want to cry. He cultivated anger to fight back the tears.

"But there must be something we can do!" he snapped.

"Uh huh," said Malcolm, shaking his head sadly. "Better get used to it."

But Alex wasn't going to get used to it. He walked briskly home, the taste of cold fury bitter in his mouth. It was dark, but there was as yet no vestige of fear on the breeze. Cactus Jack was far away. How had Kelly died? She was only fifteen? People that age didn't just drop dead, did they? She evidently wasn't in hospital, or she'd have been got up like Roger Bradley. Could she have been murdered, perhaps? But murder was hardly a commonplace occurrence in Cardenbridge. Which left accidental death, and as Alex approached the centre of Cardenbridge, a horrible idea occurred to him. Instead of cutting through the middle of town he took a more circuitous route around the ring road. It seemed a long time since he had walked this way, retracing the route he had first taken on his way with Will to the park that day, when he had fallen into 'Sticia for good. There was the police car, the skid marks behind it, and there the small sporty car with its outsized wheels, crumpled around the upright of the overhead sign gantry. It was dark, but there was enough moonlight to pick out the figure of the girl, frozen in the act of picking herself up from the road. There was pain and horror written in her features. Alex followed her gaze, and felt his throat tighten as he realised what ominous portent was written there. Twenty paces away, in the gutter, there was a dark patch. Alex crossed to that deeper puddle of darkness in the gloom, and stooped to place his trembling finger in it. It came away cold and wet and sticky. Alex turned to face the moon and its silvery touch glinted on a bloodied fingertip.

Will was standing at the gate when Alex reached home.

"Never a dull moment," he said. "Guess who's dropped in for tea… Paulo and Kelly," he said when Alex looked blankly at him.

"Oh, Jesus," said Alex. "Give me a break, I need to think this through."

"I thought you'd be pleased. About Kelly anyways," said Will, turning for the door.

"I am, sort of, but I found out how Kelly died. At least I think I know."

He told Will about the accident – and the blood.

"And there's another funny thing," he said. "In Ganymede's census return, Paulo's name came right underneath Kelly's. There was a date and a time. I guess the time they entered 'Sticia. I took special note of that, because at first I thought it was identical. But it wasn't. There was just two-tenths of a second difference. Odd that, isn't it?"

"What are you saying?" whispered Will, running his hand through his tousled dark hair.

"I'm saying it was Paulo that was driving that car," Alex said grimly. "It was him that killed her."

Will bit his lip. "Christ!" he said. "That could place a strain on their relationship if she ever finds out."

"Best she doesn't," Alex told him. "At least for now, do you hear me?" He pressed his finger to his lips. "Schtum."

"Loud and clear," said Will, following him into the house.

Paulo and Kelly were upstairs in the back bedroom with Tanya. Paulo was bragging loudly about their adventures as fugitives, but he stopped when Alex and Will came in.

"Hey, Alex, my man!" he said, as though Alex was a dear

friend of his. He got up and raised a hand gleefully for Alex to slap. Alex pointedly ignored it. "Come on, no hard feelings, man," said Paulo, toning down the enthusiasm. "I was desperate, you know that."

"Yeah, and I bet you're desperate now or you wouldn't be here," said Alex coldly. "Down to your last twenty are you?"

He was conscious of Will at his side glancing nervously at him.

"You know you are sooo wrong," Paulo told him, standing up, but there was a glint of hostility in his eye now. The way he was shifting his weight from foot to foot suggested a readiness to do violence to him, with difficulty suppressed.

"What's going on here, anyway?" asked Kelly, looking anxious, as well she might, because at that moment Alex was ready to punch it out with Paulo, however uneven the contest. A small part of him stood back and wrung its hands anxiously at this entirely uncharacteristic bravado.

"Everyone's talking about the end of the world," she said. "What with Ganymede giving everyone a week off and so on…" Her voice tailed off. She looked at Alex in a way which pleaded with him not to antagonise her brutish companion. "Tanya won't tell me a thing. Gone all sulky on me, hasn't she?"

Well, it wasn't sulkiness. The poor girl simply didn't know what to say, so she was saying as little as she could get away with. Alex shot her a sympathetic glance and sat down carefully on a pile of blankets.

"'Sticia's in trouble," he told Kelly. "And it's mostly my fault."

He explained all that had happened in recent days, since his escape from Paulo's custody, omitting from it any reference to Kelly's status as dead girl walking.

"So don't ask me to go down the offie for you," said Alex, turning suddenly to Paulo and saying slowly and deliberately,

"BECAUSE IT ISN'T GOING TO HAPPEN."

"Why not?" asked Paulo, staring back at him with his cold, pale eyes. "Seems to me if we all want to get back to Reality it's the best thing we can do. If we do enough damage to this *broccoli* place we're going to *sprout* it all up and the whole *potato* place folds. End of story. We get on with our *cabbage* lives."

"Yes, well that's all you *cauliflower* know," said Alex derisively.

"Huh?" grimaced Paulo. "What's he *cucumber* talking about?"

"I'm just saying," said Alex, leaning towards him. "That there's a few people with an interest in keeping this interstice going. And I'm not going to let you *sprout* it up."

"*Why?*" asked Paulo, an expression of distaste and mystification on his face. "*Why* is he talking about fennel vegetables?"

"Stop it," Will told Alex nervously, sensing that Paulo was getting to the end of his fuse.

"Look, Paulo," said Alex thinking hard. "If we get dropped back into Reality it's all over. Everything we've had here done with. We won't even remember it…" he lowered his voice, looking meaningfully at Paulo and then Kelly. "We won't even remember *each other*. Malcolm told me."

There was a silence. Paulo seemed to consider this, fingering his earring. Alex could pretty much see the cogs going round in his head. At last he took Kelly's hand and swung it bashfully, giving her a wan smile.

"Yeah, okay. *Peas.* Maybe you're right. *Leek* me if I couldn't do with a beer though."

Relief swept over Alex. "We'll need that cash you've got," he said, following up this breakthrough. "Taking that made a big hole in 'Sticia. It has to be put back."

"Huh?" Paulo's eyes glinted briefly like hard little stones again.

"Go on!" Kelly told him, giving him a sharp nudge in the ribs.

"Don't be so daft. What the hell do you need it for anyway? You never even bought me flowers."

"Yeah, sorry chick," he said with a leer. "I would if I could, mind. You know that."

Kelly tweaked his nose. "Yeah, I believe you… Come on – cash. Cough up!"

After a moment, Paulo reached into his pocket and pulled out a crumpled wad of notes. He extended these towards Alex, pulling them away teasingly at the last moment, before finally letting Alex take hold of them.

"You owe me one, Big Ears," said Paulo, giving him a playful slap around the head that made him see stars.

Later, whilst Paulo slept in the front bedroom, Alex was awoken by Kelly's hand on his shoulder. It was nearly dawn and the 'Stician moon was sinking to the horizon behind the bottle factory, taking with it its soft cloak of darkness. Alex, who had hardly slept anyway, looked up blearily at her.

"Can we talk?" she whispered, glancing warily back into the upstairs landing. "Outside."

Alex followed her stealthily down the stairs, past the bedroom where Will and Tanya still slept. Will, wrapped loosely in blankets, had his mouth wide open.

"There's something up, isn't there?" said Kelly when they stood by the front gate. A small stiff boy on a scooter was frozen in the act of hurtling past, an expression of determination set in his features. "Everyone's behaving funny around me."

Alex briefly entered into another fragment of the long debate he had with himself throughout the night. Should he tell her? His instincts assured him that he shouldn't, yet reason, taking the opposite view, was just about worn out with arguing. It was easier to say nothing, however, and Alex felt too exhausted to

209

do otherwise.

"It's just Paulo," he lied. "He's such a chav. Can't you tell we don't like him? What do you see in him anyway?"

Kelly seemed to accept this explanation. She shrugged and smiled wanly at him. "I don't know. He's funny and he can be really generous. He's a free spirit, you know. No one can hem him in. He doesn't see why he has to play by the rules. He makes his own rules. I don't know… there's lots of things." She cast her dark eyes upward, thoughtfully. "Maybe he reminds me of my dad."

"I thought you couldn't remember your Dad," objected Alex.

"No, but I know what he was like," said Kelly. "Mum talks about him enough. He was a bit of a rogue, too." She frowned, affecting seriousness. "Anyway, why am I telling you all this? It's none of your business, is it?"

Alex didn't answer, so she took his hand in hers, small and warm and full of life.

"Is that jealously I hear talking? I like you too," she said, with a smile and a coy tilt of her chin.

But the word 'like' held too many shades of meaning.

Chapter Fourteen

It was the Gathering later that day, so Ganymede would be tied up in the park restoring a measure of normality to 'Stician life. He gave his instructions to Alex and his friends first, making a good show of concealing his annoyance when confronted with Paulo. Paulo grinned insolently at him. Ganymede told him all his previous offences would be forgiven if he helped set things right. To Alex's relief, Paulo seemed to accept this olive branch. Kelly went with Will and Tanya to the park, to keep up the impression that things were alright, while Paulo and Alex went with Malcolm to the post office.

"Hey, dude," Paulo said to Malcolm when the angel arrived. He favoured Malcolm with another insolent smirk. "Ain't never met an angel. Funny, you don't *look* like an angel."

"He's undercover," Alex told him, whilst Malcolm looked uncomfortable. The angel fetched out his transponder and began pressing parts of its top surface.

"There," he said triumphantly at last, as a brilliant glow suffused him. "What do you think of that?"

The next moment he was authentically an angel, clear white light, streaming from him so that Paulo had to shade his eyes. Unfortunately, instead of growing into a tall majestic angel like Tony, he had shrunk into a tiny, cute, naked winged child, like those Alex had seen in Renaissance paintings. Paulo and

Alex stared open mouthed whilst the little angel fluttered on dove-sized wings before them.

"What?" said Malcolm, before glancing down at himself. "Oh!" he said, reverting abruptly to his usual be-suited shape. "Bloody Mark Fourteen. Piece o' garbage."

Alex picked the transponder from the fruit stand, where Malcolm had thrown it, whilst Paulo sniggered and made a rude gesture with a crooked little finger. Morlock and Minion looked on impassively. They had come along in case any heavy fetching or carrying needed doing.

"Let's get on with it," said Alex, taking the bank notes from his pocket and straightening them out.

Malcolm travelled back to the previous instant to take pictures for the sake of comparison. Soon the notes were replaced in the till, exactly as Alex had found them. Malcolm held his transponder over them and nodded.

"Yep, that's made a huge difference. Hell of a spike that was. Now it's hardly a blip."

Malcolm's moving to and from the previous interstice had given Alex an idea. Their next job was at a large house that Paulo had stayed in with Kelly two nights previously. There was a little green graffiti here and there, as well as the general scatter of litter associated with Paulo's occupation. Lager cans bobbed in the swimming pool. Alex took Malcolm to one side whilst Paulo helped Morlock and Minion fish these out.

"I think I know how my friend got killed," he said, whilst the angel tilted his head to one side. "Can you do me a big favour? I need you to go back again to the interstice before this one. Only this time I want you to go to the ring road. There's an accident there. If you could just have a look in the crashed car and in the gutter. There's only a blood stain there right now. Please, I'd be really, really grateful." He looked at Malcolm earnestly.

"This is outside my brief," said the angel, looking doubtful. "Is it something to do with that idiot?" he said, nodding towards Paulo, who had just thrown an empty can playfully at the back of Minion's head.

"Maybe," said Alex guardedly.

Malcolm pursed his lips. "Hmm, okay. I'll be right back."

He was as good as his word, returning almost before Alex had realised he had gone. The angel's face was pale, and his eyes darted towards Paulo at the other end of the pool, before he seized Alex's arm and pushed him behind the changing room.

"You were right," he said. "It's him, Paulo. He's the one in the car. It's a mess. Blood everywhere. He's alive though, just about." He cupped his hands over his mouth and drew them slowly downwards. "Your friend's definitely a goner though. It's like you said. She's lying in the gutter... like a broken doll. Sorry, pal," he said, putting a light angelic hand on Alex's shoulder.

Alex bit his lip. It brought him a certain grim satisfaction to be proved right, but a kind of bleak despair, too. He wanted to run up to Paulo and hurl him into the pool, hold his stupid head under until the bubbles stopped rising.

"There's got to be something you can do," he said.

"Why has there?" asked Malcolm reasonably. "You don't think I'm about to go back and start messing around with the course of Reality, do you? Even if I could. Accept it, Alex. It's better if you do in the long term."

But Alex couldn't accept it. "What would happen if you went back in time a few moments and twisted the wheel of Paulo's car so that he just missed Kelly?"

"No way! You must be joking. That would alter the course of this Reality," said Malcolm. "It would create a different future. We call it a Mod. I don't have authority to insert a

213

new breakpoint. That kind of permission has to come right from the top. I'd have to go through Mike, and I don't see Mike signing up to that one. It's not like Kelly's a big wheel in this Reality. Her getting offed hardly makes a ripple. Okay, so maybe if she was going to invent a cure for cancer something could be done. No, forget about it, Alex. It isn't going to happen."

"Why can't *I* go back?" asked Alex desperately. "If I was there a couple of seconds earlier, I could knock her out of the way."

"Uh, huh," said Malcolm, shaking his head violently. "Two major points there. First, 'Sticians don't decide when to drop back into Reality – Reality sucks them back in when their time is up. Second, you guys can't time travel. Simply can't be done. Besides, then you'd exist twice in the same instant. Think about it. There's one of you already there in the instant you want to go back to. Suddenly there'd be two of you. At the very least it would be embarrassing. Reality doesn't take kindly to being messed about. Could be catastrophic. At the very least the instant would fold and you could lose the whole of Reality. Put it out of your head." He paused, apparently hearing voices in his head and then nodded. "Okay, so now we've got other priorities anyway. I just heard from Dave in Tony's office. The meet's tomorrow. We'd better go tell Ganymede."

"What you need to understand about Tony is that he's a deeply bitter little angel," Malcolm told Alex and Ganymede that night. "He was a rising star, tipped for the top. Everyone said how gifted he was. And then there was some scandal about the allocation of resources. Nothing was ever proved, but our Tony's reputation took a nose dive, nevertheless. His junior, Mike, got the plum job he'd coveted for himself. That's how it is now. There are four Archangels, see. Top jobs in creation.

214

There's Uriel in Accounts, Raphael in Personnel, or Angelic Resources as they're starting to call it nowadays, then Gabe's in charge of PR and right up there at the top of the tree there's Mike, Head of Operations. Poor old Tony got lumbered with Intersticia, and he was lucky to get that."

Malcolm had a laugh about this and poured each of them another glass of the delicious drink he had brought with him. Nectar, he called it, and it was like a golden distillation of honey and sunlight. Drinking it made Alex want to laugh and cry and run around the room all at the same time. With difficulty he restrained himself. His fingers and toes tingled delightfully.

"But Mike's never going to rest so long as Tony's holding down any kind of responsible job. They hate each other like poison. If he can prove Intersticia's going down the tubes, he'll have an excuse to kick Tony out. He'd be lucky to get my job," scoffed Malcolm. "So Tony's under pressure to run a tight ship, what with Mike breathing down his neck, and Ganymede here letting holes get torn in the fabric doesn't exactly help his case."

"It's pretty much fixed, didn't you say?" grunted Ganymede, looking resentful.

"Sure. We ironed out a lot of spikes, but it's going to be pretty much touch and go. Have you had a look at the Moon recently?"

Alex and Ganymede exchanged glances for a moment and then crossed to look out of the window. The Moon was rising above the poplars by the football pitch.

"See anything odd?"

"Oh my god!" breathed Alex and Ganymede in unison.

There was a definite blurriness around its outline that hadn't been there before.

"Cumulative, you see," said Malcolm matter-of-factly. "Takes a while for the instabilities to take effect. You might have felt a few earth tremors, too. It'll take a while for our fixes to feed through. You'd better hope it's not too little too late."

"There's about seventy lives depending on it," said Alex.

"Rather more than that," said Ganymede grimly.

"What do you mean?"

"You're thinking of this sector, this instant. I'm thinking of the whole planet. You don't imagine this little bit of the planet can disappear without taking the rest of it with you, do you? We're talking about rather more than ten million souls here."

Alex found that he had to sit down. Suddenly the consequences of his innocent tinkerings with Statica seemed almost too much to bear. Ganymede apparently found something of interest to stare at in the fireplace and drummed his fingers on his knee.

"Yeah, well," sighed the angel. "Let's not despair too soon, shall we? It may work out okay. The problem is, Glenda is going to be presiding over this meeting tomorrow and she's one of Mike's sidekicks. If she can find any excuse to close down the interstice she'll do it. It all strengthens Mike's case against Tony."

"Yes, but this is only one tiny sector in one tiny interstice," said Alex. "There must be trillions of them in Intersticia. What difference can it make in the grand scheme of things?"

"You don't know how pear-shaped things are going in the rest of Intersticia," Malcolm told him. "Tony's made some bad appointments." He pointedly avoided Ganymede's eye. "It's all part of a bigger picture. And there's a clear trend. This sector could be pivotal for Tony if he wants to hold on to his job. He's got to be seen to be doing the right thing…"

"And what, exactly is the right thing, Malcolm?" growled Ganymede. "In your humble view?"

Malcolm took another pull at his nectar and wiped his mouth

with the back of his hand. "It isn't what I think that counts," he said, diplomatically. "It's all down to Glenda. If there's any possibility of dumping you, Ganymede, they'll have to be casting around for an alternative." He turned to Alex. "And I'm looking at him right now."

Alex glanced awkwardly at Ganymede and shook his head. "Not me," he said.

"Don't bank on it. They'll be sizing you up. You've got all the right qualities. You've got exceptional cross-dimensional manipulation skills and you're highly stable."

"Huh?" said Alex, frowning.

"He means you aren't going to fall back into Reality any time soon," Ganymede told him. "The more stable you are in Intersticia, the longer you'll stay here. Maybe hundreds of years. I've presided over eleven hundred and twenty-seven Gatherings, would you believe."

"Ganymede has a stability reading of point eight four," said Malcolm. "Yours is point eight nine. Chances are you'll be here a long time. Your friend Paulo now, his is point three five. Chances are he'll be dropping back into Reality real soon."

"What about Kelly?" asked Alex, looking from face to face and finding precious little comfort there.

"She doesn't have a reading at all," Ganymede said softly. "She'll be around only until Atropos tidies things up."

"I still don't see how all this affects me," Alex said after a moment whilst this sunk in. "What's going to happen in this meeting anyway?"

Malcolm explained that Ganymede would be asked to account for his running of the sector. He and Alex would be required to give evidence. Various other angels would be called out to comment on Ganymede's attitude and performance. It sounded like it could go on for days. Alex's spirits sagged.

"There's three possible outcomes," said Malcolm, counting

on his fingers. "They could decide to fold the interstice, they could decide to keep things as they are or they could opt for keeping the interstice but putting in a new sector head. And it all looks pretty finely balanced to me. Much depends on you, Alex. What you say and what you do."

"But I don't want it," said Alex, shaking his head. "I don't want the lousy sector anyway."

Alex sat alone in the bandstand for a while when his interview with Ganymede and Malcolm was over. It wasn't long before Malcolm joined him, arriving by traditional means this time, strolling across the lawn from Ganymede's house rather than materialising suddenly at his side.

"Hey," said Malcolm, raising a hand in greeting. Even his be-suited form had a vague glow to it when seen in the darkness of the 'Stician night. Alex hoped there was no one else around to see.

"What do you want?" asked Alex glumly.

"Some people would think that was the wrong way to be speaking to an angel," observed Malcolm, leaning next to him on the balustrade but managing to convey no serious criticism.

"Yeah, well you're not the average angel, I guess" said Alex. "And you're part of a setup that might shortly be pulling the plug on my world."

Malcolm shrugged. "Nothing personal, you know that."

"There's a big part of me that wishes I'd never come here, that wishes I could just close my eyes and be back in Reality."

"It could well happen," said Malcolm softly. "Could well happen."

"But there's another big part of me that wants to stay here and save Kelly. She's kind of… special to me, you know? There, I've said it. I guess I've got a bit of a thing for Kelly."

He had, too. Various strands of unformed thoughts and

feelings had finally coalesced into recognisable form. He felt a sudden physical weakness that seemed particularly to affect his knees and cause his heart to flutter in his breast. Malcolm made no comment, only looking at him in a wondering sort of way, as though he thought Alex might go on to elaborate upon this declaration. Alex cleared his throat, feeling awkward about this last disclosure.

"How is it I seemed to be able to get in and out of 'Sticia whenever I wanted to, at least to begin with?" he asked to move things on a bit.

"Well, you've a pretty special talent for disassociation," said Malcolm, turning to face Alex.

"Yes, I saw that word in Ganymede's register," said Alex. "I guessed it meant daydreaming. That's what I was doing each time I got into 'Sticia."

"You were right," said Malcolm. "But you only got into the upper part of 'Sticia – the part we call VISTA, Vestibular Intersticial Space Time Area. You can think of it as like a sort of entrance hall to 'Sticia proper. Each time you came in you came in a little deeper. The last time you broke through into BISTO."

"BISTO? Go on…"

"Basal Interstician Space Time Order. This is deep 'Sticia. The molecular order is much more stable here and it's much, much harder to drop out of it, particularly with your kind of attributes. Like I said, you're particularly stable down here. You could be here for centuries, not that you'd ever be aware of it. As you'll have gathered, time operates a little differently down here."

"That's right, it does. Why doesn't it seem possible to keep track of it?"

"That'll be because we have time on a thirty-day loop," said Malcolm with a wry smile. "And we do a PMW on you guys so you never realise it."

"Let me guess, a, er, Permanent, er, Mind… uh. No, I give up."

"A Progressive Memory Wipe," supplied Malcolm with a wave of his hand like a magic wand.

"Right," nodded Alex. "It sounds like you've got an acronym for everything around here."

Malcolm looked thoughtful for a moment, then he grinned. "Well, one of the performance indicators I get assessed on is my first alert reaction time. I never saw an acronym used for that."

"Yeah, go figure," said Alex with a chuckle. "And I guess a PMW means you gradually forget what's been going on."

"Exactly so, which is why nobody here knows how long they've been here. No one's memories reach back longer than three weeks or so."

"Hmm. It all makes sense now," said Alex nodding slowly. "But where do you fit into all this – angels, I mean?"

"Like Tony said, some of us get to look after Reality while some get to work with 'Sticia. It's just a job, you know." he shrugged.

"But what's in it for you?" pressed Alex. "I mean, do you get paid for it or anything? What sort of money do angels use?"

"Whoa!" Malcolm raised a hand. "Too many questions, and I'm thinking I've already spilled a few too many beans. Better call it a day for now, eh? And you wouldn't believe how many forms I've got to fill in. Bureaucracy see, the one common thread that runs through the whole of existence."

And with that he was gone.

Alex didn't go straight home. He needed to think and he wasn't going to be able to do that in the company of Paulo, Kelly, Tanya and Will. He dropped by to visit his mum, having neglected her in recent days, and spent a long time sitting at the kerbside on the ring road, glumly contemplating the fateful blood stain in the gutter. Fragments of Kelly came into his mind: her visits to him in the House of Correction, her help with his skip of water, the way she smiled, the smell of her hair, the delightful litheness of her waist. There must be something he could do. He couldn't let Cactus Jack take her. In his mind's eye he saw her kicking and fighting as Jack took her in his cold embrace, the pressure of his hand on the back of her neck. So matter of fact, like breaking a chicken's neck. He had seen a farmer's wife do it on television once, carelessly despatching the chicken whilst continuing to conduct a conversation about her daughter's wedding. But what could he do?

He was almost home, wending his way amongst the Statical traffic on Greenfield Avenue, when he came upon Mad Annie sitting on top of a Volkswagen Beetle. There was a blanket wrapped around her shoulders and she was gazing at the Moon, crooning softly to herself. Normally, Alex would have strode rapidly past, before she fastened her unpredictable attentions upon him, but tonight he was in no hurry.

"Isn't it past your bedtime, Annie?" he asked.

She appeared not to notice his presence, continuing to sing in her cracked old voice, swaying gently to and fro. Her funny Victorian-looking shoes stuck out from beneath the hem of her old-fashioned skirt. He shrugged and turned to move on, but Annie called him back.

"Fine moon tonight," she said, fixing her mad, staring eyes upon him.

"Yeah, it's a good one," agreed Alex, thinking it was exactly the same as the one last night and the one before that, except maybe a little blurrier around the edges. Could she have noticed that? This was one of the minor frustrations of

'Sticia – everything looking exactly the same. After a while the accumulation of minor frustrations became a major one. Alex had never realised how much he had appreciated the subtle variations of the skies, the soft dawns, the pyrotechnics of sunset, lying on his back in the warm grass on a Sunday afternoon, making out ephemeral whales and ships and castles in the shifting clouds.

Annie talked to Alex, as she always did, although Alex got the feeling she didn't really need an audience. Talking to herself was just fine by her, and having Alex there was an unlooked for bonus. Her conversation was as randomly disconnected as ever, leaving Alex grasping for strands to pick up and respond to.

"Course, the Moon was nicer in my time," Annie said. "Bigger, it was. Aye, bigger. Bigger than a hen's eye. Cooler than a blue shirt."

"I bet it was," said Alex, nodding slowly. "Well, look after yourself. Be good now. I'm off to bed."

Something troubled Alex about Annie, something he turned over in his mind as he turned into Cobden Road. He was at the end of Gladstone Street before he realised what it was. When he did so, he slapped his head and span round. After a moment's hesitation he broke into a run, retracing his route to Greenfield Avenue. There was something that Annie had said that had sparked a series of connections in his brain. She was gone though when Alex emerged into Greenfield Avenue. Panting, he glanced about urgently into the shadows. Was that movement amongst the play equipment in the little park by the primary school? Alex darted after it. He caught up with Annie as she was wandering down the little passage that led to the Red Lion.

"Annie," he gasped, as her silhouette turned the corner at the end of the passage and disappeared.

After a moment her shape re-emerged.

"Yes, dearie?"

Alex hurried after her, trying to control his breathing.

"Annie," he said. "What did you mean in my time?"

"What do you think I mean?" she retorted, looking sidelong at him. "Her Majesty Queen Victoria's time, God bless her. What else would I mean? Everyone today is always asking daft questions. I said to Mrs Runciman only yest…"

"Whoa!" Alex held up his hands, palms outwards. "Hang on a mo'. How did you get here? This is the twenty-first century. Queen Victoria's been dead for more than a hundred years."

Suddenly Annie's twitching face became still and she smoothed her wild hair absently with one gnarled hand.

"Snarks fixed it for me, di'n't they?" she suddenly scowled. "I told you that before. Folks never listen. If you can't attend the first time I ain't gonna tell you again." She turned and shuffled off, cursing him over her shoulder.

"Annie, wait!" Alex shouted after her, but to no avail. He stood in the gloom of the passage and wracked his brains for recollections of Annie's conversations with him; if you could call them conversations. Alex usually switched his brain off and let her ramblings wash over him. But there was one phrase that she had uttered that came unbidden to his mind now. Rode one once, she had said when they were talking about dugongs and manatees. Could that have been it? It sounded bizarre enough, but then of course there was much that was bizarre in 'Sticia.

Alex smiled grimly in the darkness. One thing was for sure – Malcolm had been wrong. Mortals could travel in time, but what had snarks to do with it? Alex didn't even know for sure that they could speak, let alone organise time travel. He would need to speak with Ganymede tomorrow. Ganymede knew about snarks.

Tanya had gone to bed by the time Alex arrived back at Gladstone Street, but Will was still up. He probably wished he wasn't, since Paulo had been making him arm wrestle with him and was now demonstrating karate techniques on him. Kelly was looking on in amusement, shushing the other two whenever their grunts and gasps seemed likely to wake Tanya in the room next door.

"Hey," said Paulo, looking up as Alex came in. "It's the Master of the Universe, Ganymede's main man, the mighty Alex Trueman." He grinned his insolent grin and raised his fists. "Come on Master," he said in what he might have thought to have been an oriental accent. "School me in the arts of angelic combat."

Alex found himself having to fend off a succession of playful but robust blows.

"Get off!" grunted Alex, reeling backwards as he tried to parry these assaults. His wrists and forearms ached. The blows had been heavier than Paulo had made them appear, and one had caught him under the ribs, partly winding him.

"Hey!" laughed Paulo, turning to Kelly. "Did you see that? *Broccoli* outstanding. I have much to learn."

"Cut it out you daft pillock," Kelly told him with a chuckle.

Alex didn't stay up much longer. Paulo was on top form, laughing and joking in a way that even Alex had to concede had a certain rough charm. There was a good deal of boasting, too, and scurrilous accounts of Paulo's many brushes with the law. When Paulo got on to bragging to Will about his driving exploits, Alex felt he had to retire to bed. He could hear Paulo through the door talking about cars he had stolen. He stood for a while, slowly clenching and unclenching his fists whilst the attractive notion of thumping Paulo crossed and re-crossed his mind. His eyes gradually refocused, and growing used to the darkness in what he now thought of as *his* bedroom settled upon Malcolm, seated nonchalantly on the edge of the bed. The angel put his finger to his lips.

"I know it's late," he said apologetically. "I wouldn't bother you again tonight, only I've got someone who wants a word with you."

"Oh?"

"Glenda," mouthed Malcolm, glancing furtively about him as though he feared being overheard.

"Oh."

"You okay with that?"

"Go on then," said Alex resignedly. He walked up to Malcolm in a way that was becoming second nature to him and Malcolm moved his hands in the air.

They materialised in what proved to be a large and well-appointed office. A middle-aged woman sat behind a large and imposing desk, toying with a fountain pen. Her considerable bulk was crammed into a tight grey suit, her hair swept back into a severe bun. The severity of her hair was matched by that of her black-rimmed glasses and her small, red painted mouth, a feature which seemed likely to be a stranger to smiles.

"Good day, Mr Trueman," she said, with the briefest nod of acknowledgment to Malcolm. "You will be wondering why I have invited you here."

Well, Alex was, but nevertheless vaguely resented being told he was. He nodded.

"I make no apology for appearing to you in my true likeness. Unlike Tony I do not favour traditional angelic manifestations except when it is necessary to overawe the ignorant or gullible. I detect neither quality in you, young man."

"Oh good," muttered Alex, shuffling his feet nervously and wishing she'd get to the point.

"I won't beat about the bush," declared Glenda. "We are seeking an alternative to your friend Ganymede, should he be deposed from his present position. I think Malcolm has already intimated as much. The case for dismissing Ganymede will be enormously strengthened should a suitable replacement be to hand." She tapped the pen briskly on the glossy red fingernails of her left hand. "Would you be interested in taking on the sector, Mr Trueman?"

"Uh… no," said Alex after a moment, this brief hesitation brought on only by the fear of upsetting this formidable woman. "No thanks, if it's all the same to you."

"You disappoint me," said Glenda, a frown creasing her smooth white forehead. "And I see much potential in you. You are young, of course, which some may regard as a problem, but you are uniquely gifted in this interstice and your youth will take care of itself in due course. You are highly stable in Intersticia and, if I read you correctly, very willing to learn. You could go far, young man, further than you could possibly imagine. If the sector goes well under your care, you could become Elect. Do you understand me, Mr Trueman? Become an angel yourself." She paused for a moment to let the significance of this interesting prospect settle in. "Many of us began as sector heads in Intersticia."

Alex tried not to give consideration to what Glenda had just said. There were other priorities.

"I'd really rather not," said Alex doggedly, sticking firmly to his undertaking to support Ganymede.

"I see," said Glenda, pursing her lips and regarding Alex stonily. Alex's eyes cast about for something to distract them, but there were no windows in the office and only one framed print on the wall, this showing a herd of white horses splashing across a river.

"I understand that a friend of yours is dead, that her

Interstician existence is likely to be cut short by Atropos in the near future. What would you say if I told you that I may be able to prevent that?"

"What do you mean?" asked Alex warily, his interest now fully engaged.

"I'm sure you are aware that all mortals are distinguished from one another by their unique DNA. This is how Atropos locates his, er… 'targets'. There is a device called a DNA mask, which allows an individual to conceal their genetic identity from others. I am informed this would work equally well to frustrate Atropos. I can make such a device available to you – if you reconsider your decision. It may make the difference between what you would think of as life and death for your friend. I urge you to think about this…"

"This is a bribe, right?" said Alex cautiously.

Glenda shrugged, almost imperceptibly, and spread her hands a little.

"You're offering Kelly the chance of life?"

"So it would appear." She pushed an envelope across the desk towards Alex. "We'll need a sample of your friend's DNA. A strand of hair should be sufficient. Then we can tailor the mask to her requirements. You may return it to me before the meeting. Would the arrangement I propose be satisfactory to you? It is a generous offer."

"I'll have to think about it," said Alex slowly and with more confidence than he felt. He picked up the envelope, his mind in turmoil.

"Very well," said Glenda, nodding briskly. "But don't take too long over it. The meeting is at eighteenth tomorrow, by your reckoning. I should like to know your answer by seventeenth at the latest. You can contact me through Malcolm." She steepled her fingers and regarded Alex stonily over the top of them. "Think well, Mr Trueman. I offer you much."

A moment later, Alex re-materialised in his bedroom. Malcolm was there, too, mouthing the words "See you later." Alex grabbed his sleeve desperately before he could finish moving his hands and disappear himself.

"Hang on a minute," he hissed. "Don't you dare leave me now. There's stuff I need to ask you."

"Right," said the angel, looking a little taken aback but sitting heavily on Alex's bed nevertheless. "More stuff. Okay. Fire away."

There were so many questions, Alex hardly knew where to start. He knuckled his forehead and glanced at the door, behind which Paulo's voice could still be heard. There was Kelly's also, raised in laughter but quickly smothered.

"What about this DNA mask thing?" he asked Malcolm. "Is Glenda on the level with that? Can I trust her?"

"Of course you can trust her," said Malcolm simply. "She is an angel. If she's offering you something you can be sure it'll be legit."

"Okay," said Alex, thinking hard. "What did you think? She's just trying to use me against Ganymede, isn't she? What's to say she won't drop me as soon as I've outlived my usefulness?"

"Hey! What do I know? I'm only a lousy technician," said Malcolm, spreading his arms wide. "I'm getting sucked into Mike and Tony's little squabble just as much as you are. First, I've got Tony bending my ear and then, next minute, it's Glenda on behalf of Mike. I'm fed up of it, I can tell you. This isn't even my interstice. I'm covering for Derek whilst he's off on a course. He must have known it was going to go belly up, crafty b…"

"You never said anything about a DNA mask before," said Alex, cutting him off.

"I never even heard of one until Glenda raised it with me

earlier on. Don't mean there's no such thing. I asked my friend Gerald in Technical. He gave me this — owes me a favour, see." He drew out of his pocket a slender chain from which hung a small, flat triangular amulet. There were three raised discs on its surface. He held it up in a beam of moonlight for Alex to inspect.

"This is the prototype," Malcolm said. "Seems Gerald was in on the project. He had this in his desk drawer. It works, too, or so he says. And it's universal because it checks out your DNA and masks it straight out. Don't even need a specialist to make an individual match, see. You just press the three discs three times each and then once all together. Then I guess you'd be pretty much invisible to Atropos."

"Wow, thanks!" said Alex with feeling.

"Yeah, well," said Malcolm, raising his hands. "Don't go over the top. I haven't finished. There is just one small problem. This sucker's only the prototype, see. It'll only work so long as its fuel cell does. Gerald says it should be good for about two minutes. After that you're back to square one." He shrugged. "I don't know, I just thought it may buy you a bit of time."

Alex took the amulet, feeling somewhat deflated. "Yeah, that's a bit of time alright. I thought you said you can't cheat death," he said.

"You can't," said Malcolm. "Course you can't, but you can sure confuse the hell out of it." He stood up, stretching and yawning. "I don't know, it's not much. I wondered if it might give you an edge sometime, you and your little friend. I'll have it back if you don't want it... I take it you're not going to go for Glenda's deal then."

"I don't know," said Alex, slipping the amulet into his pocket. "I haven't decided. I know Kelly can't keep running for ever when Cactus Jack shows up." He frowned. "Hey, look. I don't think you've been entirely honest with me."

"Serious accusation against an angel," said Malcolm, crossing his arms and tapping an index finger on his bicep.

"You said mortals can't travel in time," said Alex, looking hard at the angel.

Malcolm looked uncomfortable. "Yeah, well. It isn't permitted; that's what I meant."

"But it happens, doesn't it? Whether it's permitted or not."

Alex explained about Annie. Malcolm listened, nodding slowly when Alex had finished.

"Well, that explains a lot," he said. "That'll be that low level general disruption I was picking up."

"So what's to stop Kelly and I going back in time to an earlier instant in Reality?"

"Nothing to do with us," said Malcolm. "Like I said, we angels don't deal in time travel for mortals. Too many variables involved. You'd have to speak to the snarks. That'd be Ganymede's province. He's a big fan."

"So I gather," said Alex, thinking of Ganymede's horror when he heard about Paulo's snark barbecue.

"I'll be off then," said Malcolm, crossing to the window and looking out into the street. "I've still got to write up my report. This sector's a nightmare. Everything goes wrong in it. Ganymede's manna requisition went astray, too. I've got to chase that up."

"Eh? Hang on, what did you just say?" gasped Alex.

"Ganymede's manna requisition," repeated Malcolm slowly. "Got lost in the system. Why, what's the problem? Why are you looking at me like that?"

"Ganymede doesn't make his own manna then?"

"Nooo," Malcolm laughed. "Not likely. He has it delivered in bulk from Central Resources. What's he been telling you?"

Alex told him. Malcolm laughed so much he had to sit down.

"The crafty dog. He's pullin' your chain. That's why we got a power drain from his house the other night. He was conjuring up a pretty little fantasy for you. Quarks and mesons my sainted halo! You've got to give it to him!" He slapped his thigh in delight. "They come ready-baked on big trays and Ganymede just sorts them out into piles the day before he needs them."

Alex clenched his fists. "Damn!" he said. So Ganymede had spun him a line. "Just one more thing," he said to Malcolm. "Please take me back to Ganymede's."

Ganymede was asleep when Alex arrived in his bedroom, not that Alex cared. He grabbed Ganymede's shoulder and shook him roughly awake.

"Hey! What the…" Ganymede sat up and glared at him furiously. "What is the meaning of this? How dare you?"

"The meaning of this is that you've been lying to me," snapped Alex. "Again! And I want to know what's going on."

He explained everything that had happened to him that night, his encounter with Mad Annie, his meeting with Glenda, the DNA mask. Everything.

"What can I say," said Ganymede defensively when his manna trick was brought to light. "I *do* work like a slave for everyone. I just wanted to drive that point home." Sitting up in bed he groped for his hat and crammed it down over his unruly grey hair.

"Let me ask you a question," said Alex coldly. "Do you want to keep this sector?"

"Yes," said Ganymede softly. "You know I do."

"Well it's mine if I want it," said Alex, finding grim satisfaction in the expression on Ganymede's face as this sank in. "What do you think of that? And if you want me to turn it down, you'd better help me and Kelly get the hell out of here. Before Cactus Jack comes calling."

"What exactly do you mean?" asked Ganymede, his eyes glinting from the shadows under his hat.

"You know what I mean. Getting back into Reality – time travel. It can be done and the snarks know how to do it, don't they? Take me to the snarks, Ganymede. Take me to the snarks *now*."

Chapter Fifteen

The snarks were on the top of Micklebury Hill, standing in a semi-circle and contemplating the declining moon. Alex was exhausted by the time they reached Micklebury, but Malcolm was long gone and there was no option but to make the journey on foot. Sleep fogged Alex's brain and fatigue clawed at his thighs and calves as he trudged up the steep path that led to the summit. When they were there and clear moonlight picked out the small shapes of twenty or so snarks, he stood for a few moments clutching his sides, trying to bring his breathing under control. Ganymede marched ahead. The snarks turned slowly to face him, long snark shadows reaching across the hard packed earth. Ganymede raised his right hand, but there was no sound other than the soft sough of the 'Stician breeze through the long grass on the lower slopes of the hill. And then suddenly there was a voice *inside* his head.

"Greetings Alex," it said in clear and mellow tones. "We have been waiting for you."

"Huh?" exclaimed Alex out loud.

"Not much in this interstice escapes our attention. And you are not like the others. Approach."

Cautiously Alex stepped forward into the semi-circle of small creatures. He tried to put out of his mind his gruesome recollection of the little blackened body roasting on Paulo's camp fire.

"Do not let that trouble you," said the snark voice. They could evidently read his mind. Alex felt more naked, more vulnerable than he had ever felt in his life. "We are one mind with many bodies. We live across many interstices and realities. The loss of the occasional body matters little. Think of us as a colony, like the bees in your Reality. The hive is what counts. Individuals are expendable."

Tasty too, if Paulo's to be believed, came blundering into his mind, before he could help himself. He wanted to perform the mental equivalent of putting his hand over his mouth and found himself physically wince, his eyes squeezed tight shut. There was an awkward silence – in his head and on the hill.

"There is something you wish to ask us, is there not?" said the voice again at last. There was no hint of annoyance, or indeed any emotion. Lots of glittering little eyes were regarding him from those strange cat-like faces. Suddenly he relaxed, as though a great tension had been released. He felt a curious calmness and peace, the first he had felt for many hours.

"Yes," he said. "There is. A friend of mine is dead. In Reality, that is. She's still alive here, but Atropos is coming for her. I want to go back in time, into Reality, to the moments just before the accident that killed her… I think maybe I can save her," he finished lamely.

"That would be impossible," said the snark voice.

"Why?" asked Alex. "What about Annie? You must know about her. She's come across more than a century to be here. I only need to go back in time a few seconds."

"That was a mistake, I'm afraid" said Ganymede's rough voice. "A catastrophic error. Two interstices folded altogether, taking with them the instant of Reality between them. Ripples are still spreading out across a dozen others. Those disturbances you felt, your falling in and out of Intersticia before your final definitive arrival here, those were all caused by Annie's little time trip. Besides, it scrambled her brains. Is that what you want?"

"And the one called Annie," came the snark voice. "There was another difference, an important one. She travelled along the interstices, without touching upon the instants of Reality that lie between them. By so doing she made no impact on Reality itself – on any Reality. What you ask is different. You ask to travel from Intersticial space into Reality, and then to combine this with the backward movement in time. What you ask is problematic, although theoretically feasible. However, we have only limited ability to effect such a thing and the consequences are somewhat unpredictable."

"What do you mean, limited ability?" asked Alex.

"It would not be difficult to arrange for your transport to an earlier interstice. As you know, Annie managed it for herself, entirely without assistance. She rode a dugong. She climbed the clock tower of the town hall and leapt upon one's back as it passed beneath her. Likewise we could arrange for your transport to an instant of Reality before this one, but our reach is severely constrained. We could give you only what you might describe as seven tenths of a second. And there are many philosophical implications," said the snark. "If you return to a previous instant, you theoretically exist twice in the same period of time. One of the few basic laws we understand is the uniqueness of matter. Reality would be forced to resolve that conflict. Our best guess is that the life force you are now would merge with the life force there. For a short time the interloper would predominate, but the original would quickly reassert itself. What we are saying is this: if you re-enter Reality at an earlier point in time, you will retain your consciousness for only a short time. Within a few moments you will forget… all this, all that has happened to you since entering Intersticia. You will become once more what you once were. Your life would continue as though this had never happened. Is that acceptable to you?"

Alex shook his head, the cloying tendrils of fatigue clogging his mind. "I don't know. That's not enough time, not nearly enough. I'm well away from the road. I'm too far from Kelly to be able to do anything about it in so short a time."

"Well, who can do something about it?" demanded Ganymede. "Ask yourself that question."

It was quite clear what Ganymede meant, and the answer swam into focus in Alex's mind.

"Paulo," he nodded. "Yes, of course! If I take Paulo with us he might be able to avoid hitting Kelly. It might just give him enough time to swerve." He turned to Ganymede. "Ask them to do it Ganymede. You want rid of me, don't you? If you can't fix this for me you could be looking at the next sector head."

Ganymede frowned and glared at Alex for a few moments. "I'm doing my best, aren't I?" he said. "I brought you here, didn't I?"

"Come on," urged Alex. "You've got to do this for me."

Ganymede turned to the snarks. He appeared to converse with them, although it must all have been on a purely mental level because Alex could hear nothing. Sometimes the snarks appeared to shuffle together a little or twitch their little noses, but apart from these small signs there was no sign that anything at all was going on. Ganymede continued to stand stock still, his eyes half shut as though in a trance.

"Very well," said the snark voice at length in Alex's head. "We will do this thing for Ganymede that he asks of us. But only once. Ganymede understands that this is a gift that can never be repeated because the consequences may be hard to control, even for us. Ride a manatee tomorrow," said the snark, "If you wish to persevere with this. We concede it would be...

interesting being in the nature of a unique experiment. As you will have gathered, dugongs and manatees are more than just convenient timekeepers in a world without clocks. They travel backwards and forwards across the interstices. Dugongs travel forward in time, manatees backwards. If you can find a convenient vantage point you may leap upon one's back. We will be watching."

"How will I know when to jump off again," asked Alex, rubbing his eyes because it was so hard to stay awake.

"You will have no problem with that," said the snark. "Trust us on this."

When Alex awoke he was being dumped unceremoniously at his doorstep by Ganymede, who had carried him part of the way back from Micklebury draped across his shoulders. The tramp stretched himself and rubbed sore arms, glancing at the dawn sky.

"Better get some sleep," he said ruefully. "Big day tomorrow… today."

Alex staggered to his feet. "Thanks," he said.

"Big decisions to make," said Ganymede, turning towards the end of the street. "Sleep on it."

Once in his own room Alex slept as peacefully as he had ever slept. Perhaps he owed this to the snarks. Their presence had made him feel calm and powerful and confident in a way he had never felt before. He could see why Ganymede was so keen on them. He slept a restful, dreamless sleep and awoke around ninth to the sound of Kelly and Tanya talking in the upstairs hall outside his door. He lay for a while and took simple pleasure in those sounds and in the tiny motes of dust dancing in the sunbeams. Today was a day for decisions, as Ganymede had said. He could, should he wish, remain in

'Sticia and take on Ganymede's role in looking after the poor castaways of this strange world. Kelly would be there, too, concealed from Cactus Jack by the angelic DNA mask. In due course Paulo would be sucked back into Reality, one less serpent in paradise. It was a tempting prospect. But then it was something less than life. It was existence, but not exactly life. So much was missing. They would never know rain, or music, or cinema or even travel beyond the limited confines of the sector. So much was missing. It was less than life. But was it enough?

Alex stared at the ceiling. What was the alternative? To ride a manatee? He would need to confide in Kelly and Paulo, convince them to go with him. And then what? Paulo had nearly died. In Reality he lay in a coma. He would need to endure that last instant once more, a terrible lottery, in the knowledge that this time he may die in order to try to save Kelly's life. Would he do it? And even if he did, and Kelly survived, none of them would remember it. Their lives would carry on as though 'Sticia had never existed for them. They wouldn't even know each other. Alex pulled a blanket over his head. It was so difficult. "Keep your options open as long as you can," he told himself. He didn't have to decide yet. There was still time.

"What's going on?" asked Will later that morning. Paulo had gone out to the park with Kelly and Tanya. Alex was in Kelly's room, detaching a few long dark hairs from one of her blankets. There could be no mistaking them for Tanya's occasional blonde ones. Alex carefully coiled the hairs and slid them into Glenda's envelope.

 Alex told him all that had happened during the previous night, slipping the envelope into the back pocket of his jeans. There was a lot to tell. Will listened, his face growing paler and paler.

"Never a dull moment, is there?" he said when Alex had finished. "What are you going to do?"

"I don't know," Alex told him, sitting down to eat manna for a belated breakfast. "I'm putting off making a decision until I absolutely have to."

"I'd rather have you than Ganymede," said Will. "Why don't you go for the sector, if they're offering it you?"

"I guess I don't trust the offer," Alex said, swilling water around the bottom of his glass. "That Glenda, she's slipperier than an eel, if I'm any judge. I don't want to be a pawn in some kind of power struggle between her and Tony. This DNA mask thing may be a load of baloney."

"Quite an opportunity though," said Will, gesturing at him with a crust of manna. "It's not every day you get a chance to set your foot on the first rung of the angelic career ladder." He laughed. "I can just see you with a harp."

Alex threw a lump of manna at him.

"I should mind my step," teased Will. "Could be thunderbolts next time."

Kelly was still not back when Malcolm came to collect Alex for the meeting. Alex regretted this because it was as though getting another clear look at Kelly might have helped him to set his thoughts in order. Malcolm had Ganymede with him, so it wasn't even possible to discuss things openly with him. Ganymede eyed Alex warily. He had helped his rival find the snarks but there was no longer any trust between them. Alex wondered if Ganymede suspected that Glenda had definitely offered him the sector. Malcolm re-materialised them in what proved to be the ante-chamber for a large conference room. Through an open door a long polished table could be seen. Set upon it at intervals were crystal water flasks with glasses placed upside down on them. Along either side were tall-backed chairs with plain black upholstery. In the ante-hall, coffee was being served along one of the side tables by an angel dressed as a waiter. Perhaps two dozen angels in dark suits drank coffee and chatted as the hour for the meeting approached. Apart from Malcolm, who looked noticeably uncomfortable in these circumstances, Alex recognised only Glenda. She noticed his arrival and made her way across to him, holding a white cup in one hand. The other held a saucer with two biscuits balancing on its rim. Glancing about him, Alex drew the envelope out of his pocket. He was about to hand it to her when two things happened. First, a tall angel of distinguished appearance touched Glenda's sleeve and drew her aside. Then, Tony himself appeared next to Alex. He wasn't manifesting himself as an angel in these circumstances, but he was easily recognisable nevertheless. He removed the envelope calmly from Alex's unresisting fingers and slipped it into the inside pocket of his suit. Over his shoulder, Alex caught a glint of alarm in Glenda's eye as she was speaking to the tall angel, but then more bodies moved between them and she was lost to sight.

"Will you excuse me a moment?" Tony asked Malcolm and Ganymede. "I must have a quiet word in Alex's ear."

Taking Alex's arm in a gentle but insistent grip, Tony led him away into a corner.

"There isn't time to mince words, young man," he began, glancing over his shoulder. "Suffice to say, I know from my own sources exactly what has transpired between you and Glenda." He patted his pocket. "Glenda had no right to make such undertakings to you. Let me make a few things clear. You are, of course, an exceptional individual in this sector, but you will not be sector head. Not so long as Ganymede desires it. Various negotiations have taken place and the outcome of this meeting is not in doubt. I have noted your activities in the sector since last we met, and enough of the damage has been undone for this interstice to be saved. Ganymede will be cautioned but allowed to retain his post. I have secured enough support amongst Council to be able to tell you this with confidence. We must dutifully go through the motions, but the outcome of this enquiry is not in doubt. All that is required from you is that you give your truthful testimony when required."

Someone rang a little hand bell, its musical tinkle cutting through the conversation. Angels began drifting through into the conference room.

"Come on," said Tony smugly. "We may as well get the formalities under way."

It was the longest, dullest meeting Alex had ever attended. Tony, Head of Intersticia, sat at one end of the long table, with Glenda, Head of the Enquiry Team, at the other. A number of angels sitting along the sides of the table were required to give reports on aspects of the sector and the interstice in general. There were technical reports, historical analyses and even a psychological assessment by one elderly female angel with the most monotonous voice in creation. After a lengthy and wearisome discussion of Ganymede's conduct and behaviour she concluded that he was not actually insane. This must have come as a relief to Ganymede, who stared at her throughout as though he wanted to throw his glass of water over her head. Malcolm was called forward to make his own contribution. He was talking confidently about spikes and anomalies when his voice suddenly seemed to falter and he raised a finger to his ear. Then he glanced at Alex and swallowed hard.

"Everything all right, Malcolm?" asked Glenda, her head

cocked to one side.

"Uh, yes… fine," said Malcolm taking a sip of water, but after this his delivery seemed to have lost its previous confidence. Alex felt an odd sense of foreboding. He was due to give evidence next, but by common agreement the angels adjourned the meeting for coffee. Malcolm slid up next to him as they streamed out into the ante-chamber.

"Trouble," said the angel out of the side of his mouth.

"What?" asked Alex, feeling a sudden dryness in his mouth.

Malcolm leant close to him, his eyes grave beneath his lank hair.

"Atrop… I mean Cactus Jack's back in the sector," he said. "I just heard."

"Jesus!" The world seemed momentarily to whirl around him. He felt unsteady on his feet. Malcolm's face swam in and out of focus."

"Mind your language," muttered Malcolm. "Remember where we are."

"I've got to get out of here," said Alex urgently. There was no Plan A now. There was only Plan B – and time was running out for that one. There had been no time to talk to Malcolm about last night's arrangement with the snarks. He quickly told the angel what he had in mind to do.

"Best of luck," Malcolm told him, leading him behind a large potted palm that shielded them from the rest of the room. "I can't come with you, you understand that. I've got to give more testimony. You're on your own, pal. I'll do what I can to cover for you, if it's needed. Time operates differently with us, so you may not even be missed."

He held out his hand. Alex shook it. The air shimmered and Malcolm's hand disappeared. The air reconstituted itself into the form of Gladstone Street. After a moment to re-orientate himself and gather his wits, Alex ran for the front door. It was almost dusk, the light of day beginning to fade as 'Stician night approached and shadows lengthened in the streets.

Chapter Sixteen

Inside, there was what Alex's mum might have described as an 'atmosphere'. Will and Tanya were sitting with their backs to the wall. On the other side of the room sat Kelly, her eyes red-rimmed. It was immediately clear she'd been crying. There was a small white handkerchief clutched in her hand. Alex glanced quickly from face to face.

"Kelly and Paulo had a row," said Tanya, before Alex could open his mouth to speak.

"What? Where's Paulo now?" demanded Alex, regarding Kelly anxiously.

It was ironic in its way. Ordinarily, at any other time, Alex's response to such tidings would have been a desire to leap and skip from one end of the street to the other. Now though, he only felt panic clutch at his heart. Paulo was a vital part of his plan. And Paulo was missing.

"I don't know," said Kelly with a shrug. "And I don't care either."

"We've got to find him," said Alex. He stood for a moment and looked at Kelly, his brain working frantically.

There had to be an easy way of breaking the news to someone that they were, well… dead, but in reality it wasn't a problem that often cropped up, and Alex had no idea where to begin. He decided there was simply no time for the subtle approach. Brutal honesty would have to do.

"Kelly, we have to get you out of here," he said, squatting beside her. "Cactus Jack is coming."

She turned to face him, alerted perhaps by something ominous in his tone. Her face was pale, blotched with red around the eyes. She regarded him seriously, her dark eyes wide.

"He's coming for you," he said simply.

She continued to hold his gaze, her eyes twitching a little wider.

"Huh?"

"You're dead," said Alex, placing his hand gently on her forearm. "You were killed in a road accident, the one on the ring road."

He told her about his visit to Ganymede's house, his furtive look at the census return and the grim details it contained. He described his interviews with the angels and his meeting with the snarks. Kelly believed him. She saw that she had no choice but to trust in the snarks.

"It sounds crazy," she said. "But what else can I do? I guess I have to give it a go. But you don't have to do it, Alex. You're safe here."

"I want out of here," he told her. "And I don't care how risky it is. If there's any chance of getting my life back I'll take it. This isn't life, Kelly. It's only existence."

She placed her hand on his. There were so many other reasons, so many other things he wanted to say but couldn't bring to utterance. His throat was tight. His eyes stung and a sense of helplessness and self-loathing came over him. "Besides, Ganymede wants me out," he managed to say. "I'm a threat to him so long as I'm here. So he fixed it with the snarks for me. Ganymede loves the snarks and the snarks love Ganymede. That's the way it is."

There was one crucial detail of the story that he left unspoken until the end.

"But why do we need Paulo?" she asked him, absently pulling back strands of hair from her face. "Can't we just go and leap on a passing manatee?"

Alex closed his eyes and took a deep breath.

"We need Paulo because… because he was the one that killed you," he said softly after a moment.

Kelly's grip slackened on his wrist. Her other hand flew to her mouth.

"No!" she groaned. "He didn't," but there was no conviction in her voice.

"Yes," he said. "Paulo was driving the car. He doesn't know. The snarks are going to place us back in time, an instant before the accident. I'm just hoping you'll have a moment to dodge and Paulo'll be able to swerve to avoid you." He rubbed his eyes. "I know it's a long shot but it's all we've got."

"I'll miss you Kelly," said Tanya in a small voice.

Alex had almost forgotten that Will and Tanya were present.

"I wish we could take you," he said, turning to them.

"Not me," said Will, shaking his head. "Sound's risky. I'm happy to let nature take its course, or whatever."

"I think Paulo might be with Chad," said Tanya. "He was talking about him earlier."

Alex was about to reply, but at that moment there was a little flutter of fear within him. It was like a shadow passing across his soul. He knew at once what it was. So did they all. The four of them exchanged nervous glances.

"Cactus Jack," breathed Tanya.

"Come on," said Alex, stumbling to his feet. "We've no time to lose."

"Where are we going?" asked Kelly, grabbing at Alex's arm when they were all out in front of the house.

"We're going to find Paulo," Alex told her.

"Not me," said Kelly, her face reddening. "I've finished with Paulo. I'm not going crawling to him now."

"What?" Alex was aghast. "Of course you are. Your *life* depends on it."

"I'm not begging him," declared Kelly adamantly, digging in her heels as Alex tugged at her.

"Come on, Kelly," urged Will, jumping up and down with anxiety. "This is no time for amateur dramatics."

"Stop it, Kelly," cried Tanya. "You're scaring me."

But there was a set to Kelly's jaw that Alex read as potentially fatal stubbornness. "Okay," he said, recognising defeat. "Will, you come with me. Kelly, Tanya, get yourselves to the insurance office. You know, up by the old library. The manatees pass just beneath its south face and it's got a nice flat roof. I reckon if we can get up there we've a good chance of making it."

"What if we meet Cactus Jack?" asked Tanya, her eyes round with terror.

"He walks," Alex told them. "He doesn't run. You should be able to out-run him in the short term, but he wears you down – that's how he operates. If you see him, run like hell. Lead him round in a big circle, round the block will do. Keep a look out for us. We'll meet you by the front entrance as soon as I've got hold of the Vegetable King." Alex frowned, groping in his pocket. "Wait a mo," he said, drawing out the prototype DNA mask. "Put this on."

"What?" Kelly looked suspiciously at the amulet, but took it from his outstretched hand.

"Just put it on. I haven't got time to explain properly now, but it may help to hide you from Jack."

Kelly shrugged and slipped the chain over her head, shaking out her hair.

"Thanks," she said.

"Don't mention it."

Then Alex was away, running as fast as his legs would carry him, with Will puffing and panting behind. Will reckoned Paulo might be in the park, as Chad more or less lived there lately, according to Will. It was a mile or so from Gladstone Street to the park. After the first few streets Alex realised he wasn't going to be able to continue running flat out, so he settled instead for a steady jog. He found himself wishing he'd worked a bit harder at cross-country running. The school version of this form of torture usually found him dawdling at the back of the field amongst the bronchitics and the fat wheezy boys. Even this pace was too much for 'Sticia's own fat wheezy boy. Will lagged further and further behind as Alex's pounding legs ate up the distance.

"I'll... catch... you... up!" he heard Will's plaintive call from behind him.

Running past the end of Gordon Road, Alex caught a glimpse of something that filled him with a rising tide of panic. At the other end of the street, marching in the opposite direction, there had been a flash of white. The glimpse was too momentary to be definitive but the cold sensation of dread in the pit of Alex's stomach left no doubt that it had been Cactus Jack. Alex put on another spurt, turning in through the park gates and heading down the parade towards the bandstand, glancing about in all directions. The bandstand was empty. Where was Paulo? He called Paulo's name. Again and again he called. Alex was desperate. Stitch seared in his side as he lurched across the bowling green and down past the tennis courts. There was no sign of Paulo. Down by the pool he tripped over a small dog and fell headlong on the path, grazing hands and forearms. Cursing, he staggered to his feet and carried on, calling again, over and over, his voice swallowed up in the 'Stician silence.

He found Paulo by the children's play equipment, perched on the bottom of the big slide whilst Chad dangled off a climbing frame.

"Hey, Big Ears! I thought that was you calling," observed Paulo laconically, as Alex ground to a halt in the bark chippings in front of him. "What's your problem?"

Alex had to waste precious instants controlling his breathing, composing his thoughts, before he could speak coherently.

"You've got to come," he blurted out between gasps. "Kelly needs you."

"Yeah? Well Kelly can *Brussels sprout*," said Paulo through an infuriating grin. "I've had it with that *potato courgette*."

Alex, rather than putting his fist straight through the infuriating grin, tried reason.

"No you haven't," he said. "You've got to understand something… Kelly's going to die, you've got to help her." He grabbed Paulo's sleeve by way of encouragement.

"*Peas!*" snapped Paulo, knocking Alex's hand away. "What the *cabbage* are you talking about, man? You're round the *turnip* twist." His eyes were narrowed and his mouth was set in a tight line now. He made to stand and walk away, calling to Chad, who had dropped from the climbing frame and was rubbing his hands together underneath. Whatever Paulo had intended to say died in his throat, because at that moment Alex rugby tackled and felled him like a pole-axed bull. His PE teacher would have been pleased and surprised by the power and determination in this show of aggression. Paulo was equally surprised, although somewhat less pleased.

"No you don't!" Alex snarled into Paulo's thigh as Paulo tumbled in his grasp. "I haven't finished with you!"

It was as though some slender thread of control parted in both of them. A thin veneer of civility was stripped away and naked anger burst from beneath. Each disliked the other with a raw passion that now found expression in a flurry of kicks and punches as they wrestled, grunting and cursing amongst the bark chips. Paulo, being larger, older, heavier and stronger, got the better of it, but Alex had the advantage of pure, heedless rage that blinded him to any other consideration but wounding Paulo in any way possible. Within seconds, Paulo had a split lip and a row of Alex's teeth marks in his arm, amongst other wounds. Alex found himself lying on his back, with Paulo astride him, whilst Paulo's granite fist pummelled his head.

"Stop it, bro!" Alex heard Chad yell. "You'll kill him."

"You killed Kelly," Alex screamed, his mouth salty with his own blood. "You killed Kelly, you…"

"What?!" Paulo's fist paused as he raised it for a fresh assault. Suddenly both of them were motionless, Alex panting, Paulo looming over him, one hand holding a fistful of shirt, the other poised ready to strike once more. "What do you mean?" he demanded. "What the *spud* are you saying?"

Alex told him, gasping out the story as the hot blood trickled from his nose and crept into the corner of his mouth.

"You can save her," he sputtered. "You can swerve! Just one little tug on the wheel, that'd do it. You can live that last second again."

"What about me?" said Paulo slowly, wiping his split lip with the back of his hand and studying the resulting red smear. "What about me, eh? I might get *cauliflower* wasted this time."

"You shouldn't have done it," Alex told him with cold indignation. "You shouldn't have nicked that car and you shouldn't have driven it like a mad idiot. Kelly's dead and it's your fault. I'm giving you a chance to take that back. You'll never get another. I don't know if you've got a conscience or whether you're too stupid. I certainly wouldn't want it on mine."

Paulo glared at Alex, who thought for a moment he might be in for another bout of violence. But instead, after a moment, Paulo put his head in his hands and groaned. Then he rolled off Alex and looked around him in apparent confusion. His gaze fell upon Chad.

"What are you *carrot* looking at?" he demanded. "*Cour-gette!*"

With a shrug, Chad turned and walked slowly away, just as Will came panting around the boating pool clutching his sides.

"You care for Kelly, don't you?" tried Alex desperately, struggling to get up. "You do, don't you? And I know she cares for you."

"Leave me alone!" said Paulo angrily. "Just leave it… Leave it!"

"No," said Alex stubbornly, shaking his head. "You'll have to kill me before I leave you alone. I'm not going anywhere until you come with me. Cactus Jack's coming for Kelly, for God's sake. That's *it* for her. End of story. You can't let that happen, not if you feel anything for her at all."

"I've *parsnip* had it with Kelly," snapped Paulo. "And she's finished with me. She likes you better than me anyway, for *sprout*'s sake, because I'm scum and you're *cabbage* Holy Joe. You think I'm scum, don't you? Don't you!"

"Prove me wrong then!" shouted Alex, where a simple "yes" would have sufficed. "Show me you're a hero. Save Kelly's life."

"Alright!" roared Paulo after a moment, his chest heaving. "Alright."

He and Alex stood face to face, eye to eye, whilst overhead the twenty-first manatee glided silently above the tall beech trees that rimmed the park.

"Alex…" said Will, pointing after it.

"I know," said Alex, glancing upward. "Time's running out.

Come on."

They ran, Alex stumbling and limping from some of the wounds Paulo had inflicted on him. Soon though, he was hardly aware of them. It was almost a race. Paulo was heavily built but he was strong and fit. Alex, for the first time in his life in any running-style activity, was determined not to get left behind. His lungs ached. His thighs and calves were throbbing, seething masses of torment. Will, however, was doomed to this fate and soon he was trailing, his plaintive appeals echoing along the silent streets.

They came out on the ring road at its junction with Darford Street – and there was Cactus Jack, plodding steadily towards them along Greenfield Avenue, a spot of white amongst the stiffs and the stationary traffic. Glancing up the hill towards the fateful accident, Alex picked out Kelly and Tanya outside the insurance offices. It was too early. It would surely be a while before the fateful manatee arrived there.

"We've got to do something," Alex panted. "Too early… Got to lure Jack away, slow him down or something."

"Okay," Paulo looked grimly around him. "That skip, see the one in front of the dance school? Get me that piece of angle iron."

Alex nodded. He clambered up on the skip and hauled at the length of steel. It was easily the heaviest thing he'd ever tried to shift from Statica and it took every ounce of his strength to budge it. He heaved on it until his eyes bulged, but at last it came free, sliding from under an old door and a broken window frame.

"Good, now chuck it down here," said Paulo grimly.

Alex jumped down and followed the Vegetable King as he strode out towards the approaching Cactus Jack, the length of steel held before him like a spear.

"What are you going to do?" demanded Alex, fear already clutching at his throat, as Jack drew nearer.

"I'm going to *cabbage* kill the *aubergine*," snapped Paulo over his shoulder.

"What? You can't kill Death."

"Yeah? Just *fennel* watch me."

Paulo raised the steel and charged at Cactus Jack, roaring like a lunatic. Alex's feet seemed rooted to the ground with fear, but he forced himself to follow. Cactus Jack showed no sign of alarm at Paulo's approach. He seemed to notice nothing around him, so focused was he on homing in on his victim. Perhaps he had never previously been attacked by a maniac with an iron bar. A minute later he was an old hand at it. Paulo swung the bar with all his strength as Jack passed him by. With a sickening thud that set Alex's teeth on edge, the bar connected with Jack's midriff. In Alex's mind's eye he anticipated the creature folding in two, stumbling broken to the ground. Instead, he saw the bar rebound harmlessly from Jack, who strode on heedlessly as though nothing had happened. Cursing, turning to follow his victim, Paulo drew back the bar once more and swung it at the back of Cactus Jack's head. Another crunching impact. Jack should have been decapitated, but on he marched, shaking his head a little as though an irritating insect had troubled him. Paulo came after him, jabbing and swinging, but all to no avail.

"Trip him up," cried Alex, jigging with excitement and anxiety. The fear had subsided now, replaced by adrenaline-fuelled desperation.

Nodding, Paulo thrust the bar between Jack's long legs. This at least Cactus Jack could not ignore. He tripped, half-turned, clawed impotently at the air and crashed to the pavement. Before he could stir himself, Alex and Paulo were on top of him, Paulo thumping Jack's face with his pile-driver fists, Alex doing his best to pinion his legs. It was hopeless. Cactus Jack clambered to his feet, shaking off his assailants like a dog shakes off water. Calmly he swatted Paulo away, sending him careering through a hedge.

"And again," shouted Paulo, stooping for the bar. "*Do* the *beansprout*."

Over and over again they tripped Cactus Jack and brought him down. Each time he calmly righted himself and carried on. Paulo and Alex were exhausted.

"It's no use," panted Alex. "We've got to lead him away."

It was easy enough to outpace Jack, but both of them were nearing the limit of their endurance. They found Kelly and Tanya hiding in the entrance of the insurance office, peering along the ring road towards where Jack's long legs were eating up the distance between them.

"Run!" called Alex when they were within earshot. "Come on, down the High Street. We'll lead him round in a big circle."

Even from this distance he could see Kelly's pale face, wide-eyed with fear. She and Tanya sprinted across the ring road, dodging amongst the Statical cars, with Paulo and Alex in hot pursuit. They paused for a moment at the top of High Street for Paulo and Alex to catch their breath.

"Sorry, chick," said Paulo to Kelly, taking her by the arm. "Sorry about everything."

They looked hard at each other for a moment and then Kelly rushed into his embrace. They hugged, he stroking her hair with his big, bruised hands. It struck Alex as an inadequate apology for having mown her down in the morning of her life, but it seemed enough for Kelly. There was a little shriek from Tanya, who pointed to where Cactus Jack had emerged from the passage between the bank and the dry cleaners.

"Come on!" urged Alex. "Time to go."

They ran once more, a brisk jog sufficient to keep them in front of their grim pursuer and gradually increase the distance. A brisk jog was all Alex felt he could manage by now. Paulo was also perhaps beginning to regret smoking all those cigarettes. He was puffing and blowing as hard as any of them as they rounded the corner into Market Street.

"He can't cut us off, can he?" asked Kelly when they slowed down for a moment. "What if he cuts through The Talbot Arms?"

"Let's hope not," said Paulo. "Let's *parsnip* hope not."

There was no sign of Cactus Jack in front of them. They hurried along Market Street to its junction with Worcester Road, re-joining the ring road once more as it curved around towards the insurance office.

"What do you reckon?" asked Paulo, nodding up at the eastern sky. "Manatee must be about due now. Getting dark over there."

"You're right," agreed Alex, walking briskly. "Better get into the offices. It might be hard to break in, and we don't want to get trapped out front."

They ran once more, picking up the iron bar from where they had earlier discarded it, just in case Alex needed it to smash his way in. Will was waiting anxiously in the doorway. Everyone else stood helplessly as Alex flung himself at the double glass doors. The first time he rebounded painfully, rubbing his shoulder ruefully. The second charge ended with the same result. He placed his shoulder against it, braced himself against the doorstep and pushed with all his strength.

"Wrong side," called Will suddenly. "Look! There's someone just gone through it."

Will was right. Cursing, feeling a fool, Alex transferred his attentions to the other door.

"Hurry up, for *sprout*'s sake," grunted Paulo.

"I can see Cactus Jack," shrieked Tanya, who was keeping watch from the pavement outside. "He's just come out past B&Q."

At last the door gave way. The party burst through into the foyer, glancing anxiously around at the scene of Statical activity thus revealed. A receptionist laughed at a joke she was being told by a young man leaning over the desk towards her. A cleaner uncoiled the lead of a vacuum cleaner. A man in a hurry twisted to grab at two sheets of paper that had slipped from the stack of files he was carrying. One of the two lifts stood open, and instinct almost led Alex to run into it. He checked himself just in time.

"Stairs," said Kelly, reading his mistake. "There must be stairs."

There were, just along a short corridor to the rear of the lifts. Alex forced open the door and they rushed up the stairs, taking them two at a time, their feet clattering in the echoing concrete stairwell.

"Oh God, please don't let the door at the top be locked," said Alex to himself as they made their way to the top of the building. It wasn't – it was a fire exit with a push bar latch. Alex hurled himself at it and the door burst open. They ran across the flat terrace of the roof top towards the parapet and made for the side nearest to the decaying Victorian temple to literature that had once been the old town library. From here they could look back along the west side of the ring road to where the tiny shape of a manatee could be made out, gliding painfully slowly towards them.

"Come on, come onnnn," fretted Will. "Is it always that slow?"

They all cast anxious glances back at the lift head at the open door that marked the top of the staircase. Paulo was still holding the iron bar. He and Alex looked at each other and then at the door. They had the same idea at the same moment.

"We could wedge the door shut," said Paulo.

Alex nodded. "Worth a try."

They hurried to the door, slamming it shut and wedging the bar between the handle and a crack in the slabs that made up the roof surface. They weren't an instant too soon. The next moment the door shook as Cactus Jack placed his weight against it. Alex and Paulo sprinted back to the parapet. Kelly was trembling, ashen white, doing her best to console Tanya, who was weeping on her arm.

"It's still a way away," reported Will, leaning over the parapet. "Maybe thirty seconds."

Alex didn't know if they had thirty seconds. He found himself shifting his weight anxiously from foot to foot. The door was vibrating now with great thundering crashes and the bar was beginning to slip.

"I'll hold it in place," said Will, taking off his glasses. His small, weak eyes held a world of terror, but he hurried to the door, slapping Kelly's and Alex's outstretched hands in passing.

"Good luck," he called to them over his shoulder.

"It's going to be alright," Kelly assured Tanya, cradling her head in her hands, but she didn't look like she believed it.

Paulo put his arm around Kelly and drew her to him, causing Alex a moment of the sharpest anguish. They climbed up onto the parapet and faced the void beneath, a void into which they must surely leap in seconds now as the manatee slid past B&Q. Alex felt Kelly's arm snake around his midriff as the three of them stood poised on the parapet edge and the slow seconds dragged past.

"Tell us when," said Kelly to Tanya, who had moved a little further along to watch.

"I can't hold it," cried Will from the door, struggling to hold the bar in place. The door burst open and Will fell on his back as the bar toppled to the floor with a loud clang. Cactus Jack strode through.

"Quickly, Kelly, the mask," said Alex, snatching at the amulet that hung at her neck. He fumbled with the buttons. At first nothing seemed to happen but at last, when Jack had covered half the distance between them, it began to glow. For a moment all four of them froze, watching helplessly as Cactus Jack ground to a halt.

"It's working," breathed Tanya.

"Shhhh," hissed Paulo. "Shut the *sprout* up!"

Cactus Jack stood only a few metres from them, his head turning slowly from side to side, his nostrils flaring as he sniffed the air. Then he took a slow, faltering step towards them, pausing again to sample the breeze.

"He's still getting a whiff of you Kell'," said Paulo, drawing her closer to him as though he thought he was going to be able to protect her from Jack. "Now what, Alex?"

There was desperation in all of their eyes as they regarded him. Alex shrugged, and then his hand brushed against a small, hard object in his trouser pocket, even as Jack took another cautious step towards them. The manatee was close now, no more than a hundred yards. Inspiration struck Alex. He drew Tony's pager stone quickly from his pocket and squeezed it hard, picturing Tony in his head.

"What are you doing?" asked Kelly.

Before Alex could even begin to answer, Tony materialised in front of them. He was still dressed formally, as though dressed for the meeting from which Alex had absconded. There was a look of severe irritation on his face.

"This had better be important," he managed to say before realising who had summoned him. "What? You!"

Almost at the same instant he realised that Kelly, Tanya, Paulo and Alex all had their eyes fixed firmly on what was immediately behind him. He swivelled, even as Cactus Jack suddenly bore down upon him.

"Huh! Atropos, what are you doing here? Hey, unhand me at once."

Cactus Jack had taken hold of Tony. The angel's panic-stricken hoots rang out across the rooftop as Death's delegate tried to get a good grip on the back of Tony's neck. "What are you doing? Get off!" grunted Tony as the two of them wrestled.

Alex realised with a jolt of delight that Tony still had a sample of Kelly's DNA in his jacket pocket. Confused and desperate for his kill, Jack must have homed in on that. Tony was strong, possessed of angelic power indeed, but every time he went to make those special signs in the air, Jack's hands seemed to interrupt the movement – and Tony was getting more and more anxious. "No, help! This is all a mistake. Aah!"

There was no time to watch any more. Tony's unwitting intervention had bought them a vital few seconds and now the manatee was gliding beneath them. It was the moment they had waited for.

"Now!" cried Tanya.

With a last glance at each other, they jumped. Alex's stomach flinched upwards. He caught his breath. Air tugged at his hair. The grey bulk of the manatee loomed towards them and he braced himself for the impact.

But there was none.

Suddenly they were falling not onto but through it, as though a hole had opened up in the fabric of 'Sticia. Alex's last impressions were of Kelly's mouth, open in a silent scream, Paulo flailing at the whirling darkness, Tanya's pale face over the parapet, diminishing to nothing. There was a brief dizziness, a lurch and suddenly Alex was back in Wardworths, a vacuum flask and a bowl in his hands. The world sprang into motion and sounds assaulted his ears as though a switch had been suddenly flicked. Flask and bowl dropped from his nerveless fingers. There were impressions, loud voices, expressions of concern from those around him. His mum turning towards him, a loud bang somewhere. Heads turning. It was bizarre. Memories were leaking from his head like water streaming through a colander. He fought to hold on to them. Will, Ganymede, Malcolm, Paulo… and Kelly. They were all getting away from him. Ignoring the momentary confusion behind him and his mum's call of alarm, Alex ran for the doors. He pelted through jostling crowds along the passage that led to the ring road, desperately trying to hold on to the diminishing image of Kelly in his head. It was hopeless. She faded like a wisp of smoke until she was gone, even as he joined the press of onlookers at the kerbside.

The traffic had stopped. A police car was drawn up with its lights flashing and its doors hung open. One policeman considered the wreckage of a small car, shattered against the side wall of the insurance office, and spoke urgently into his radio. Another was walking back along the road waving his arms to stop the traffic as it swung round the bend. More policemen were rushing out of the police station and somewhere in the distance the siren of an ambulance could be heard. Alex felt numb. He worked his way to the edge of the kerb. What might have been an off duty doctor had joined the policeman by the car and was leaning in through the shattered windscreen. He came out again, shaking his head. The policeman spoke into his radio again. A colleague ran across with a green medical bag. The medic signalled that this would not be necessary. It was clear that the driver was dead. Alex felt a sensation of sadness so acute he had to look away. Why had the death of a stranger affected him so? His eye fell upon two girls standing awkwardly on the other side of the road. One was rubbing her elbows and rolling up one trouser leg to rub at her shin. The other was smaller, dark-haired, pretty. She had the lower part of her face covered by her hands, only her eyes exposed, staring fixedly at the wreckage of the car. A policewoman took her gently by the arm and began to lead her back across the road towards the police station, fending off enquiries from the drivers of various stationary vehicles.

"What on earth are you doing?" rang Alex's mum's voice from behind him, and then "Oh!" as she took in the scene of the accident. The two girls were led past Alex. He gaped. There was something so familiar about that girl, and as she passed their eyes met. There were tears in hers – anguish, shock – and then as she passed by a glimmer of recognition. Alex almost called out, but what was there to say? Then she was gone, her head turned away once more as the crowd swallowed her up. His mum was scolding him, grabbing at his arm, but Alex hardly heard. He remained frozen, watching until the two girls vanished inside the police station. Then he allowed himself to be drawn away back towards the High Street, letting his mum's complaints wash over him.

"... out of your pocket money," she was saying. "Great clumsy clot. And running off like that. What on earth did you think you were doing?"

A stranger appeared at Alex's side, a young man with a struggling goatee beard and a kindly face. He wore an ill-fitting suit. Before Alex could react, the stranger had taken his hand and pressed something into it. Alex glanced down. It was a page torn from a jotter with a name and a telephone number scrawled upon it. Alex looked up.

"Come on," called his mum impatiently from up ahead.

But the young man had gone. Alex glanced wildly up and down the street. He looked at the paper again. 'Kelly' was the name.